WHERE DARKNESS SLEEPS . . .

The living room was almost black, devoid of life. The embers of the fire glowed like a miniature landscape of hell. Amid the glowing ruins, something stirred. The balled-up portrait of Emily, blackened, began to open, as a rosebud opens in a time-lapse film. The portrait rose over the hot coals and burst into flames.

Miles away, the stately old Hamilton Home for the Aged faded in and out of the night like a colossal blot through thick milky blue fog. On the third floor, the halls were empty and nearly black. Behind a locked door, strapped to a narrow bed, Charity Francis, aged and pain-wracked, was coming out of a deep, drug-induced sleep. Into her imagination came a face, the face of a girl, looming before her, golden but taking on the dimensions of real flesh.

The girl.
Emily Jordan.

WHERE DARKNESS SLEEPS

BRIAN RIESELMAN

St. Martin's Paperbacks

WHERE DARKNESS SLEEPS

Copyright © 1995 by Brian Rieselman

ISBN: 0-312-95682-7

Printed in the United States of America

St. Martin's Paperbacks edition/December 1995

10 9 8 7 6 5 4 3 2 1

For Ricardo

WHERE DARKNESS SLEEPS

Chapter One

SEPTEMBER MORNING

After a long journey of many hundreds of miles, there is a moment when a body must seem to finally come to a complete stop. Emily Jordan felt that settling sense of arrival, and found it oddly terrifying.

"Please have a seat," the young nurse said to her, and sniffed again. She had a vicious cold. "You won't be kept waiting too much longer."

The nurse, in her soft white shoes, stepped quietly through the open door, which she now closed behind her with painstaking slowness. The inevitable springy hollow click of the latch bolt seemed forever in coming, but at last Emily was alone in Eugenia Temple's stately office on the ground floor of the old hilltop mansion.

Emily shrugged off her moth-eaten brown bomber jacket and sank into the soft padded chair opposite a grand antique desk.

She looked around. The chamber was old-fashioned,

a parlor converted into a business office. Heavy oxblood curtains were drawn from the high lattice windows, which looked out over the tree-lined hilltop, valley, and expanse of green country miles. Through the translucent glass in the office door, Emily saw human shapes move past. Voices were soft. Even the occasional bleat of a telephone was barely audible.

At last Eugenia Temple opened the door. With a long-legged patrician gait, she entered the room, her eyes locking on Emily's.

Emily stood up, feeling herself perspiring a little. Officials didn't exactly frighten her, but they made her uneasy. This woman was tall, ramrod straight, silver haired. Her handshake was firm.

"It's a pleasure to meet you, Emily," Eugenia said, smiling, taking the chair behind her desk. Her voice was deep and calm as a dead lake. She opened a file folder, put on a pair of small metal-framed reading glasses, and scanned the papers before her. Emily looked at Eugenia's long white fingers and noticed the rigidity of her body, clad in a conservative navy-blue suit. Eugenia projected strength and vitality, an energy that obscured her obvious maturity. Emily could not quite place her age.

At last Eugenia looked up from the papers. Her face was unusually handsome, but cold, as though carved of some sleek sea-bottom stone. The silver hair was upswept, perfect, a delicate widow's peak demarcating her high forehead. Now she smiled warmly, and her soft voice belied the icy facade.

"You'll be performing mainly menial tasks here at the Hamilton Home for the Aged," she said, looking Emily in the eye. "I've compiled a list of the sorts of things you'll be expected to tend to on a regular basis. Housekeeping and the like. In addition to the items on this list"—Eugenia handed a mimeographed paper across the desk—"you will be expected to help the nursing staff whenever called upon to do so. The main thing is to be helpful, professional, and cheerful."

"Yes, of course," Emily said in a voice that was smaller than her usual one. She tried to manage a smile. She felt it flicker from her face.

"You are to have no unsupervised visits with the residents, though you are expected to join in planned group activities whenever called upon to do so."

"Yes, Miss Temple."

"Federal guidelines require that our little home be inspected by the state at least once every fifteen months. These are surprise inspections, as it were. We have never had one in the winter, due to our very remote, tranquil location and the harshness of our northern Wisconsin winters—something I would expect a young Californian will take some time getting used to."

Emily smiled politely at her comment.

"At any rate, you are not to speak to any person about your business here—or ours—either in the home or outside of it, without checking with me first."

Eugenia folded her hands on the desk. She paused, letting her words settle before going on.

"We are dealing with human lives here, Miss Jordan. Many of our residents are barely functional. Don't be surprised if some of them tell you outrageous stories, or engage you in malicious gossip, or even tell you they are being kept here at the Hamilton Home against their will."

"Yes, ma'am."

"We provide exceptional care to our residents. We have almost zero turnover of staff. We provide a full range of religious services, right here on the premises, including funerals. You may have already heard that we have a cemetery on the grounds, a final resting place for our residents."

Emily said nothing.

"And that brings me to a delicate point, young woman. You will have, on occasion, contact with the sick and the dying, and even the dead."

Emily listened intently.

"I expect you to be brave in these circumstances," Eugenia said. "Growing old and sick is perfectly natural. Death is, of course, a part of life. What I'm asking for, Emily, is respect for the work, the institution, and the *mission* of the Hamilton Home."

The warm smile returned to her face, and she handed Emily a brochure titled "A Place For Rest: The Historic Hamilton Home, Blackburn County, Wisconsin."

"You'll find the history of this magnificent, if slightly worn, old house in here. In a few minutes I'm going to introduce you to a young member of our part-time paid staff, Beth Hanes, who lives in the village of Leonora, is a senior at Leonora High School, and who has been recently hired under our new Youth Program. She is your age exactly—seventeen, correct?"

"Yes."

"You'll both have essentially the same sorts of tasks."

"I look forward to meeting her," Emily said.

"Beth will show you where the white coats are kept. You'll wear one at all times on the premises, along with your name tag. We encourage camaraderie here, so I hope you'll like Beth. Oh, and another thing. Beth doesn't know that you're a volunteer, so to speak. I strongly advise you not to mention to her the nature of your *terms* here at the home. We have had others in your position. I am not making any personal judgments, mind you. But discretion is a valued code of conduct here—and in life in general."

Emily nodded and looked down at her hands, folded in her lap. Her black hair, parted on the side and thick as a horse's tail, fell over her eyes. She brushed it back and tried to smile, looking up again with wide-set blue eyes at this strange woman who was going to help her.

"Thank you," she said to Eugenia.

Her "terms" here: two-hundred hours of court-ordered community service. The judge's banging gavel echoed in her memory. Emily sighed inwardly. The alternative might have been jail, or a California girl's institution, had her father, with his name and his money, not swept into San Francisco at almost the last moment to offer this arrangement.

Eugenia rose from her chair. "I expect that at some point you will meet our chief physician, my brother, Dr. Herbert Temple. I regret he's not here today, as he has taken ill."

"I'm sorry," Emily said. She stood up now, too.

"In the meantime, there are plenty of people to meet, and lots to learn." Eugenia extended her hand. She was framed in the tall, sun-glinted window behind her, a window that looked out over leafy tree tops and down to the lonely curving stretch of an empty rural highway.

Eugenia gave Emily a little smile. Emily smiled back and shook the woman's hand.

* * *

Emily was to meet Beth in a basement laundry room, where Beth would give her a white coat to wear and a name tag. It had taken Emily almost ten minutes to find the laundry room. There were so many corridors in the basement, many of which led to dead ends and locked doors. Now she feared she'd missed Beth all together.

Emily folded her second-hand bomber jacket, purchased months ago at a thrift shop in San Francisco's Mission District. She hung it over the back of an orange plastic chair and sat down in the brightly lit room piled high with white linens. The homey smell of freshly laundered towels and bedding filled the air. The machines created a din.

Emily read through the brochure, with its brief history of the Hamilton Home.

The Great Hill, as it was known throughout Blackburn County, had been the favored building site of more than one wealthy European settler. A timber baron by the name of Orion Hamilton, having defeated his rivals in acquiring the property, had built a great mansion on this spot. It burned shortly after he'd moved his family into it. He built again. The home burned again. The third try was the building she was in now.

A grainy black-and-white picture of the Hamilton patriarch glared out at her from the brochure. The odd size and shape of his head and his deep cadaverous scowl spooked her, as antique portraits sometimes did. The full history and weight of the home was literally above her head. And the laundry room was deserted. Emily cleared her throat and turned the page.

After the Orion Hamilton family left the house—

no reason for this departure was given in the brochure—the county took it over and converted it to the local poorhouse. There were orphans, some of them retarded, who'd spent their entire lives under the Hamilton Home's black eaves. Then they were buried in the backyard, in the potter's field.

An odd fate for such a splendid home. Perhaps it was too magnificent—and too remote up here in the north of old Wisconsin—to ever attract another wealthy buyer, Emily speculated.

She looked at the high ceilings, the pipes crossing overhead. Down here, you felt the dark soul of the industrial age: the coal furnace and steam engine grubbiness hidden beneath the Victorian charms. A truly Dickensian place, she decided.

Sometime in the 1930s the house for the poor was restored to its "lovely original state" and turned into a home for the aged, the brochure promised.

"Emily," someone said from behind her.

Emily dropped the brochure to the concrete floor and turned, rising quickly to her feet. Before her stood a girl about her age, on the plump side, with long red hair and striking green eyes. She wore a white coat and held another one in her hands. She offered the coat to Emily.

"Didn't scare you, did I?" the girl said. Her voice was raspy and tomboyish. She was smiling. "I'm Beth Hanes. Did Temple tell you I was supposed to show you around this dump?"

Emily took the coat. She slipped it on. "Yes. She gave me this to read," she said, stooping to pick up the fallen brochure. "Kind of creepy."

"Creepy? The home, or Temple?"

Emily smiled. "Well, both, I guess." Though in truth Emily felt that Eugenia Temple had seemed pretty nice during the interview. Benevolent but serious minded.

"You don't know the half of it," Beth said mysteriously. "Come on."

They took an elevator up to the main floor. Along the way, Beth told Emily that she was a senior at Leonora High School—a hellhole—and she'd taken this job—a shit job if there ever was one—so she could afford an apartment in Madison next year. She planned to attend Madison Area Technical College for a couple of years, and then if possible transfer to the University of Wisconsin's mammoth Madison campus. She wanted to be an architect or a psychologist. But mostly she wanted to get out of Blackburn County.

When they stepped out of the elevator Beth asked Emily what her zodiac sign was.

"Sagittarius," Emily answered.

Beth withdrew a paperback book entitled *Understanding the Zodiac* from the big pocket of her coat. She opened the book at a certain page. "I'm a Leo." She scanned the pages. "I guess we're compatible." She closed the book and tucked it back into her pocket.

"What did you mean back there in the basement, about me not knowing 'the half of it'?" Emily asked as they entered the sunlit lounge off the main entryway. The home had its grandeur and Victorian charms, Emily had to admit.

"What? About how creepy this joint is? Where shall I begin? That brochure sure as hell doesn't tell the whole story, especially the part about the murders."

"The murders?" Emily said, alarmed.

"The entire Hamilton family, except for the old man, Orion. Throats slashed in their beds, even the little children. Of course, everyone thinks Orion Hamilton did it, but it was never proven. The county ended up taking over the house because nobody who had enough cash to buy it would ever touch it."

"Charming," Emily said. "But that's practically ancient history."

"Yeah, well, the place might as well be cursed. These days they positively rob the residents here. They have Medicaid and Medicare scams going like you wouldn't believe. Who do you think actually gets the Social Security checks that pour in? People drop dead here, nobody much cares. You're *expected* to do that in a place like this. It's really awful."

"Beth, shhh! Aren't you afraid someone will hear you?"

"In this place? Sweetheart, you practically have to scream to attract their attention."

Emily grinned. "But how do you know about all these scams? Do the residents tell you?"

"No way. The residents are all scared shitless of Eugenia and Herbert, her brother. Meet the good doc yet? A real treat, let me tell you. No, the residents never complain; they just grow older and sicker and eventually take their secrets to their graves. The scoop on this place comes from the outside. My mother could tell you all about it." Beth blew a small pink bubble, popped it, continued chomping. "This place has a bad reputation among the locals. Most everybody in Leonora knows enough to die first and skip the terminal lounges of the old Hamilton Home. But say you're from Boston, you're loaded, and you've got some annoying old relative you'd like to dispose of . . . welcome aboard!''

"But you're basing your conclusions on rumors, right? Is there really any proof?" Emily touched the wood paneling of the corridor as they walked by. She liked the feel and sound of her nails tracing along the gleaming wood. "If the townspeople are so suspicious, why don't they investigate? Or are they afraid of the ghost of Orion Hamilton?"

Beth frowned. "Nobody does anything because this is a small-town community where people gossip for a living, and everything begins and ends with gossip. If people around here wanted trouble, they'd move somewhere else."

They entered a grand room with a high ceiling and a great red carpet with dusty gold fringe. A long window overlooked the valley. Old people sat at tables and chairs, some nodding off, others glancing through magazines. Most wore bathrobes, though a few were dressed in regular street clothes. Everyone wore slippers.

Emily told Beth roughly where her father's country house was located, near the old mill, a good distance from the village of Leonora. She told her she'd be living there at least until Christmas, probably longer.

Beth knew of the old mill, but the name Patrick Jordan meant nothing more to her than his association with his parents. The old Jordan place. The Jordans' boy. That's who he was. Not a nationally known and respected painter whose work was represented in some of the greatest museums in the world. Perhaps that was one of the reasons Patrick liked it here so much, Emily thought, why he'd moved back here from New York after he and her mother divorced, when Emily was four. People here really were fairly oblivious to the world outside their own experiences. That meant they left you alone.

"So, you're a high school dropout or what?" Beth asked.

Emily smiled. "Sort of. Actually, I kind of finished early. I'm starting a class at Leonora Community College—tonight, in fact."

"Oh, hold everything," Beth said, her voice lowered.

She pointed at three white-uniformed nurses. They were coming into the room. Other than their hair color, the nurses were almost indistinguishable to Emily. They were quite fat, in their late forties, she guessed.

"Who are they?" she asked.

"The biggest bitches in the entire place. I call 'em Patti, Maxine, and Laverne 'cuz they always travel in a pack. They don't get out much, if you catch my drift."

"Beth!" cried one of them, the one Beth had identified as Maxine. "Beth, I need you to run a fresh set of linen up to Mr. Hogan's room."

"Sorry," Beth said in an oversweet, somewhat sarcastic tone of voice. "Miss Temple has me training the new girl."

The old nurse looked Emily up and down. "Christ," she grumbled. She grimaced at her own hands, with their clawlike purple nails. "Guess I'll have to climb the goddamned stairs myself."

"Why don't you take the elevator?" Emily said.

The old nurse scowled at her. "New girl, eh? We'll see how long *you* last around here." She tottered off.

"God, what was that supposed to mean?"

"It means stay away from Patti, Laverne, and Maxine," Beth said.

At the center of the Hamilton Home entryway, beneath a chandelier, a great, wide staircase carpeted in gray rose to a mezzanine. Beth started the "tour" of the home on these stairs, and for the next hour she showed Emily the features of each floor.

Beth spiced her instructions and advice with gossip and humor.

"They put the crazies over here," Beth said, pointing. "The complainers are up one floor. The living dead are mainly on One. They're not good climbers."

On the third floor they entered an open "lounge," where an old TV set glowed green and several old men sat smoking cigars.

"If you want to smoke, you can usually sneak one in here," Beth said. "The old guys won't rat on you."

A decrepit man with a mouselike face came clanking by, his walker in front of him.

"Good afternoon," Emily said as he passed her. He nodded, watery bloodshot eyes taking her in as he moved on. Another man, this one bigger but with rounded shoulders and wearing a worn plaid bathrobe, followed on his heels.

The bigger man looked at Emily. "What the hell is so good about it?" he hissed.

Emily was stung. People really were crabby in this place.

"What's eating you?" Beth said to the old guy in a matter-of-fact tone of voice.

The other old guy piped up. "He's been robbed of his youth," the mousy man said.

The bigger fellow turned toward his comrade. His eyes widened. "Charlie, you're a goddamn fool!"

Both men shambled off, and as they did, Emily had another shock.

She turned to see a tall younger man with sunken eyes and patches of white in his hair. His hands were freakishly huge. He glanced at her like a wary wolf, then lumbered by. Emily felt as though a rash had erupted beneath her skin, and her stomach rather turned.

When the ghoulish, hulking young man was out of earshot, Beth said, "That was Ned Fox." She pulled gently at Emily's arm, leading her down another hallway. "He's Eugenia's chief henchman, and they come no weirder."

"Henchman? I feel sorry for him," Emily blurted out. "What sort of life could be he possibly have here?"

"Yeah, well, your life isn't going to be a whole lot more fun as long you're stuck here in this place, so get used to it."

Emily turned to Beth. "You know something, you've really got an attitude, kid," she said.

Beth shrugged.

They stopped at the end of the hallway, cordoned off with a velvet rope. Hanging from the rope was a sign marked OFF LIMITS.

"Now what?" Emily said, tired, cross, the weight of her situation descending on her. She was miles from home, miles from her mother.

And miles from Danny.

Danny. Better not think about him right now. Or

about those fast rides to Marin, clutching his leather-clad torso on the back of his cycle.

Emily sat down on the step. She could feel Beth's presence looming behind her.

"I'm sorry," Beth said.

"Forget about it," Emily said. "I didn't mean to snap at you."

Beth remained standing.

"No, I mean it," Beth said. "I didn't mean to come off as such a bitch."

"It's okay. And you didn't. I've been enjoying your company, for the most part. Okay?"

"Okay. But tell me something. What are you doing in this place?" Beth asked. "Really. I mean, I could tell you didn't belong here the minute I laid eyes on you."

Emily sighed. "Sit down. How about that cigarette? Can we have it here?"

Beth sat down and they lit up, daringly sneaking a smoke together.

Emily told Beth about the community service hours she'd been "sentenced" to, and a little bit about her father, who'd arranged it all.

"He and my mom are divorced. Have been for years. I grew up with my mom, in San Francisco. My father hit the big time, dropped out of New York, and built his dream house up here in Blackburn County, in the valley where he grew up. That's my home base for a while. It's a gorgeous place, secluded, quiet. Perfect for an artist, especially an antisocial one."

"But not so perfect for you?"

Emily shrugged. "I was what they call an accessory

to a crime. The prosecutors considered a motion to waive me into adult court. I'm lucky to be free."

Beth's eyes widened. She dragged on her cigarette. "And your crime?"

"Well ... My boyfriend—my *ex*-boyfriend, Danny—is a chemist, or was a chemist ... a straight-A genius with a bright future at Cal. At least until he started cooking up batches of ecstasy in his kitchen in Berkeley. It became very lucrative for him. He was what the prosecutor called a designer drug lord of the San Francisco nightclub scene." Emily rolled her eyes. "I, of course, thought he could do no wrong."

She felt a sting of rejection. She thought of Danny with his dark mane of hair, his cool good looks.

He'd not once tried to contact her after their arrests. She'd learned through her lawyer that Danny had actually tried to shift the blame onto her, saying that it was her school friends who'd created the demand for his wares.

Emily's defense lawyer argued otherwise: Emily had gotten innocently caught up with the brilliant and older—at age twenty—Danny and his crowd of computer hackers and designer-drug enthusiasts. She'd been seduced by Danny and his scene, the motorcycle trips he'd taken her on, and the overall "spell" this dangerous boy had cast over her.

What nobody had mentioned was that Emily had really loved him. And when she'd learned the extent of Danny's "business," she'd thrown herself deeper into the relationship, not turned away to run. She'd seen what she wanted to see.

And now, for what amounted to taking down a few

phone numbers in a nightclub ladies room, she was two thousand miles away from her home, from her mother . . . and from that boy who, she now had to admit to herself, did not really love her at all. And maybe never had.

"He's doing hard time now in a real prison," Emily said of Danny. "He's not as lucky as I am."

"Hoo-boy," Beth said with a grin. "I just knew there was something different about you." She slapped her thigh.

Emily felt a sting of shame. What a fool I've been, she thought. And now I have a record. And a past.

All the "good times" were supposed to be behind her. And here was her reprieve: an old folks home. She was supposed to redeem herself here, start a new life where others ended theirs. She sighed heavily and shrugged her shoulders.

"So are you through trying to scare me?" She said with a smile.

Beth shook her long red tresses. "I may exaggerate a little, but the truth is, weird things do go on around Blackburn County. Girls disappear. Most young people move out the first chance they get. The ones who stay don't have much work to do, and people drink and drive like it's mandatory. Between you and me, I think this community has some kind of death wish."

Emily watched the end of her cigarette, the red-hot ash consuming with a tiny hiss the paper and tobacco.

"Come on," Beth said. "Let me show you around the grounds."

Outside, the warm sun felt good on Emily's face. They walked around the building, which commanded the high hill. In the distance, beyond the valley with its cornfields and farmsteads, were the distant blue hills Emily had seen on her way from the airport yesterday from her father's car.

She now looked up at the massive four-story redbrick structure, with its black mansard roof and four brick chimneys, its gables and turrets. The grand front door, black, was centered in a wide, white column, two stories high. A portico surrounded the first floor, and on it sat empty rocking chairs, as many as fifty of them by Emily's quick count. To the left of the entrance, a porte cochere was constructed of the same red brick with ornate black wooden trim.

It was real, just as her father had described it to her. Her father had explained to the court in San Francisco about the home, and about the arrangement he was making to take her away from the bad influences that had led her—a good student who had never been in serious trouble before—to possible incarceration. (Emily's mother, Cathleen, seeing no alternative, had agreed with every detail of Patrick's plan. An attorney herself, she had helped map out the strategy with Emily's lawyer.)

Even Patrick's description of the Hamilton Home didn't quite capture the shock and surprise of it. Emily hadn't expected the stately building she was looking at now.

It was an antique mansion of impressive size and design. Even in San Francisco she'd not seen a Victorian structure of such stern, buttoned-up grandiosity. It was strangely beautiful.

A few men worked in the yard, pushing wheelbarrows and carrying rakes. One of the men had a stubby, unlit cigar planted between his teeth. He looked sourly at Emily and then went on his way.

Emily looked back up at the mansion. Sun glinted in the windows, where reflections of clouds drifted by.

The rest of the afternoon was easygoing. Emily helped out in the "activity room," where her job consisted of helping one of the nurses photocopy events schedules. The nurse was about sixty and wore her hair in an enormous dyed-brown beehive. Her name was, in fact, Bea.

Bea and Emily then posted several flyers on each floor. One of the flyers announced an upcoming visit from State Senator Allan Pullman. Emily had never heard of him, but the nurse in charge told her Pullman, though relatively young, had represented the district for years, as had his father before him. The event was advertized as a "town hall meeting" with a question-and-answer period. It was to be held in the old ballroom.

When they had finished posting the flyers, Bea and Emily came back to the activity room and poured orange juice into fifty paper cups. Old people milled in to drink the orange juice, which came out of giant cans and which to Emily's taste was rather thin and watery. Patti, Laverne, and Maxine also enjoyed a cup or two of the juice, then carried off tray after tray.

When it was time to clean up the activity room, yet another strange old woman came rushing in. She had a terribly concerned look on her face, a lost look. She had stooped shoulders and wore a colorful scarf on her head, which gave her a gypsylike appearance. She covered her open mouth with a gnarled hand. Tears pooled in her eyes. Emily rose at once to see if she could help.

"Have you seen Maria Kraus?" the old woman asked, seizing upon Emily. The woman had a deep, raspy, chain-smoker's voice.

"I'm sorry," Emily said. "It's only my first day here."

"My name is Hazel Stern," the woman said, "and I'm not crazy. Do you believe me? I'm not!" She tugged on Emily's hands.

"Of course I believe you," Emily said.

"People are missing," Hazel said. She turned to the others in the room, "Have any of you seen Maria?"

It was as though the others had not heard Hazel. Emily thought perhaps they hadn't. But it seemed more likely that they were actively ignoring her. One old man covered his face with his hand and turned his head. Emily supposed there were several explanations for this, among them the desire not to get involved, or perhaps, sadder, the wish not to be disturbed by the frequent outbursts of an erratic person.

"You could be next, any one of you!" Hazel cried shrilly.

"Be quiet," someone said.

"They won't let us use the telephones," Hazel said to Emily, her voice growing even more broken and terror filled. "They listen in to our conversations."

Beth entered the room now, having heard the commotion. She looked sympathetically at Emily, in whose hands Hazel's cold and trembling ones now shook.

"You must be quiet," said an old woman with tight blue curls.

A kind of light seemed to die in Hazel's faded blue

eyes. She turned her face away, withdrawing her hands from Emily's.

"Ma'am," Emily said as Hazel began to walk slowly from the room. "Miss Stern? Is there something I can do to help?"

Hazel turned swiftly. Her look of desperate pleading turned hard and angry. "Run from this place," she said. "Get away while you still can."

Then she turned and left Emily standing there.

Beth came over and put her arm around Emily's shoulder, giggling. "You have to have a thick skin here," she said. "Now do you understand why I'm looking forward to getting the hell out?"

"We should help her find her friend," Emily said. "Shouldn't we?"

"Emily, listen to me." Beth looked into Emily's eyes. "Hazel is crazy. Everybody here knows that."

"Crazy," Emily said, still a bit rattled. Well, yes, of course Hazel was crazy. She had spoken a lot of nonsense. Obviously everyone was used to her acting this way. *Be professional*, Emily told herself. "This job is going to take some getting used to," she whispered

"Come on, kid, it's almost time to pack it in," Beth said.

Emily traded in her white coat for her own leather jacket, and she headed for the door. Her father would be would be waiting in the drive for her.

"I have a car," Beth said. "It's a beater, but you're welcome to catch rides with me whenever you want."

Beth wore a tattered blue-denim jacket. She looked pretty, and Emily thought that Beth was probably one of those girls who is often told how cute she'd be if she lost fifteen pounds. Nobody needed to hear that.

"This will sound really idiotic," Emily said, glancing at her watch, "but I have to check with my dad. At least for a while."

All at once from the hallway behind them there came a loud crash and a scream. Emily and Beth both spun around, surprised. *Now what?* Emily thought. Someone had taken a spill, judging by the sound of it. The girls ran around the corner, and there in a heap was a most decrepit looking old woman.

"Charity!" Beth cried. She bent down to try to help the woman up.

Emily was surprised by this woman's appearance. Her hair, flecked with gold and silver strands, and even some red ones, was very long, matted, and wild, and her face was smudged like a chimney sweep's. Her clothes were ragged, in layers like a homeless woman might wear. If Emily hadn't known better, she would have thought this Charity woman was dead drunk.

"Wow, they must have you on heavy meds," Beth said. Her zodiac book fell from her jean jacket pocket. She hoisted Charity Francis to her feet.

Emily reached out a hand to help steady the old woman, and was alarmed when Charity's hand suddenly grasped her wrist.

Help me!

The voice was as if spoken, but Charity had not spoken. Her fiery green eyes were like penetrating beams.

Help us, Emily! Help us!

Was she imagining this? She had to be. It was the oddest thing.

Another hand reached out and abruptly broke off the connection. Emily looked up into the stony face of Eugenia Temple. Ned Fox stood close behind.

Emily felt the hair rising on the back of her neck. She felt a little faint. But she fought it. *Don't do this,* she told herself, *don't be ridiculous. That voice was only your overactive imagination. You're being as silly as crazy old Hazel Stern.*

"Get a chair for Miss Francis at once," Eugenia said, not looking at Ned. "Wheel her back to her room."

Patti, Laverne, and Maxine were hovering over the scene now, too. For once they looked sheepish.

"Charity should not be wandering about on her medication," Eugenia warned. "She might have fallen down the stairs and broken her neck."

Ned arrived with the wheelchair. Charity was placed rather roughly into it. She looked up into Emily's eyes. Her cherubic face fell in agony. She opened her mouth, and Emily expected to hear a kind of gasp, but nothing came forth. Her eyes widened as she was wheeled away. Her gaze never left Emily.

Beth and Emily stood before their chief supervisor. Eugenia's hands were clamped onto her hips, her head cocked. Emily stepped up to her.

"Miss Temple, why are Charity's clothes so dirty and her hair matted like that?" she asked.

Eugenia looked genuinely pained. Her eyes misted.

"How many times I've offered to brush her hair," she said and pursed her lips together. "She refuses my help. It just kills me that I can't assist her. At least not yet. She doesn't trust us yet.''

Emily nodded.

''We don't force, we only offer gentle suggestions,'' Eugenia said. ''I've tried to tempt Charity to take a soothing hot bath. As you can see, she prefers to go around looking unkempt. I dare say our gentle approach has its down side, at least as far as appearances go. Yet, if we sent the poor dear off to a state mental hospital . . .''

Emily looked on sympathetically. It clearly hurt Eugenia to explain this.

Eugenia's voice had trailed off. Her pursed lips trembled. She took a breath. ''No, she's not going off to a mental institution at her age; she's staying here, messy or not. This is her home!''

''That's right,'' one of the nurses said.

''Mm-hm,'' said another.

''I hope this hasn't left you with the wrong impression, Emily,'' Eugenia said in a pleasant tone of voice, her confidence returning.

Emily shook her head. ''No, now I understand,'' she said.

''The residents here come first. Their care and safety are our primary concern. Rest assured we have few fatal falls here at the Hamilton Home. And no one ever died of knotted hair.'' She smiled. ''Thank you for your help today, Emily. We're so happy to have you with us. Things are going to work out splendidly.''

Eugenia and a few of the nurses left through a door that led to the business offices.

From the hallway, Emily saw two formidable older

male orderlies looking at her, and at Beth. One, the menacing-looking thug with a crop of thick black hair, had a cigar in his mouth, unlit. He was the one Emily had seen outside, from a distance. He wore a leer on his fat face.

"Let's get out of here," Beth whispered.

They walked from the main entrance to the back service door, where a trail led to the caretaker's house. This house was a sizable white-frame affair, modest next to the behemoth that was the Hamilton Home. Eugenia and Herbert Temple lived there.

The early evening air was crisp and pleasant. Clouds hung like gray strands of smoke against the purple sky. A few stars twinkled. Emily could see the lights of the white BMW, where Patrick, her father, was waiting.

"Here's my number," Beth said, pressing a piece of paper into Emily's hand. "I'm outta here."

The classroom was barely a quarter full at six P.M. when the instructor, Gloria Munson, called the ragtag group of young students to order.

Emily had been dropped off by her father, who promised to be back in an hour. They'd stopped for burgers at the A & W, and Emily had told her father about the weird events of the day.

"Think you'll be able to stick it out?" he'd said, wiping ketchup from his graying beard.

She'd turned to him and, not for the first time since she'd arrived in Wisconsin, felt a cold pool of anxiety spread through her chest. She suppressed it as best she could and took a deep breath.

"Of course I will," she'd answered.

And though she'd been feeling somewhat disturbed

by the lost souls at Hamilton Home, she felt a certain affection for them. This surprised her. She'd long considered herself mature, a young woman. But in contrast to the aged human beings she'd seen today, and the lives these people were essentially forced to live, she felt she'd not lived much at all.

Now, sitting in this big classroom, she felt a pair of eyes boring into her back. She turned to see a young man staring, a big-eyed boy with a head of wavy brown hair. He sported neat sideburns, and wore a blue-plaid shirt, open, with a white T-shirt beneath it. When he saw her looking back, he blushed and looked away.

This muscular jock was too clean-cut for words, Emily thought. But handsome in an odd way. He had a low forehead, full lips, and a strong chin.

She turned away and looked down at her blank notebook. She felt a mixture of embarrassment and what she had to admit was a dash of vanity. Around Blackburn County, where everybody knew everybody, she knew she would be cast in the role of the "the new girl," whether she liked it or not. Naturally she'd be noticed. Especially with the way she dressed: leather jacket, clunky black shoes, urban. Different from most of the farm kids.

The classroom quieted down.

Gloria Munson had slightly graying dark hair, loosely tied back. She wore a black sweater and jeans. Her figure was trim, athletic. Emily imagined Gloria a brilliant scientist, a refugee from the big city, like her, only from Boston or New York. East, not west. In this fantasy, Gloria had come to northern Wisconsin to live in the country, miles from the secret underground factories where the government had paid her to build bombs, Emily concocted. Now she was living a simpler life.

The reality was only a little different. Gloria told the class a bit about herself. Emily soon learned that Gloria was actually from Madison, where she'd grown up. She was divorced. No kids. She and her ex-husband had founded a genetics research firm, where they engineered the creation of juicier oranges and spicier tomatoes.

"I got tired of fooling Mother Nature," Gloria told the class, a wry smile on her face.

She liked teaching, she said. But mainly she liked the solitude of the rural north. "And raising horses," she added. "It's my passion. At the semester break, this winter, you're all invited out to my farm. Sleigh rides, cider, ice skating by torchlight on the pond, the whole bit."

"What, no beer?" someone said.

Gloria laughed along with the others. Emily looked back and saw the smiling wise guy who'd made comment; he was sitting next to the handsome guy who'd been looking at her earlier. This one was a curly haired blonde.

"If you're twenty-one, it's entirely up to you," Gloria said. Nearly everyone groaned. Of course the class was composed mostly of Leonora High School seniors, most of whom were still seventeen or eighteen.

Emily's eyes met with the guy's again. Neither smiled. She turned her attention back to her teacher.

"So, let's begin," Gloria said, and she wrote the name GREGOR MENDEL on the blackboard. She then drew crude stems with leaves attached.

"Pea plants," Gloria said. "Copy them into your notebooks; they're very important to the study of genes."

Emily forgot, at least for a while, about the boy with the sideburns. She poured herself into the lecture, concentrating on the figures and diagrams that filled the board, were erased, filled the board again, and vanished in clouds of chalk dust as the night wore on.

At the end of class, Emily gathered up her coat and went to speak with Gloria. She was asking about a problem when she felt someone else's presence.

It was the guy with the sideburns again. Emily felt mildly annoyed, but seeing him up close also confirmed to her how attractive he was. They looked briefly at one another, then away.

Gloria went on at length, answering Emily's question, and when she was finished, the room was empty except for Emily, Gloria, and the guy with the sideburns.

"I see," said the guy next to her, as Gloria finished her comments. He repeated much of what Gloria had been explaining. "The theorem is thus. . . ." he said. He was trying to impress the teacher, Emily thought. She was embarrassed for him.

Gloria smiled. "I don't believe I got your name," she said to him.

"Kerry. Kerry Thornton," he said. He smiled nervously at Emily. He extended his hand to Gloria and then to her.

Emily smiled and shook his hand, which felt too warm. Kerry was showing off. He hadn't needed to repeat Gloria's lecture to her.

"And you are . . .?" Kerry said.

"Really late," Emily said with a smile. "My father's waiting for me."

Patrick cleared his throat.

Gloria looked at up Patrick, whose large frame filled the doorway. Emily smiled at him. He was wearing his small, wire-framed glasses and a long black leather coat. He looked like a German spy from an old movie.

"We won't keep her any longer," Gloria said pleasantly. She turned to her students. "I hope I've answered all your questions sufficiently, Kerry—and Emily. If not, my home number is on the class syllabus, stapled to the last page of your first assignment. I've got to be going home now, too. My poor dogs must be about to burst their bladders."

She took her coat from the closet and put on her big floppy black hat. Emily followed her out as Kerry grabbed his coat and backpack.

"'Bye, Emily," was the last thing she heard as she left the classroom. She turned and glanced back at Kerry. He tried to smile. He wore a letter jacket.

It all seemed so corny and innocent. What did he know about a young woman like Emily? He could never have guessed in a million years all she'd been through. It was hopeless. Yet she found herself waving, mouthing, "Good-bye."

At home Patrick had a fire going. From the CD player, Miles Davis's horn wove its way into the brightly lit room. Emily loved her father's house. It was beautiful—in some ways rustic like a cabin; in others, a designer's Prairie school-influenced dream, composed of cedar and glass, elegantly and sparsely decorated.

Navaho rugs were draped over chairs and hung on the wall next to African masks and Native American spirit dolls.

The living room, where Patrick and Emily were relaxing after Emily's first day of work at the home, had an impressive cathedral ceiling. One room spanned into another, to a large kitchen, a den with a satellite-fed TV, and a plant-festooned breakfast nook by a high bay window.

Emily lay on the big white sectional sofa. She wore a large, baggy sweatshirt and faded navy-blue sweatpants. Blue, Patrick's golden retriever, lay on the floor beside her, occasionally licking her hand for attention.

She sipped kiwi juice with mineral water, having just finished a grilled-chicken sandwich Patrick had made for her, along with marinated vegetables on the side. He was going to extremes to please her, she thought. And she was enjoying it.

"I'm dead tired," she said and yawned with a smile.

"But you keep moving," Patrick said. He stood at his easel, where a small lamp was clipped, brightly illuminating the paper. In his hand he held a pencil, the point of which he touched to a portrait he'd just composed, to the lips, which he darkened.

"I'm not moving at all," she said. "I'm the world's best model." She kicked her legs and waved her arms like a dancer. The couch squeaked beneath her. Then she jumped to her feet.

"I'm Audrey Hepburn," she said. "In *Funny Face*." She walked down an imaginary runway. Then she dropped to her hands and knees. She moved her hands across the plush gray carpet, and looked off blankly into some hazy distance. "Now I'm Audrey in *Wait Until Dark*."

Patrick chuckled. But then he frowned at the picture.

"What?" Emily said, going back to the sofa for a swig of juice.

"It's not right," he said.

"Oh, Dad. Maybe if you weren't such a perfectionist . . ." But she let her voice trail off. Maybe what? Maybe everything would have been a lot different in their lives?

He snorted, rubbing away a line with a soft, gummy eraser. She came over to look at the picture.

"Christ," Emily said. "You make me look like a little kid. What's with the big eyes?"

"The eyes . . . I thought it was the mouth I'd screwed up."

Emily grabbed the portrait from the easel.

"Hey," Patrick said. "Be careful with that."

"You know what?" Emily said. "I think you still see me as a little girl. That kid in New York."

He took a reflective draft from his green bottle of beer.

"You can't see me as an adult," Emily said.

"You *are* my little girl," he said, looking at the picture. His glasses had slipped a bit, toward the end of his nose.

She handed the portrait back to him. He considered it; then to her surprise he crumpled it up. He let it fall to the floor. "Let's try again," he said. She watched her father carefully. His eyes retained their sadness. Something resigned about them. Emily wanted suddenly, desperately, to see him happy.

"I remember when you used to draw me in that tiny little apartment in the Village," Emily said.

He started sketching in a few lines. "Yes, I remember it, too. I hope you don't think I'm trying to live in the past. I know we've both changed."

She thought of the ordeal they'd been through in the past month. How he'd come to her rescue, arranged for her to move to Wisconsin with him, after all these years. How he'd tearfully confessed to her his own history of drug problems, cocaine, in his case.

Emily looked at the crumpled ball of paper on the floor. She picked it up. Then she walked to the fireplace, which had died down to hot red embers. She dropped the paper onto the coals. It just sat there, refusing to burn.

She turned to see her father's reaction, but he looked away, as if absorbed in the new sketch. Another sketch of her, she saw, when she came over to his easel.

This drawing was more abstract. He was creating it in violent, swift strokes. But she recognized her unsmiling face. It was turned upward in a somewhat defiant gesture. She liked it. Despite herself she sighed, and it turned into a yawn.

"I'm really tired," she said. "Will you forgive me if I turn in a little early?"

"Of course, honey," he said. He continued to make black strokes on the paper, this time making her hair a violent mess that, she felt, must be the way he saw her now.

The more violent, weird strokes he added, the less it resembled Emily. The other portrait, now perilously close to the flames in the fireplace, had been in some ways a better likeness. As if sensing her disapproval, he put his pencil down and stood back. She kissed him goodnight on the cheek.

Emily climbed the short flight of stairs. At the top she listened as her father put away his paper and his easel. She saw the last lights go out. She went to "her" room, decorated especially for her, closed the door, undressed, slipped on a big T-shirt, and lay down on the sleigh bed of blond pine.

She took some deep breaths, thinking about the strange, beautiful room she was in, trying to imagine ever thinking of this place as home.

Home.

Of course, thoughts of San Francisco—her real home—led to thoughts of Danny.

Once she'd thought he was beautiful, in spirit as well as in his physical nature. They'd met and become lovers three years ago. A sense of heaviness pooled in her chest. For a moment she thought she might even cry.

"I'm tough," she said, closing her eyes, settling her head on the smooth pillow. She slid over onto her side, enjoying the sensation of cool, clean sheets in a strange bed. She was not going to cry. Country stars twinkled over a country landscape outside her window.

She sighed. "I'm a girl with a past."

Patrick Jordan's living room was almost black, devoid of life. The embers of the fire glowed like a miniature landscape of hell. Amid the glowing ruins, something stirred. The balled-up portrait of Emily, blackened but not consumed, began to open, as a rosebud opens in a time-lapse film. The fire glowed through the paper, which whitened, revealing the drawing. Flames licked behind the wrinkled face and wrinkled features of the girl. The portrait rose over the hot coals and burst into flames.

Miles away, the stately old Hamilton Home for the Aged faded in and out of the night like a colossal blot through thick milky-blue fog. All that emerged on the hillside for a lonely passerby on the highway below to gaze up at was the faintest impression of a hulking mansion. As if sketched ethereally by a sidewalk picture artist in chalk and pastels, the mansion seemed more spectre than real, its distant rows of glowing yellow windows illumined through the gauzy brew of night and mist.

On the third floor of the home, the hallways were empty and nearly black. Outside the closed doors, canes rested against the walls. An empty wheelchair by a window shone with glints of fog-muted moonlight.

Behind a locked door, strapped to a narrow bed, Charity Francis, aged and pain racked, was coming out of a deep, drug-induced sleep. Her matted hair covered most of her face. A dream had consumed her sleep, as fire consumes paper. And as she woke, she strained with her body and her mind against the straps that held her fast. But the straps wouldn't budge.

Into her imagination came a face, the face of a girl, looming before her, golden but taking on the dimensions of real flesh. Black hair and flame-blue eyes, curving lips—features that were strangely familiar.

The girl.

Emily Jordan.

Chapter Two

Kerry opened his locker with a crash of metal. Then he hopped onto the bench and stretched wide his arms and yawned with a smile. "Do you believe in love at first sight, Joe?" he said.

"Of course not," Joe said with a snort. He'd been listening all through gym class to his friend go on and on about the new girl in town. He sat down beside his friend on the bench and untied his gym shoes. "Get real. How can you really fall in love someone you don't even know? Physical attraction—that I can understand. But love? You have no idea who she really is."

"But I feel as though I do . . . like I've been waiting for her all my life."

Joe rolled his eyes. This conversation was too much for him. Love and romance were, in his skeptical view, just a silly spin on the biological hard wiring that made all guys lusting robots.

Kerry was still dressed in his gym shorts, while most of the other guys in the locker room were already undressed and heading to the showers. He sat beside Joe on the bench in front of the row of lockers.

"This is just like last year," Joe said, "when you had the hots for Sue Cates, and the year before, when you swore you were in love with Cheri Freund," Joe said.

"This is different. Those girls wouldn't even look at me," Kerry said, pulling his shirt off.

"Of course not. Why do you always fall for upper-classmen?"

Kerry worked his shoes off, toe to heel. "This time I'm not. This time I'm falling for a total stranger—a real brain, by the way." He stared off into the distance. "I've got to get to know her. Body and soul."

Joe wrapped a towel around his waist. "A brain, huh? She doesn't sound like the type who'd be very impressed by your wrestling trophies."

"How would you know?" Kerry said.

"I know more about her than you think."

Kerry pulled off his shorts and jockstrap, and wrapped a towel around his waist. He and Joe walked to the shower together. The sound of water raining down hard on tile echoed through the locker room.

Kerry stepped into the steamy communal shower. The hot blast of water felt good over his head and back.

"What do you mean, you *know* about Emily?" Kerry shouted to his friend.

Joe's blond curls were matted down with water. He squeezed a green gooey glob of shampoo into his hand.

"Beth Hanes works with her at the Hamilton Home," Joe said. "She happened to tell me about the new girl in town. Putting two and two together, I figured it out."

"An aide at an old folks home," Kerry said wistfully. "Kind, generous, caring. She'd be good at that," he said.

"You don't even know where she's from."

"Well, where's she from?"

"San Francisco. But her dad lives here."

Kerry nodded. He rinsed off and stepped out of the shower, drying himself. He kept thinking of Emily. Maybe love was a strong word. Maybe she'd be frightened off knowing he was going on about her, talking with friends, acting like some sort of nut.

"What I really want is to be friends with her," Kerry said, drying himself off in front of his locker. "For starters, I mean. To get to know her."

"That's a crock," Joe said.

"*Best* friends," Kerry said, not checking to see the reaction in Joe's eyes.

Later that morning, Kerry strolled into the school library, books under his arm, and he looked around for Beth Hanes. He'd never known her well, despite growing up with her in a small community and having her in several classes ever since kindergarten. She hung out with a different group than he did, a more bookish crowd, yet one with a slight antisocial bent to it.

But Leonora High was a small school in a small town. Out of a few thousand townspeople, Beth's face was naturally familiar, as were the faces of her siblings and even her parents. At last he spotted her among the book stacks. She stood in front of a shelf at the far wall of the library, the industry and sciences section. Beth wore ripped blue jeans and a faded blue cotton work shirt, untucked. Her long red hair was loosely pulled back in a ponytail.

"Hi," Kerry said, positioning himself directly in front of her.

Beth blinked and looked up from an oversize book she'd been paging through, a picture book of the buildings designed by the architect Louis Sullivan. "Oh. Hi," she said.

"I hear you have a new friend," Kerry said. "At the Hamilton Home."

The librarian, a blue-haired older woman in white-frame cat's-eye glasses put her finger over her mouth and shushed him.

"Sorry," Kerry whispered. Now he whispered to Beth. "Emily."

"Who?" Beth said, as though she couldn't quite hear him. "Emily? . . . Emily . . . Oh! Emily Jordan. I hear you're desperately hot for her."

Kerry swallowed, and he could feel his face filling with blood. "I guess rumors travel fast."

"Guess so. Emily and I have only just met, actually. I guess you want to be my friend now, too." She turned, looking at a row of books lined up on a shelf. Her eyes scanned over the call numbers. "My, what a friendly little town this has become."

"Maybe you could just give Emily a message."

Beth turned and looked at him. "What is this, Cyrano De Bergerac? Won't you see her at the tech school?"

Kerry sighed. "Okay, if you're really that offended, forget it." He turned to leave.

"Wait a minute."

He turned and saw that Beth was looking at him. She was a serious looking girl, he noted. A lot more mature than many of his friends. Of course, he'd never really noticed much about her before, never even looked at her twice. She was, he thought, strangely pretty. But then, he was suddenly noticing beauty in all sorts of unexpected places. Was he really in love?

"I only want to get to know her better," he said. "I'm not a bad guy. I think she would benefit from knowing me."

What had he just said? It had come out wrong.

She laughed. "That's the most conceited thing I've ever heard anyone say."

He felt defensive immediately. Then he felt embarrassed, and a little angry, too.

"Look, Beth. Just forget it."

"No, wait a minute. Don't go. What's the message? Maybe you should try for something sort of specific."

"Tell her I'd like to know if she'd see me some time."

Beth rolled her eyes. "More specific."

Kerry gulped. Why was this so difficult?

"You'll see her at class three nights a week," Beth said. "Come on. Just ask it. Where and when."

Where, he wondered, did Beth get all her knowledge about dating?

"Tell her we should all do something together this weekend," he said. "Saturday! You and me and Emily and some of the other guys. We'll go out driving, maybe see a movie. We could get some beer and go to the Hamilton Hill graveyard."

"Not bad." Beth said. The Hamilton Hill cemetery was a favorite place for lovers and partiers—despite its proximity to the home. It commanded a great view of the valley and the stars. Beth picked up her backpack. "We accept." She started for the door.

"Hey, wait a minute," Kerry called after her.

The librarian emitted another loud *shssh*.

"Sorry," Kerry said. Beth was out the door by the time he looked back across the room for her.

Emily sat back on a big flat rock that jutted out of the grass, near her father's cedar-and-glass house, and puffed on a cigarette. She was wearing jeans and boots, a white shirt, and her leather jacket, though the sun had warmed the ground enough this morning for her to discard it. She shook it off.

"Come along, Emily," Josh Webster called. Webster was a tall, slim handyman and gardener in his sixties. He'd farmed the land he and his wife lived on, some forty acres to the west, bordering the Jordan property. For the past four years he'd managed properties and tended to the real estate owned by newcomers and quasi-newcomers such as Patrick Jordan. He was a kind-faced cowboy, and Emily instantly liked him.

She crossed the yard to the flat open parcel of the Jordan spread (as some called the three-hundred-acre property). A gravel drive wound its way out to the highway. Weeping willows shaded the yard and the steep path uphill up to the barn.

Emily felt exhilarated this morning. The view was spectacular. The cool September air was clear and golden lit, and high above the tree-lined hills a few majestic clouds drifted slowly across the hard blue sky.

"Did you sleep well?" Webster asked. He opened the gate inside the barn where the horse, a golden palomino named Amber, snorted expectantly. The shaded barn was at least ten degrees cooler than the sunny lawn, and Emily felt the drop in temperature as she walked in.

Webster dipped a plastic bucket into a bag of oats, and the mare clopped over for an eager munch.

"Straight though the night," Emily said. She came over to stroke Amber's muscled neck and felt the horse's blast of exhalation though its nostrils. Amber's ears flickered back, and she looked at Emily with huge liquid brown eyes.

"I found a litter of kittens over there the other day," Webster said, pointing. "Fine, healthy babies, long as their papa don't find them."

"Can I take a look?" Emily said.

"Sure. Follow me."

Emily stepped over the slats of the floor. She passed a window with a magnificent view of the house.

Emily looked beneath a dilapidated old dresser, stored in a dark corner of the barn. Sawdust had been shored up around a black female cat with a white patch around one eye. Kittens suckled at her nipples. She mewed at Webster and Emily.

Emily counted seven kittens. Four were as black as their mother. Two were striped. One, a particularly fat-bellied fellow, was orange.

"I'll have to ask Dad if he'd like a new house pet," Emily said. Then she added, "I didn't hear Dad get up."

"Well, that's not unusual," Webster said. "He's an early riser."

Patrick always rose at about four-thirty each morning, Emily knew. Weather permitting, he conducted his usual routine. After only a few days, she knew it by heart. He told her it seldom varied. At sunup, he went for a jog up the gravel road, dressed in sweats. When he returned, he worked out with weights in the room he called his gym, in the basement. Then he changed into his paint-spattered pants and sweatshirt, and went up to the attic studio.

By that time the sun would have crawled up over the hills and ridges above the valley. Light would filter though the white parachute silk affixed over the sky-lights in Patrick's studio, spilling over the still life of flowers and paint cans and oddments discovered around the spread. A creature of habit, Patrick Jordan painted each morning until about eleven. If the weather held, he'd have his coffee outside, with a newspaper, or he'd visit with Webster. If it was raining he'd sit in the kitchen.

It was almost eleven now. Emily thought of heading back to the house to see him. Amber snorted. High above her head, light shone through the slats of the old roof. Barn swallows had built a nest on one of the crossbeams.

"This old barn could use some work," Webster said, looking up at the roof. "Are you handy with a hammer? Afraid of heights?"

"I could learn to use a hammer," Emily said. "But I don't much care for heights." She was wondering about her father's progress, up at the house.

When a painting was finished—and Patrick's paint-ings were big and could take months—it would be wrapped in plastic and stacked with others in a storage room, off the studio. Patrick had a lot of artwork stored in this storage room, which was big and windowless. He had cabinets with rows of thin drawers, and the drawings and sometimes paintings of dozens of artists, collected over the years, were stored there. Other paintings and drawings were framed and displayed on walls all over the house.

Once a year—sometimes more often, occasionally less—a truck would come to the farm, and the paintings would be carefully loaded on board by shippers and driven to Patrick's agent and art dealer in New York City. Patrick would board a plane shortly thereafter, and attend an opening of his work. In fact, a showing of his work was planned for later in the fall.

Happily, sales had been steady and lucrative, after years of struggle. Patrick had every reason to be happy. He was, Emily knew, quite set in his ways, and they were not bad ways. He was also, however, alone, except for Webster and Webster's wife and Blue and Amber and the guernsey cow, who grazed the yard along with Amber and whose name was Sally.

Emily followed Webster back to where the horse waited, neighing for more oats. Emily obliged, filling her hand with the oats. Amber's powerful neck strained as she gently chewed.

Webster had given Emily a few tasks, one of which was feeding Amber her oats. He apologized several times for giving Emily these chores, as if he was forced to be some kind of slave driver. But she kept assuring him that she'd wanted some work to do around the "farm," as she called it. It was hardly a farm. Patrick kept a small garden. His "salad garden." That was the extent of the Jordans' farming.

"You have enough work to do with your schooling," Webster said, walking beside her through the tall grass that led to the orchard. In the orchard were dwarf apple trees, dozens of them. They looked to Emily as gnarled as the collection of ancient residents at the old Hamilton Home. The apples they collected were small and hard and tart, their skins splashed a shiny green and blush red.

"I can handle hard work, Webster," Emily said.

Everyone called Josh Webster by his last name.

"And that Hamilton place," Webster said with a wince. "That's no place for a pretty young girl to spend her time." He spat tobacco juice on the ground. "Hell, that's no place for anybody. I hope when I die—many years from now, God willing—that I go quick. Wouldn't want to linger on there as some folks do."

Emily bit into a tart apple. "It's mostly women who linger on at places like the Hamilton Home," Emily said. "We live longer than men, but it hardly seems worth it for some of us."

"Don't I know it. I wished we could'a kept my own mama at our place," Webster said. Emily heard the sadness in his voice. "She ended up at the Hamilton Home, and she was right miserable there. I tried to get her out, near the end of her life. I had a terrible time doing it. That woman runs the place, she put up a fight. Miss Eugenia Temple."

"Eugenia Temple is the one who helped Dad get me my job at the home," Emily said. "She takes her job seriously."

"My mama died before I could bring her home. That was in 1959."

Emily almost choked on her apple. "Temple has been there that long? What, she started as a teenager?"

"She seemed old even back then. Something strange and cold about her, and about that weird brother of hers."

Emily shrugged. "I've already seen some sad things at the home, but I've been warned to expect it." They approached the house. Patrick was sitting out at the picnic table in the yard, sipping coffee from a steaming mug.

"This community is too full of strange things, Emily," Webster said. "Be careful."

"Don't tell Dad," Emily said. "He thinks Blackburn County is heaven."

"I thought so once, too," Webster said. "I grew up around here, you know. I expect to die here, on these lands. But not up on that goddamn hill."

Patrick looked up from his day-old *New York Times*. "Good morning," he said. "How's the new hand working out?"

"Right capable," Webster said.

Emily sat down next to her father, and he smiled at her.

"Have an apple?" she said, and he took one of the tiny apples and bit into it. She could see from his expression he found it sour. But he chewed it up and swallowed.

After his break, Patrick disappeared again into his studio. Emily spent the rest of the morning studying her genetics text. Then she read for a while from a novel called *Giovanni's Room* by James Baldwin, which she had been given by a friend, Tony, before she left San Francisco.

Thinking of San Francisco reminded her it was about time to call her mother.

The receptionist at the Cathleen Jordan law office put Emily on hold for two minutes before asking Emily who she wanted to speak with. That happened a lot.

It was a busy little office. Emily never pulled rank on the secretaries. She just politely asked to be put through to Cathleen. Two out of three times she called she actually got right through. She never left messages.

"Baby, I was wondering when you'd call me."

"You're not that easy to reach," Emily answered.

"Sorry, snookums."

Cathleen had what she called "endearments" for people. She had trunks of them.

"Listen, honeyplum, are you hating it?"

"The farm? No, I actually like it a lot."

"I still think the whole deal was a farce. The 'war on drugs' my ass! I could'a got you off, sweetie. Who says mothers can't defend their daughters in a court of law? I think it would have gone beautifully."

"Mom, I could have ended up in prison. Would you have wanted that hanging over your head?"

"But you're innocent! It was guilt by association. So help me, if I ever see that Danny bastard again, I'll pull every lock of hair from his head!" The tone of her voice shifted dramatically to a conspiratorial whisper. "You don't still have a *thing* for him, do you?"

Emily sighed. "I don't think so, no."

"Good! Then the therapy helped."

"Yes, Mom. The therapy, the money—it all helped!"

"I shudder to think what might have become of you dear if . . . What—I'm on the—Huh? Emmy, sweetheart, can you hold a minute? I swear to God . . ." She often trailed off in the middle of a sentence. Emily was switched to "hold." After a while the clicking in her ear stopped, and Cathleen came back.

"So . . . where were we? Are you keeping yourself busy?" Cathleen asked.

"I've already started the community service job, you'll be happy to know," Emily said.

"Just stay the hell away from nightclubs. Nightclubs are your downfall, Emily. They were almost my downfall, too. Look what they did to your father. He's not still sniffing coke, is he? Wait, I didn't mean that. Gads. If the judge had gotten one whiff, so to speak, of Patrick's history—poof! His whole scheme to get you to Wisconsin would have vanished."

"Daddy's been great, and as for nightclubs . . . there isn't one for miles." Emily switched the phone to her other ear. "Listen, I just wanted to say hi. I really have to run now."

There was a pause before Cathleen cleared her throat. "I miss you, hon."

"Yeah, I miss you, too. But things are going to work out. I know it."

"Oh, I hope so, pickle."

The afternoon was consumed with wanderings. Webster was off doing his work, driving away from the property in his old Ford truck, returning, leaving again. Emily picked a switch from a young hickory tree and with Blue walked to the rolling hills above the fields of dry yellow corn.

It was a beautiful day, and the view from the hilltop was majestic. Blue sat at her feet and panted.

Sometimes Emily wondered why her father had never remarried. Cathleen had married again for a time. A guy named Bart. Emily had actually liked him. He was funny. He was a banking executive in San Francisco but had pretensions to a more bohemian lifestyle. Bart played clarinet in a jazz band. Cathleen had always loved jazz, the more abstract the better.

Cathleen's marriage to Bart didn't last long. Emily hadn't been terribly surprised the day she came home and Cathleen told her Bart was moving out. By that time Cathleen had owned her own house on Russian Hill for several years; Bart had never sold his Corona Heights condo. It was like he knew he'd need a safety net to fall into.

Emily scratched Blue behind the ears. The young dog looked up and licked Emily's hand. As sweet a gesture of acceptance as she could have hoped for on this pristine fall day.

When she tired of watching clouds drift by, she rose and brushed the dry grass from her pants. Blue stretched, then followed her home.

Later in the day, Emily came back to her room and took a shower in the bathroom located conveniently off her new bedroom. She dressed in a clean pair of jeans and a dark blue T-shirt. Then she had a cigarette and read James Baldwin for a while.

When it was almost time for Beth to pick her up, as arranged, Emily tiptoed up to her father's studio. Schubert's Eighth Symphony boomed majestically from the CD player.

Deep in thought, Patrick took several seconds to look up from his painting, having finally sensed another's presence in the room. He smiled at her.

"It's beautiful," Emily said, coming closer to the big canvas. Bursts of dazzling fresh color, ultramarine and aqua, put her in mind of some fantastic seascape.

"It's coming along, all right," he answered. He was wearing old black-framed glasses, and he slipped them off. He rubbed his moist, red-rimmed eyes with a single paint-free finger.

"I'm headed out," Emily said.

"Are you sure you don't me to drive you?" he asked.

She shrugged. She knew he would have preferred to.

"Hey, I'm making friends," Emily said. "Good, clean friends."

"Oh, what a bore. Maybe you'll meet some good dirty friends." He waved paint smeared fingers at her as she descended the stairs. "Wait," he suddenly said, reaching into his pocket. He pulled out his wallet and handed her some bills.

She felt slightly awkward. She wasn't sure why. She'd always accepted money from him before.

"Dad, you already gave me fifty dollars the day before yesterday. There's nothing to spend money on around here."

"Keep it with you anyway," Patrick said. "Really, I insist."

A car horn sounded. Beth had arrived.

"What, she's not coming in?" Patrick asked. "Don't tell me she's too shy to meet your family."

"She seems pretty fearless to me. How about I invite her in next time?"

On the way to the car, Emily looked at the money he'd handed her, quickly counting thirty dollars. She noticed a streak of fresh red paint over Abraham Lincoln's face.

✳   ✳   ✳

Beth drove Emily to the home for the evening shift. The drive should have been soothing; the scenery was splendid. But it wasn't pleasant knowing you were going to a place like the Hamilton Home, even if you could leave again in six hours. The days were getting shorter, and the woods and fields seemed strangely somber to Emily. The trees were mostly green. But a hint of inevitable winter was in the air. The failing light, the slight chill, and a smell of dry leaves were all impressed upon the strangely spooky atmosphere.

Emily decided to ask Beth about Kerry. He had, she admitted to herself, been on her mind.

"Kerry . . . do I know a Kerry?" Beth said. "Oh, of course, Kerry Thornton." She smacked herself on the head.

"That's the one."

"So, you met him?"

"Yeah, in my genetics class."

"He's really cute, wouldn't you say?" Beth swerved to avoid a chipmunk.

Emily put her hand up on the dash as the car zipped back into its lane. "He's kind of cute. I'm not sure he's my type."

"But you're a little bit interested, right?."

"Minimally interested."

Beth cracked up. "I suppose I should tell you," she said, amid her giggles. "It's all over school."

"What?"

"Kerry has a major crush on you, but of course he's not really admitting it yet. Listen, this is a small community. Gossip travels like wildfire."

"But it's not even gossip yet. Nothing's happened."

"Not yet, anyway," Beth said.

They entered the sloping drive that led up to the home, and Emily looked at the forbidding redbrick facade. As they drove up to the little parking lot, Beth told Emily that Kerry was a "great catch," with lots of potential girlfriends, though he'd yet to choose one.

"He's chosen you," Beth said. "You could do worse."

Emily didn't like the sound of that, somehow. She would do the choosing if any choosing were to be done. And she wasn't at all sure Kerry was the choice she'd make. Even as a friend, much less . . . much more.

Inside, Emily and Beth signed in at the workers' station, then donned their white jackets. Patti, Maxine, and Laverne were waddling around, and Patti waddled over to hand Emily a name tag.

"Wear it with pride," Patti said, a frown on her face. Her blond hair shimmered in a glaze of hair spray.

Emily affixed her name tag to her jacket.

Checking her list of tasks, she entered the community room and came upon a strange scene. Something was wrong. A man was bent over one of the patients, who was crying inconsolably.

The man turned and gave Emily a nerdy, sympathetic smile. It hardly seemed to be any time for smiles, Emily thought. He wore a shiny name tag.

His name was Dr. Herbert Temple.

Dr. Temple wore a neatly pressed dark suit. A stethoscope dangled from his neck. His head was bald and smooth and gleamed under the light, which shone in his odd little round glasses.

"We haven't met," he said in a chirpy voice, and he extended a waxen hand. It was cold to the touch. Emily softly said her own name.

"Some of our residents drift in and out of hallucinations," Herbert said. Light flashed in those glasses as he nodded his head. Hazy light filtered in through the big bay windows. A TV flickered in one of the corners, where a group of old people sat in its sickly green glow. The sound was barely audible.

"Is there anything I can do?" Emily said, looking at the poor woman, who was the victim of a bad perm among other indignities. She was crying about someone.

"She was fine yesterday!" the old woman with the frizzled perm wailed.

"You didn't even know her, Miss Ellsen," Herbert said, a trace of annoyance in his voice. "What makes you think you're fit to judge her condition?" The woman seemed not to hear a word anyone uttered.

Herbert turned again to Emily.

"We lost a patient last night. Pulmonary embolism. It happens. In a place like this, you expect it. But there are people here who are pathologically fixated on death. Someone dies, and it terrifies them. So they find ways of involving themselves. To rationalize their response, I suppose."

"I loved her!" the woman wailed.

Herbert turned to the old woman again. "You barely knew Hazel Stern," Herbert said. "Come now. Pull yourself together."

Hazel Stern. The woman Emily had spoken with yesterday. Dead?

Herbert turned his face slowly to Emily. His eye-brows rose in an expression of sympathy. "See what I mean?" he whispered.

She knew the Hamilton Home line. Death. It's part of the job.

She turned away with a shudder.

Hazel Stern had been in distress yesterday, she knew. But she had been on her feet. And she'd been fighting mad. Today she was dead.

One of the male attendants, the one who always had an unlit cigar in his mouth, helped the poor old woman into a wheelchair, and wheeled her away.

"You must be brave, my girl," Herbert said, turning back to Emily. Again he gave her an appraising look.

"I'll try," Emily said. She turned away from his penetrating gaze. *I'm not your girl, butthead.*

She excused herself and went to a bathroom, closing the door behind her. She noticed that the lock on the door was broken. She splashed some water on her face.

Hazel Stern looked *fine* yesterday. She was upset about a missing resident. What was the name she mentioned?

Maria Kraus.

Emily closed the lid of the toilet and sat down on it. She took some deep breaths, telling herself that everything was going to be okay, not to jump to conclusions.

Someone pounded on the door, giving Emily a start. Emily jumped up, turned on the water in the sink, and opened the door a crack. It was Beth.

"God, you frightened me," Emily said.

"I saw you come in here," Beth said. "Is everything

all right?" She looked at her watch. "I think we'd better get moving. We have to help serve dessert in the cafeteria tonight."

Emily pulled Beth into the bathroom and closed the door. The bathroom was windowless. It had a chemical-cleaner smell.

"Did you hear about Hazel Stern?" Emily said.

"Yes. Awful."

"Awful? It's worse than that. She was on her feet the last time we saw her. She was fine."

"Emily, she wasn't fine. She had a bad heart. I didn't know her well, but you do pick up on these kinds of things. I could tell you the life expectancy of any number of the residents. Hazel was eighty-four with a bum ticker."

She reached out and gave Emily's shoulder a pat.

"What about that missing patient?" Emily said. "Maria. The one Hazel was asking for?"

Beth smiled. "I saw her on a roster this afternoon. Maria is recovering from some kind of operation. She was probably at the hospital, and Hazel just freaked out about it." She sighed. "Emily, I know it's not easy, but you've got to steel yourself a bit if you're going to survive here."

Emily closed her eyes and counted to ten. Maybe she was overreacting. That talk this afternoon with Webster. A strange new environment. And the ghoulish Dr. Temple.

"You're probably right," she said. "I'm not a wimp. I grew up in the in the big city, remember. You'd really be surprised how tough I am."

Beth smiled again. "I grew up in the sticks. I saw a pig butchered when I was five." She shrugged and grinned. "Life is strange. Why should death be any different?"

"It's just that I wasn't expecting . . ." Emily stopped. "I'm beginning to dislike this place," she said.

"Welcome to the club. But it beats jail, right?"

The cafeteria was alive with activity. Residents in bathrobes scooted in and out with their dinner trays. Emily helped serve ice cream to about seventy of them. Seeing them joylessly devouring the sweet dessert gave her a lump in her throat.

After supper, Beth and Emily folded towels in the laundry room. The smell of soap and clean fabric filled the air, and the steam from the washers raised the temperature and humidity. Emily felt thirsty.

Beth asked her if she was feeling better. Emily nodded. But she didn't feel exactly wonderful about being here. Hazel Stern was dead.

"You said the Temples are running some kind of money scam," Emily said. "Obviously they could get rid of residents who became suspicious, or whose families start asking questions?"

Beth shrugged. "I wouldn't doubt it," she said with a laugh. "But seriously, Blackburn County isn't exactly famous for crimes against its elderly citizens. It's the missing girls that people think of when they think of the crimes in our lovely community."

Emily held a warm folded towel to her cheek.

"Actually, the most recent person to disappear was a young mother named Jan Schmidt," Beth said. "That was two years ago. She just vanished. For two years you'd see signs in grocery-store windows with her face on them. But she never turned up. None of them ever turn up."

''How many have been missing?''

''I don't know. Maybe three since I was a kid. Maybe more before that. The disappearances don't happen that often, and people just seem to forget about them. They told us in junior high sex ed that the girls ran off to Milwaukee and became prostitutes and drug addicts. But that's probably bullshit. You know, people just can't think of their tranquil little county as anything but safe. It's lily white, there's not much crime—if you don't count the missing girls.''

Emily and Beth made plans to see Kerry and some of his friends that weekend. Kerry would pick them up in his Mustang. It was understood that this wasn't really a date, just a group outing.

''I feel like I might be making a mistake,'' Emily said. ''Leading Kerry on, you know?''

''Relax,'' Beth said, ''It's just a ride in a car.''

That settled it.

Near the end of their shift, Emily and Beth were taken to the kitchen by Patti and given sealed boxes to take to the caretaker's house, where Eugenia Temple lived with her brother, Herbert.

It was long past dark.

The cobblestone path wended from the Hamilton Home past the hidden part of the hill, where Emily could see the iron fence that surrounded the graveyard. The hilltop commanded a spectacular view of the valley. It was cloudy tonight, with rain expected before morning. The dew-covered hill shone with a silvery glister.

At the door of the house Herbert and Eugenia shared, Emily was greeted by yet another old woman. Despite her age, this woman had raven-black hair, pulled back fiercely and arranged in a tight bun on top of her head. She wore an apron. Her face was gaunt, her body skeleton thin.

"Hi, Gretta," Beth said.

"Good evening," Gretta answered. "It won't be necessary for you to come in; just leave the boxes on the steps." From inside came a crash of plates, and the sound of shouting, muffled by walls and ceilings. Gretta anxiously looked inside, then turned to Beth and Emily. Beth made introductions, but Gretta did not offer her hand. She bowed her head slightly instead. Another roar came from somewhere in the house. Emily glanced at Beth.

"Thank you for making the delivery," Gretta said "You must go now."

She closed the door, leaving them to return to the home.

"Bizarre," Beth said.

"Yeah. And then some."

Inside the caretaker's house, Gretta moved quietly on tiptoe through the gloom. The room was furnished with tasteful antiques, photographs in ornate frames, glass bric-a-brac. The lighting was kept uncomfortably low, so much so that Gretta feared she was losing her eyesight.

The quarrel upstairs showed no signs of waning. Gretta went to the kitchen. She closed the door behind her, checking to be sure it was secure.

Up the dark stairs, the voices grew louder.

"You grow more paranoid with every passing year, Eugenia," Herbert said. "I've come to expect it from you. But now you're getting a little out of hand." He was wearing a white sleeveless undershirt. His arms were muscular, and the veins stood out on them. He was seated in a shiny-leather wing chair the color of eggplant, a glass of brandy on the table at his side. The bottle next to it was nearly empty.

Eugenia paced the floor, still in her usual uniform: a dark jacket and skirt, white blouse, and a strand of pearls. "I've made too many mistakes in my life to *not* be worried," she said gravely.

Herbert was boiling a strange amber mixture on the flame of a small gas burner. Glass oddments stood like soldiers on a small table next to his shooting works. "Do you propose I commit an atrocity? A murder or two? Just what is it that you want, sister dear?"

"I only want my survival—*our* survival! And don't use petty words like 'murder.'"

"Poor Eugenia," he mocked. "Still a frightened little child."

She crossed her arms over her chest and paced the room. "It's Charity Francis. She's got me spooked. It's as though something at the home has changed in the past few days. I'm terribly concerned I'm losing my grip."

Herbert outstretched his arm and wrapped a length of yellow rubber tubing around it. He made a fist. "She is powerless," he said. "She's a madwoman, a homeless drifter. Don't be daft."

"A drifter? She has a great deal of financial support," Eugenia said.

"Good, we always have to keep the funds up. Charity is valuable to us, as you know—with a good dose of sedative in her blood, mind you. And besides, she's well restrained. Helpless as a kitten."

Herbert aimed the syringe at a fat, blue, wormlike vein in his arm. He inserted the needle and sighed. A teardrop of red blood was extruded. The glowing amber liquid entered his veins.

"Almost the last," he said, unsticking the needle. He placed a square piece of gauze over the needle prick and crooked his arm.

Eugenia threw off her jacket and rolled up her sleeve. Herbert removed the rubber hose from his arm and handed it to Eugenia, who quickly worked it around her arm. She flexed and relaxed her hand repeatedly.

"Give it to me," she whispered.

He injected her.

When he was finished, he lay back in his shiny-leather wing chair, and he tasted his brandy. "Let's not argue any more about trivia," he said. "We are safe. That old hag is worthless to us. It's the young ones we ought to keep our focus on."

Eugenia's eyelids drooped. "We have to be careful."

"Yes, but we have to survive, as you just said. I see great possibilities with the new girl."

"I don't know. . . ." Eugenia said. "The little criminal could end up attracting outside attention if anything happened to her. Our situation here is perfect. We can't run again . . . we must remain hidden."

"And the fat girl," Herbert said, his tongue poking out, wetting his red lips.

"Yes . . ." Eugenia said, drifting off to a dream of moonlit tides. "Possibilities . . ."

"We're home free, Eugenia. We've known it for . . . for a long time. Calm yourself and just accept it."

Eugenia's shoulders relaxed, and she seemed to let go, easing back into her chair. The sound of her rapidly beating heart, so loud in her ears a moment ago, ceased. Color returned to her tired flesh. She looked at her brother, for whom the effects of the strange injection were visibly less dramatic.

"Charity Francis," Eugenia said, slurring her words. "I have a feeling she won't live too much longer."

Chapter Three

Emily soaked in a hot bath all afternoon, excitedly anticipating her evening out with Beth and Kerry. The weekend had arrived at last.

Like the rest of the house, the bathroom was elegant and spare in design. High ceilings with skylights let in plenty of mid-September light. Potted palms and fig trees thrived, lush and green against the white walls. The bathtub itself was big enough for two people. With the switch of a button, massaging jets of air pulsed through the water. Emily had played with that device for a while, then settled for calm, lilac-scented hot water. She paged through *Newsweek*.

Tonight was to be her first real outing since she'd come to Wisconsin. She and her father regularly went into Leonora for burgers or, occasionally, a big plate of spaghetti at the family-operated Italian restaurant. But going out with her father wasn't the same as really going *out*.

Patrick was a good cook who truly enjoyed preparing meals for his daughter. For him it seemed there was no pressing need to go much farther than the kitchen and the yard. He had his own perfect, self-contained world right here.

Emily was feeling that old excitement. She wanted to meet other people. She realized she was becoming quite attached to Beth. The days they didn't see each other at the home they had long conversations on the phone.

Beth was sure she wanted to go to San Francisco immediately after high school. College could wait. Madison could wait. Emily's homesick descriptions of the Bay, the hills, the rows of lovingly restored Victorian houses, with their exotic flower gardens and palm trees, aroused Beth's interest and curiosity.

Kerry was headed in his own direction—a straight line to Madison, where he said he wanted to study electrical engineering. His level head and good looks practically assured his success, Emily thought. He was bold and confident—or so he seemed during the first five minutes of any conversation. Yet he as often as not dissolved quickly in uncertainty, made lame jokes, or simply stared at her.

She knew—from Beth—he was from a humble, country background. Her own upbringing had been a wild swing from bohemian poverty in the late 1970s in New York to the lavish success that came from her father's sudden wealth as a hot, newly successful painter and her mother's thriving law practice.

Her mother had gone to law school in California after the divorce. Divorce had taught Cathleen about the power of the law, among other things, and she wanted to tap into that power source. Not that she had been screwed in the divorce proceedings. She had gotten a decent settlement from Patrick. He'd been so coked up at the time it was hard to say if he was being generous or just indifferent to his money. The lawyers for both parties made a killing.

Cathleen had been a painter, too, and it was her work as a commercial artist on Madison Avenue that had gotten the family through the hardest times in New York. Patrick had driven a cab, tended bar, unloaded trucks. Yet it had been implicit that he was first and last a painter.

Emily hadn't seen her mother pick up a paint brush or pencil in years. She was a handsome, businesslike, nose-to-the-grindstone type lawyer. Emily doubted that her mother's business associates could ever have imagined Cathleen as the hip beatnik girl she had been in Greenwich Village.

Her parents maintained a cool friendship. And Emily wondered if perhaps they didn't still love one another. Maybe they did. But she had no doubt in her mind that they'd made the right decision about not being able to live together. Patrick was far too passive, a kind of hermit. Quite antisocial. For him, humanity could be kept an arm's length away.

Cathleen had discovered an activist streak in her nature, and she liked being in the thick of things. She liked the grit of life among people, lots of people. As a lawyer, she often dealt with humanity at its worst. She seemed to enjoy working through the muck.

She would never leave San Francisco. She loved the town, and the town seemed to do right by her. She was well established in the Bay area. No other family ties tugged from the East. Emily's grandparents were all dead. Emily's family, such as it was, was small indeed.

It was assumed that Emily would return to California and attend school at Berkeley, though she was unsure of a major at this point. Science had always interested her. And for a time she wanted to be a dancer. But she'd let that go. Maybe she'd be a physician. Here she was in Wisconsin taking a genetics course, a first taste of college life. She felt this was a good start. Whether she went to school in California or Wisconsin was not her primary concern.

Emily dressed in jeans and a white cotton sweater with a V-neck opening. She put a delicate gold chain around her neck. Then a dab of perfume, an expensive name brand that was sexily advertised in all the magazines.

She brushed back her wet hair. These days she wore little makeup, no nail polish or earrings. Seeing herself in the bedroom mirror, she thought she looked rather conservative—for her. This did not displease her. At the corners of her mirror she'd taped a few photographs. She took a quick inventory of them. Her mother's face smiled out at her. A shirtless boy from an ad torn from a magazine. The smiling faces of her girlfriends back home, under the big redwoods, their raincoats glistening.

When she'd finished dressing, the bedroom windows had darkened. The sky was purple, deepening to black. The brightest stars twinkled in the twilight. She took a last, surmising glance at herself in the tall mirror by the door. No answers came from the girl in the mirror, but then no specific questions has been posed to her—just a brief, pleading and rather vague look.

No time for this now. She switched off the light as she left the room.

Downstairs, her father had the CD player going, a collection of Ella Fitzgerald cuts. A fire burned in the fireplace, and the reflection of the flames danced in the sleek black wood of the long coffee table. The living room was theatrically lighted, as if it were the set for a magazine ad for some expensive brand of liquor, or some hotel penthouse bar. High spotlights made rows of beams, illuminating paintings on the walls, and lighting a portion of the sofa where Patrick paged through an oversized magazine. He was freshly showered, dressed in soft white pants, clean cream-colored socks on his feet. On the coffee table was his usual whiskey with ice and twist of lemon peel.

"Well, look at you," he said and smiled.

"I'm going out with Beth and few people from Leonora High."

He nodded.

"You're staying in again, huh?" she asked him.

"That's the way I like it," he responded with a chuckle. "Most nights, anyway."

He walked her to the door.

"Have a nice time," he said.

"Thanks. 'Bye."

Patrick watched her through the front window. She was illumined in the beam of Beth's headlights.

When the girls had driven off, Patrick set his magazine down on the coffee table and finished the last of his drink. He usually allowed himself only one. But tonight he went into the kitchen and reached for the high cabinet where he kept his liquor, and he made a fresh drink.

He'd been thinking lately about Wanda, the woman he saw whenever he was in New York. Not a girlfriend, exactly. An old friend, but something more. The woman he slept with. Once a year. A woman he supposed he once loved.

The phone calls between them—between his home in Wisconsin and hers in New York City—had grown infrequent. She wrote to him often, sending newspaper and magazine clips she thought he would find interesting, often about the art world. She always had plenty of gossip. And whenever Patrick spoke to Roger, the dealer who represented his work, Wanda's name was mentioned. She was a part of his link to New York, though barely a lover anymore.

Once he thought he would marry her. Now he felt lonely, thinking of the relationship. She had told him—rightfully, he acknowledged—that it was time for her to see other people. She wasn't exactly cutting it off with Patrick. She was simply opening the door for someone new to come along.

So far, no one had. At least not that his friends in New York had reported to him.

He picked up the telephone and dialed the area code for Manhattan. Something stopped him. Inertia, dread—free-floating anxiety. Or was it simply that whatever it was he needed to say—to someone—Wanda was not the one to whom he could say it? He put the receiver back in its cradle.

Outside, the boughs of the trees waved in his windows. A storm was coming.

* * *

Up at the old Hamilton Home, most of the residents had already retired for the evening. But in one of the rooms, deep and hidden, a male attendant prepared to administer a sedative to a wild-haired old woman.

He turned her arm around, searching for an appropriate vein.

"Geez, you got more tracks than a pin cushion," He said to her. "You don't have any good veins left. All popped."

Charity Francis looked into the attendant's deep brown eyes. He was a young man, not yet thirty. He had a cap of curly black hair, and a patchy beard and mustache. On his bare forearm was a tattoo. HARLEY DAVIDSON, it said.

"They've been giving me sedatives for weeks now," Charity said. "I won't tell if you skip me just this once."

She felt a little groggy, but that was an improvement on her usual stupor.

"The doc said this is important," he said. "You could hurt yourself if you ain't calmed down. And if I didn't give you the dose, Herbert Temple would have my ass."

She nodded, hoping to appear sympathetic to his problem.

"I need the sedative," she lied. "But there's no reason I couldn't take it orally."

"The doc says he wants me to shoot it."

"But as you've said, I haven't got the veins for it. You don't want to hurt an old woman, do you?"

He frowned. "Course not."

"So if you give me an oral dose of my medicine,

you haven't exactly gone against the doctor's wishes.
At least not one hundred percent. It's like a white lie."

"I don't know. . . ."

She touched his hand, looked into his eyes. Her
powers were weak now. With this young attendant, she
concentrated hard.

"I . . . suppose," he said.

Maybe it was just the power of suggestion, or the
compelling look in her eyes. She wasn't sure. But he
removed a standard oral tranquilizer from his cart and
gave it to her in a small paper cup. Then he handed
her a another, slightly larger, paper cup filled with cool
water. He watched as she put the bitter-tasting pill into
her mouth and drank the entire glass of water.

She sighed, handing him the empty cup. "Thank
you."

"You're welcome," he said hesitantly. He crumpled
the cups and rolled his cart down the hallway, to the
next room on his list.

When he was gone from the windowless room—a
room somewhere in the Hamilton Home—Charity
didn't know where; she'd been drugged and bound
when they'd brought her here—she spit the sedative
into her hand, then hid it in a crack in the floor under
her cot.

She needed to think. She closed her eyes to concentrate. Help was what she needed. She needed to find
out if Maria Kraus was still alive.

She hadn't seen Maria since the night Eugenia and
Herbert had confronted them about the letter. The letter
they had tried to send to Senator Pullman. A letter they
hoped would shut this hellhole down.

A poor strategy, Charity now admitted it to herself.

Eugenia had managed to intercept the envelope. Instead of an investigation by the state of Wisconsin, a thorough and brutal interrogation of the two old women had ensued. She remembered it now.

It *was* a memory, wasn't it? Yes, she told herself, though her mind was weak. These were not delusions—the paranoid delusions the Temples had claimed Charity and Maria had shared. These were real memories. They had to be.

They say I'm paranoid, Charity thought angrily. *That I have a . . . what did they call it? Oh yes, a "persecution complex."* Her head throbbed when she thought of these accusations.

She tried to concentrate hard on all that had happened. Terrible things had happened that night. . . . Eugenia had been unforgiving, fierce, staring with those crowlike, angry eyes.

Worst of all, Eugenia'd had her huge assistant, Ned Fox, rifle through Charity's things. He'd come upon the old silver pocket watch, that tarnished, ancient thing with its strange moon engraving. Junk, Eugenia had pronounced, failing to distinguish the watch from the other oddments Charity had traveled with for so many years—the stubs of old white candles, the baby alligator claw. Not that Eugenia would have recognized the watch; she'd never seen it before. Yet the power Charity believed it contained, *that* would have been of paramount interest to Eugenia Temple.

These weren't delusions, Charity assured herself, shaking her head. Her eyelids slid down over her eyes. The remains of the previous day's sedative was still coursing through her veins. Her thoughts skipped from one idea to another, like channels changing on TV. No continuity. But she'd be better soon, she told herself. She'd tell the senator about all this, too.

Eugenia had ordered Ned to burn all of Charity's things, and off he went with them, not knowing what he had. She remembered it now.

Had he destroyed the watch, as Eugenia ordered him to? Charity didn't know for sure, but she had always assumed, with a mind she knew was failing and often irrational, that she would perish with it.

No, she told herself, *the watch survives, somewhere in this house.*

But what about poor old Maria Kraus, her partner in rebellion?

The thought that her friend might be dead made her feel as though her heart were being squeezed violently. Just then the girl's face floated into her mind's eye again. And a name. Emily Jordan. She would need the help of Emily Jordan. Emily was no ordinary girl, this was coming clear.

Charity felt pity for the poor girl. Was she bound for the same destination as Maria—and Charity herself? A fate unknown?

She only knew that all were in great danger.

Old Cemetery Road wound through the trees at a steep grade. It ended at the cemetery gates, behind the Hamilton Home. The Home stood beaconlike against the night sky. Chill winds blew over the hill tonight, and clouds began to gather.

The group Beth and Emily met up with had built a bonfire several hundred feet from the farthest-back corridor of the old cemetery. They could not be seen here from either the road, where their cars were parked, or from the home.

The beer was flowing when Beth and Emily arrived. She spotted Kerry right away, talking with his friends. He was handsomer than ever in the light of the fire, his brown eyes gleaming. He had his jacket zipped up to his throat.

"Hi," he said finally. "I've been meaning to call you."

"Really?" Emily said. Beth, a little drunk, giggled beside her.

"Yeah, I wanted to know if you'd like to get together to study sometime."

Emily thought about that for a second. "I'd like that," she said.

After a few minutes of talking, Emily noticed that the others, Beth included, had moved to the other side of the fire, out of earshot. Beth was talking with one of Kerry's friends.

"Want to go for a walk?" Kerry asked.

"It's warm right here," Emily said.

Kerry reached over and took her hand gently in his. His skin felt hot. "Let's take a look around the old cemetery."

Emily's heart pounded. A gust of wind blew over the hill, sending a shower of sparks high into the air. She let go of Kerry's hand, then stood and stretched. She started out toward the cemetery gate.

He caught up with her and slipped his hand back into hers.

"Careful," someone called after them. "You don't want to become the next Jan Schmidt, do you?" Laughter erupted behind them as they moved into blue darkness.

Jan Schmidt. The missing young mom. Emily walked over to the graves, now safely away from the other guys but in a place that was positively creepy. The home loomed overhead, its lower windows like glowing yellow teeth in a leering skull. She squeezed Kerry's hand.

Dry twigs snapped under their feet as they slowly walked amid the old tombstones. "Let's sit down," Kerry said, and he led her to a wooden bench that creaked when they sat on it. He put his arm around her shoulder.

"When did Jan Schmidt disappear?" Emily asked. She leaned her head toward his. He smelled good. A cedar smell in his clothes mingled with a clean scent of soap.

"A couple years ago. I'm not sure."

"It seems like this area is filled with all these atrocious crimes, and everybody just conveniently forgets them."

He rubbed her shoulder through her coat. "Why dwell on the awful?" he said. "Girls disappear around here, and any number of things could have happened to them. They could be runaways. Or they could be dead."

"They could be locked up in basements somewhere," Emily said, shuddering. "Tortured and enslaved."

Kerry moved his face in close and he kissed her lightly on the lips. It was nice. She leaned against him, and they kissed again, this time deeply. Warmth spread through her, from her lips deep into her body.

When they parted, she noticed that he was grinning.

"I can't believe I'm actually kissing you," he said.

She shrugged. "If the town gossips are correct, we're meant to be together," she said.

He smiled, eyes sleepily closed. "I've never kissed anyone like this before," he said. He opened his eyes. "Have you?"

She rolled her eyes. "Does it matter?"

"No." He squeezed her hand. "I only wondered, because . . . This really is my first time kissing a girl . . . like this." He looked away. "I'm glad it's with you."

She looked at him. It was surprising that a boy as cute as Kerry had not kissed more girls. Was he some kind of puritan? Impulsively she said, "I lost my virginity when I was fourteen."

She didn't look over right away to see what his response would be. She listened to him breathing. Then she turned her head and looked into his eyes. He was not looking at her.

"Wow," he finally said softly.

"You weren't expecting to hear that?"

"No, it's not that," he said. "It doesn't matter. You didn't have to tell me."

"But you were thinking . . . otherwise. Weren't you."

"I suppose. And you were thinking—"

"You as much as said—"

"That I'm a virgin?" He made an odd smile, not at her, but at the night sky. Emily noticed wisps of fog on the trail at their feet. The fog snaked along its path as if picking up scent and information, hurrying on its feathery way to the graves and fields that lay beyond.

"Well. I've come clean. So . . . are you a virgin?" she asked.

"Sort of," he said. "Yes, I guess so."

"What do you mean, sort of?"

He still had his arm around her. He raised his hand, gesturing in a shrug, and let it fall back on her shoulder.

"I guess I mean yes. I've never . . . But tell me about what happened with you, if you don't mind talking about it. I'm kind of curious."

"I haven't much to tell. And it's kind of hard to talk about. I had a boyfriend in San Francisco. An older boyfriend. Over eighteen, I mean. We went out together for a while, almost three years. We were in love . . . I was in love. He's in jail now."

"Jail," he snorted. "For child molestation?"

"Of course not. Anyway, it's over now." She looked at Kerry. "It's history."

He looked away. "I don't have any history," he said, looking up at the sky. "Not a real history, anyway." His head was tilted back. He swallowed, and she watched his Adam's apple glide beneath the skin. "I mean, I'm normal. I think. But I've done some weird things . . . Oh God, I can't believe I'm actually telling someone this. Telling you. But I want to."

"Then tell," she said, and she squeezed his hand. He squeezed back.

"I mean I've sort of *experimented*, I suppose, too," he said quietly. He looked at his shoes. "I'm not completely inexperienced. But I'm still a virgin. Technically," he added. He turned to look at her, gazed intently into her eyes. "Anyway, this is embarrassing, and I guess I don't want to talk about it after all."

She let that sink in. She wasn't at all sure what he was getting at.

"Oh," she said, quietly. "You didn't hurt anyone did you?"

"No," he said quickly. "I mean . . . I don't know what I'm talking about. Let's skip it."

"Fine, let's. But maybe you shouldn't be so ashamed. . . . It can't be all that bad, can it?"

"I just really, really want to have normal sex with a girl," he blurted.

She looked at him. "What's normal? You keep using that word."

He looked a bit spooked. But then a smile played over his lips, and he grinned. "You're asking the wrong guy."

Emily smiled. She leaned toward him, and he leaned toward her. They kissed again.

They kissed for a long while. He put his hand inside her coat and over her breast, and then on her lower back. He slipped his fingers under the waistband of her jeans. She shuddered at the coldness of his touch.

He removed his hand from her clothes and pulled at the waistband of his jeans. He was trying to adjust his erection. It was an elaborate operation. At last he got himself into a more comfortable position.

She looked into his eyes. "You said you'd never kissed a girl like this before, but you kiss pretty good."

He blushed, turned away. "What I meant was, *exactly* like this. With someone I want to be with. Of course I've kissed before. It wasn't like this," he said, and he put his hands on her shoulders and kissed her again. "It was never like it is now, like a trillion volts going through us."

"Us?" she said. "Was it a trillion volts?"

"Wasn't it?" he said.

"I'm still thinking."

"We could go to my car. I have a condom."

She moved backward, out of his embrace. Had he really said that? "That's kind of rushing things, Kerry."

"But we've been speaking so frankly," he answered. "I thought I should be honest and say it. And besides . . . you've done it before."

She was speechless.

He smiled and jumped up on the bench. To the night sky he shouted, "I want to make love to Emily Jordan!"

She stood up and tugged at his coat. He tipped to the left and lost his footing. Down he came from the bench with a crash and fell—*whoooooosh*—into the dry leaves. Aghast, Emily rushed to where he lay in a crumpled heap. But she found him smiling, reaching for her. He pulled her close and kissed her.

She pushed herself from him, frowning. "If I did it before, with somebody else, it has nothing to do with you, or with us right now," she said. "And if I didn't know better, I'd say you're just in a hurry to find out if you can do it."

"Maybe I *am* in a hurry," he said. "But I want to be in a hurry with you," he said, picking himself up. "You . . ."

He winced, having bruised his knee in the fall. He touched her hair, ran his hand gently down to her neck. Now his hands were warm.

"Kerry, please—"

He kissed her quiet. Then he said, "I only know

that I've wanted to be with you since I first saw you in the lecture hall."

She pulled free of him and took several steps back. In a way she felt relieved. Nothing more was going to happen. She knew that now.

"We should go back to our friends," she said. "It's getting cold. This place gives me the creeps."

"Can't we at least talk some more? You've set me free, Emily . . . Emily?"

She wasn't listening to him. She was already hurrying back to the others.

Gloria Munson handed back the first big test of the semester, which she said she'd been correcting all weekend. The clock on the wall ticked, making practically the only sound in the brightly lit classroom.

"Very good," Gloria said, near the back of the room, as she handed a corrected test to one of her students.

Emily was sitting next to Kerry. Actually, he'd come in and sat down next to her, she hadn't sought him out. They hadn't really talked since the night in the cemetery. He'd telephoned a couple of times. She'd been merely polite. He was dressed in jeans and brown boots and a flannel shirt, and as usual his hair was combed to perfection.

Kerry's test came and he looked at it. A bright red B was marked at the top.

"That's a relief," he whispered.

Gloria moved around the room, then returned to Emily. Emily's heart pounded. The suspense was almost unbearable.

"Excellent," Gloria said, laying the paper in front of Emily. She had received an A. She smiled.

"On top of all your other qualities, you're brilliant," Kerry whispered. She folded her test in half and put it in her book bag.

Emily enjoyed the class with renewed vigor. Success had engaged her in a subject for which six months ago she would not have had the slightest interest. She was grateful to have this to think about—school, the possibility of a career someday—not to worry about Kerry or some other complicated love. Gloria let class out a half hour early. Standing outside the classroom door, one of Kerry's friends from Leonora High, Ralph, came over and showed off his test score: an A-.

"Not bad," Kerry said, "but look who got an A." He pointed at Emily.

Ralph said, "I'm way impressed." He zipped up his jacket. A 35mm camera hung from his neck. His blond hair fell to his shoulders.

"Thanks," Emily said.

Ralph gave Kerry a gentle shove. "Come on," he said. "Let's go get a beer."

Emily paid little attention. She didn't know many of the other students in her class yet, though she was impressed with Ralph's A-.

"Hold on a minute," Kerry said. He turned to Emily. "You want to hang with us tonight?"

"Yeah, come on," Ralph said. "I've got some great bud, too."

She slung her bag over her shoulder. "Thanks, but I'm not in a party mood. Gonna hit the books instead." She smiled coolly and started to walk toward the pay phone, to call Patrick. He was once again playing taxi driver. Kerry followed, leaving Ralph waiting.

"I'd really like to talk with you tonight," he said, taking her arm.

"I have to get home. My father gets up early in the morning," she said. "I don't want to keep him up late tonight waiting." She gently took her arm back and buttoned up her jacket.

"I'll drive you home," he said.

She was about to shake her head when Gloria Munson walked out with her coat on. She smiled as she passed them. Emily smiled back. Gloria was really a wonderful teacher. *Maybe following in her footsteps wouldn't be such a bad career path*, she thought. *Emily Jordan, science instructor . . . Emily Jordan, professor of genetic research.* She turned to Kerry.

"Thanks, Kerry. Not tonight."

"Well, just come outside and have a cigarette with me."

"I quit smoking," she said.

"Since when?"

"I just decided to, a few days ago." Webster, who had told her about the spot on his lung, had been a great motivator.

They stood at the entryway, and Kerry tried to talk to Emily into going out.

A few minutes later Gloria came back inside. "Great," she said. "My car's dead. Think I can get a tow at this hour?"

"I could give you a lift," Kerry said. "I'm already driving Emily. You could get a mechanic out here tomorrow morning."

Emily opened her mouth to say something, but Gloria spoke first.

"It's sweet of you to offer, but I live quite a ways out in the country," she said.

"I don't mind a bit," Kerry said.

Gloria smiled. "Thank you. I'd love for you to see my place. Will you stop in for a piece of cake? You, too, Emily?"

"I'll tell Ralph to take a rain check," Kerry said to Emily, before she could answer.

On the ride to Gloria's, Emily was silent. The truth was, she wanted to get to know Gloria better and was excited to be able to see her home. Kerry did all the talking. He wanted to know about the genetic research Gloria had been involved in.

"It was mainly botanical," Gloria said. "Agricultural. But we moved in an interesting community. Research on everything from how to make a sweeter strawberry to the genes that influence aging."

Emily listened with fascination. She decided she would call Patrick from Gloria's house, a little later.

Gloria's home was a traditional farmhouse, rehabbed and gentrified. The maple floors had been sanded and varnished to a high gloss, the walls painted white. Various black-and-white photos in sleek, blond-wood frames were hung on the walls, the largest of which depicted the great white sail of a boat. And everywhere were books. Gloria lived alone, with her cats and an Irish setter and a terrier. Outside in the barn were three horses. Gloria moved around the small downstairs rooms, turning on lamps.

Then she served steaming mugs of hot cider and large pieces of a fresh carrot cake she had baked that morning. It was delicious. Emily sat down on the sofa and Kerry sat next to her. He pressed his knee against hers. She did not pull away.

Eventually the conversation came around to Emily's job at the home.

"I know very little about that strange old place," Gloria said. "But I think the building is gorgeous. It really commands its place on the hill."

"The interior could be beautiful, too, if they would bother to fix it up," Emily said. "It's a mix of old-fashioned furnishings and fixtures, but with computers thrown in and big stainless steel refrigerators in the hallways, filled with medicine and God knows what."

"Do you feel the residents are properly taken care of?" Gloria asked. Kerry was polishing off a second piece of cake.

Emily took a deep breath. She didn't want to say what she suspected because so far she hadn't any proof. "I don't know," she said. "The people who run the place are very strict. But I see so many women there, and men, too—though fewer men—who all seem so forlorn and frightened." Emily thought of Charity, and she felt a tug at her heart.

"I really think we need a better way of caring for the elderly," Gloria said. "Institutionalizing people, warehousing them, really is a nineteenth-century hold-over."

Emily nodded. She enjoyed the company of this woman who spoke to her as an equal. Had the A on her test accomplished this? Did Gloria choose her friends based on their brainpower? Or would she have invited any of her students over if they had happened to come to her rescue instead of Kerry and Emily?

Gloria took a pensive sip of cider. "You know," she said, "Oscar Wilde once said that a school ought to be the most beautiful building in a town. A place where children are really happy to go to every day. Certainly that standard should apply to a place where people spend the last days of their lives. The Hamilton Home is, after all, their *home*."

"I'd rather be dead than be in a place like the Hamilton Home," Kerry said.

Gloria smiled. "Yes, I've heard people say that about old-age homes in general. But the fact is, we are all, if we're lucky, going to grow older—more of us now than ever before, what with medical advances. We're going to age to a point where we will need help. Rather than just wishing we were dead maybe we ought to work to make that future a better place."

"You said you knew about some work being done on genes that influences the aging process," Emily said. "Maybe someday we'll have the option of not growing old."

Gloria sighed and nodded. "The pharmaceutical companies would make a fortune on that, wouldn't they? Just think of the products you see on TV these days—promises to women that they can erase lines and wrinkles, tighten skin, enrich hair, strengthen bone. You notice that far fewer of those sorts of products are advertised to men."

"Men get the car ads," Kerry said. "And beer."

"Feelings of youth, rather than the mere appearance of it," Gloria said.

"They say men age better than women," Emily said. "More gracefully."

"So they say," Gloria replied. "Think of all the

money to be made off of the concept of what a woman's face should and should not be. Look at my face; it's not young. I've got mascara on, a bit of lipstick. I'm vain to an extent. But I don't dye my hair, or hide my wrinkles. But someday I might, and Madison Avenue turns on that."

"Will the money go out of the youth and beauty market if we can genetically alter the aging process?" Kerry said. "What if we could genetically control a person's looks, from birth?"

Gloria poured more hot cider into Kerry's mug. She smiled. "The profits will shift to the medical community—as if they need more money, the poor dears. Only the plastic surgeons will suffer. Plastic surgeons will have to put away all their knives and files and vacuum hoses, and form bread lines around the block," she said. She offered the hot cider to Emily, who declined.

"Maybe we all need to better accept the process of aging as natural," Gloria said. "Rather than aping youth, maybe we should ask ourselves, What is so objectionable about an old woman?"

Emily thought of the women at the Hamilton Home, the women in homes like it all across the country and the world. Hidden, warehoused, corraled to meals, forgotten, and eventually buried. It was, in overwhelming numbers, the women who inhabited this aged world. As with everything, if you were poor, the more desperate your situation.

The insults of old age were compounded at the Hamilton Home. You ended your days bossed by the likes of the nurses she and Beth called Patti, Maxine, and Laverne. Emily wouldn't have been at all surprised to know that many of the old women resented that their bodies had clung to life—if living to a ripe old age meant a kind of living death at the Hamilton Home.

As the night wore on, Emily lost track of time. She found Gloria's conversation engaging. Here was a woman leading a life Emily had never imagined possible, a country life filled with books and with a mission: teaching the young. What seemed to be missing was a man. Emily wondered if Gloria had a lover. Of course she would never ask. When she finally glanced at her watch and saw it was past midnight, she jumped to her feet.

"Can I use your phone?" she said to Gloria. "I should have called my father hours ago."

Kerry rose, too. "I'll give you a lift."

"Okay," Emily said. "But I still better call home. God, he's been waiting up for hours. He probably thinks I'm already one of the missing girls, with my face on every telephone pole in town."

She could hear the tremor in Patrick's voice when he answered, "Hello . . .?"

"Dad, its' me."

"Em! Where are you? Are you all right?"

"Yes, fine. I'm at my professor's house. I got an A on the exam. I kind of lost track of the time, sorry."

"Emily . . ." he began, but whatever he was going to say was choked up in him. She could hear the anger and fear in that void. "Look," he finally managed, "where are you?" I'm coming to get you."

"I have a ride—"

"Just stay where you are. I'm on my way. Now, what's the address."

With Gloria's help, she provided directions.

"That will take me about twenty minutes," he said. "Stay right there." He hung up the phone.

"Well," Emily said to Gloria and Kerry, who had been next to her through the entire conversation, "he's upset."

Gloria gave Emily a sympathetic look.

"I screwed up," Emily said.

"He's kind of overprotective, isn't he?" Kerry said.

"He's a worrier," Emily said. "I just wish I'd called him earlier."

Gloria offered to make coffee. Emily looked through Gloria's record collection and found an old dog-eared Abba album. She put it on the turntable. She and Kerry helped Gloria bring the dishes to the kitchen. They were all in the kitchen, with the faucet running and fragrant soap bubbles drifting over the sink, when the doorbell rang. Emily put her dish towel on the counter. Gloria, drying her hands, went to answer the door.

"Hello," she said, offering a slightly wet warm hand.

Patrick grunted something that sounded like "Hi." He looked past Gloria. "Let's go," he said roughly to Emily. He looked tired, but not necessarily angry.

"Dad, I want you to meet a couple friends of mine," Emily said as she slipped her coat on. She introduced him to Kerry first. Patrick looked at the young man, not quite with disdain but with something close to it.

"I'm really honored to meet you, sir," Kerry said.

Patrick nodded.

"And this is Gloria Munson, my genetics instructor."

"I assure you your daughter has been in safe hands

all night," Gloria said. She smiled at him, but Patrick didn't offer a smile in return.

"Do you often make a practice of fraternizing into the night with your students?" he said to Gloria.

Emily was certain he hadn't meant it to come out as haughty as it had. Gloria wasn't fazed. She smiled.

"Yes, of course I do, Mr. Jordan. I appreciate the company of good minds—wherever I find them." She put the white cotton dish towel over her shoulder.

Patrick exhaled sharply through his nostrils.

"Dad, look, I'm awfully sorry," Emily said. "It was my fault, really." Kerry looked on shyly.

"No, it was mine," Gloria said to Emily. "If my car hadn't died, I would never have needed you and Kerry to come to my rescue. But rescue me you did, both of you, and I'm eternally grateful."

Gloria handed a couple of books to Emily, novels Emily had been admiring on the shelves earlier in the evening. "You have a wonderful daughter, Mr. Jordan," Gloria said to Patrick. She turned to Emily. "Keep these as long as you like," she said of the books. "And please do come visit again."

They rode home in silence. Once inside the door of the house, Patrick didn't bother to turn on the lights. He removed his coat and started wearily up the stairs to his bedroom. Emily watched him climb.

"I really didn't mean to scare you, Dad," she said.

He stopped. He turned, and she realized that from where she was standing, in the dark, he couldn't see her.

"Emily?"

"Right here, Dad."

Patrick came down the steps quickly and kissed her forehead.

"I'm so sorry you have to put up with your worry-wart old man," he said. "It's true I dread anything bad happening to you. I don't want to lose you again."

"You never lost me, Daddy," Emily said.

"I lost a little girl once," he said. He touched her cheek. "I don't ever want to lose her again."

She hugged him.

"I love you," he said. And as he turned, she saw the gleam of tears in his eyes. He went upstairs and closed his door softly.

Emily sat down at the foot of the stairs. How very lonely her father must have been. On the surface, he led a life of comfort, ease, and abundance. Yet the weight of all his years alone had been present in his face a moment ago. She rubbed her arms up and down, feeling suddenly cold. A draft of night air pushed at the front door. And outside, through a front window, she saw the branches of the trees swaying against the night sky.

At last it began to rain.

Chapter Four

Maria Kraus's wounds had healed, but not well. Still, she was certain they had reached a stage where they weren't going to get any worse. The acute pain had given way to a general dull throb throughout her head and body. This modest progress revived her somewhat. She knew that whatever energy she had stemmed directly from a burning desire for revenge.

Her chin trembled more than ever, and attempts at walking had been disastrous. She had found her glasses this morning, but the medicine she'd been given made her vision blurry.

Yet, she noted as she slipped the glasses onto her nose, she felt better than she had since the night Herbert had amputated most of her tongue.

That was not a dream, she reminded herself. Not a hallucination. What was that word Herbert had used, trying to discredit her? Oh yes, *Co-delusional*. She and Charity Francis were supposed to be co-delusional. That meant you were nuts, sharing persecution fantasies, and not to be taken seriously.

Holding a hand mirror in her good hand (the other, the left hand, had been broken by the thugs when it was determined she had written the desperate letter to the state senator—though Dr. Temple had told her she'd broken her hand in a fall), she examined her face. Was it possible another line had actually formed? There were so many already it didn't seem possible, but there it was, a deep crease on her forehead. Her hair was white and brittle, mere wisps. *I must look at least one hundred years old*, she thought.

Was that some kind of delusion, too? Screw *that* noise, she thought.

Her arms were bone thin. She guessed she couldn't have weighed much more than ninety pounds, if that.

She took a deep breath and sat up in bed. Trying to put thoughts together was difficult, with her mind consumed in a thick cloud of pain killer. To her, the most amazing thing was that she was alive. She'd expected to be killed. The few other patients who had dared to stand up to the Hamilton Home were all dead. Some had committed suicide. That was not so uncommon in an old-age home, Maria knew, though she wished she didn't know a thing about such places— this, or any other.

She tried to remember what it felt like to be strong. Maybe if she thought about it, some strength would come back to her. Yet the truth was, her body was ravaged. She was terribly weak, and her broken fingers pained her terribly. And the absence in her mouth . . . damn then for that, she thought.

Yes, it was the thought of blood revenge that was keeping her alive, sparking her recovery.

And something else. She was convinced that Charity

was alive, too. Charity, whom she thought now of as a kind of rebellious sister.

When you've got one friend in the world, and your life depends on her, you may as well think of her as your sister. Or, hell, your whole family.

It took a long time to get out of bed. It took half the morning to get dressed. She wore a pink-flannel nightgown under a fuzzy green-and-white striped robe, and black slippers.

After a struggle, Maria was able finally to get to the door of her tiny room. She discovered, giving it a push, that it was unlocked.

What an insult! How timid did they imagine her to be? They had drained the very life from her, hacked her apart, imprisoned her. But they still counted on her lack of rebelliousness, her timidity, her childlike fear.

Over the past several months she'd needed the support of a cane to walk, when she *could* walk. But this morning her legs had some renewed strength in them. They shook, but compared to her hand they were almost pain free. So she pushed out into the hallway. Her first thought was that she would walk to one of the fire exit doors, she would find a knife and stab a nurse in the heart if she had to, but she would walk out the door and down the hill and into the town of Leonora. Even if it took her a month through lashing rain.

But she didn't have that much strength, and she knew it. Real revenge called for a better plan. So she listened to the tiny voice in her head. She didn't know if it was real, or the product of the poison that had been administered to her. The voice called to her. And she followed.

It was coming, she guessed, from the deep basement.

Maria . . . it called to her.

Maria knew that if she were to be caught in the hallways, she would be promptly returned to her room and probably chained to her bed. Maybe even killed.

No matter. Having nothing more to lose she'd take any risk.

Almost as soon as she thought this, she caught a glimpse of dark blue; like a spectre it hovered at the end of the corridor. The towering figure came into focus. Maria heard the deep voice.

It was Eugenia. Her head was bent, and she was giving instructions to some poor cowering nurse. Maria backed away. She stole another glance, and realized with glee that Eugenia had not seen her, was not chasing down the hallway after her.

Maria charged—inasmuch as she could—down another hallway. The walls and ceilings blurred in her vision. She could hear the sound of her slipper-clad feet whisking along the carpet. Her heart pounded fiercely in her chest. The extra exertion taxed her lungs and heart. At last she rounded the corner, giddy. Home free, she thought.

But as she turned the corner, she caught sight of something that took the smile right off her face.

Dr. Herbert Temple had just stepped off the elevator. And although he was looking at a file folder in his hands, he was headed right toward her.

Beth arrived right on time at eleven in the morning. Emily was just finishing her breakfast of an apple and a bowl of corn flakes. She watched Beth get out of her car and come to the house. The sun had burned off most of the morning mist from the fields.

"Ready for the salt mines?" Beth said.

"Ready as I'll ever be," Emily said. "Coffee?"

Patrick came down the stairs to greet Beth. He was dressed in his paint-splattered clothes. "Ah, my own Florence Nightingales, off to tend the sick and dying."

"Hello Mr. Jordan," Beth said.

Beth had on her oversized denim jacket. Her nails were painted bloodred today. They were short nails on small plump hands. Emily handed her a mug of coffee, and Beth blew the rising steam over the brim before taking a tentative sip. She then sat down at the table and picked up the newspaper.

Emily rinsed her dish in the sink and loaded it into the dishwasher. Patrick grabbed an apple from the bowl on the table and headed toward the living room. Beth lowered the newspaper.

"Emily, I thought you should know something," Beth whispered when Patrick was safely out of earshot. "It's Kerry. He's a mess. He's carrying the biggest torch in the history of Leonora High for you."

Emily frowned. "Well, I hope he doesn't get that big torch accidently slammed in a car door," she said.

Beth said, "Huh? What's that supposed to mean?"

"Never mind. I can't worry about Kerry's problems. I have my own concerns."

"You talk like he isn't the hottest guy in the county."

Emily turned to Beth. "Do you really think he's that hot? Maybe you're carrying a torch for *him*."

Beth grimaced, her face flushed with blood. A direct hit on a raw nerve.

Emily didn't tell Beth that she had already made a "date" with Kerry and Gloria for pizza, after much insistence and repeated phone calls from the former.

And it wasn't so much a date as a payback from Gloria, for giving her a lift home the other night when her car wouldn't start.

Why she kept this secret from Beth she wasn't exactly sure. But because she hadn't made up her mind about Kerry, she didn't want to feed anything into the gossip mill—or into Beth's overactive imagination.

Beth shook her head. "He's hot, but he's also stuck up. I can't stand cool jocks who think they're God's gift. I prefer outcasts."

Patrick walked into the room.

"I'm much too old for you Beth," he said. She laughed. He set his apple core on the counter. "Have a nice day out at the wrinkle farm," he said. He headed out of the room, to the stairs and his studio.

Emily sighed.

"To the mines?" Beth said.

"Let's go," Emily said.

Maria emerged from behind the door of the utility closet, looking carefully around for signs of Herbert, who had just passed by.

She'd successfully dodged him. And the calling voice seemed to call out all the louder now.

Maria navigated her way down the old dank staircase off the kitchen. She passed the furnace room, where a roar was muted by a heavy steel door, and she passed the laundry facilities, where a couple of young girls folded towels.

"Can we help you?" one of them called.

"Are you lost, dearie?" said the other, a skinny thing with a geyser of blond curls.

Maria smiled at them and shook her head. She felt

a little like Harpo Marx, Groucho's silent brother. She pointed down the hallway, made walking legs of her fingers as she smiled and widened her eyes. The girls just stared blankly, then looked at one another.

"Out for a little stroll?" the blonde said.

Maria nodded.

They gave her a "thumbs up" and went back to their folding. Maria pushed onward, relieved.

At last she found the room she'd been looking for. It was near the end of the hallway, next to an unruly shelf, where terra cotta pots and trays had been roughly stacked. Charity Francis was behind this door, she had to be. Maria knocked, and soon heard a voice: "Who's there?"

Maria cried out. She could not form words.

Through the door came the muffled voice: "Maria! You heard my plea! I knew you would!" The voice was unmistakably Charity's.

Maria knocked rapidly with her good hand, and her heart pounded.

How to get in?

It was perhaps a measure of Eugenia Temple's arrogance that she left keys to rooms, even rooms where people were imprisoned, in likely places. As if, Maria thought, no one would have reason, or nerve, to go snooping around.

Maria found the proper key to the door in the third terra cotta pot she reached into.

She opened the door, and Charity embraced her hard. Both women tried to fight their tears. Charity, smiling through a stream of unstoppable tears, pulled Maria all the way into the room and closed the door.

"Thank goodness you're alive," she said. She sat

down on the cot and pulled Maria beside her. Maria kept her head bent. She didn't want to face Charity.

"They hurt you," Charity said. Maria felt Charity's hand on her trembling chin. Gently her head was lifted, and a tear rolled down her cheek.

With all the strength she could muster, Maria opened her mouth for Charity to see what Eugenia and Herbert had done.

Charity rose to her feet and closed her eyes.

"Damn them!" Charity screamed in a whisper. Her hands were clenched into fists that turned her knuckles white.

Slowly Charity turned, and Maria saw that the face so many residents at the home had considered ugly and witchlike was, in fact, filled with compassion and beauty. Brilliant green eyes glittered in the soft light.

"I wish I could protect you, Maria," Charity said. "I wish I could undo all that has been done. But without a strong ally, I fear we are lost."

Maria hung her head in despair. Charity sat down beside her and took Maria's injured hand in her own. She held it lightly.

"They broke your fingers, too? Because of the letter?"

Maria nodded.

"They won't get away with it. I know there must be someone who can help us. That strong ally."

Maria looked at Charity, uncertainty in her eyes.

"Herbert and Eugenia are far more wicked than I had ever supposed," Charity said. "But I can't quite believe they've made a prisoner of *me*."

Maria patted Charity's hand.

"I'm sorry," Charity said, dabbing at her eyes with a white handkerchief. "I don't want you to think I'm giving up. We may be living in old, tired bodies that are failing us, but we aren't beaten yet."

Maria felt happy hearing this. She'd known since Charity's arrival that she'd found help, her own strong ally, a comfort in the storm. And maybe even a way out of it.

Slowly, Charity reached into her pocket and pulled out a folded piece of green construction paper. She handed it to Maria, who unfolded it. It was one of the flyers announcing the visit from State Senator Allan Pullman. His visit was only days away.

"I ripped this off the bathroom wall when I was alone," Charity said. "No one saw me."

Maria looked at Charity. And Charity held up another item, fished from her pocket.

A pen.

Emily switched on the Hoover and started vacuuming a hallway on the third floor of the Hamilton Home. The carpet was old, and its peach color had faded to mostly gray. The paint on the walls, too, was more gray than beige. A strange, cold draft blew down the hallway.

She was alone, or thought she was. The vacuum cleaner was loud, and above its din she thought she could hear voices. An argument of sorts, with shouting, and things being smashed.

She switched off the Hoover and listened. Now it was quiet; the eerie quiet of a deserted house.

She switched the Hoover back on, and she was backing down the hall, vacuuming diligently when something crashed into her from behind with such great force that she was lifted off the ground.

Emily went sprawling, as did someone else, someone who'd been running at high speed. It was Ned.

Emily struggled for her breath. Her shoulder hurt. Ned gaped at her. He looked frightful. His lip was bleeding. His gray eyes winced in pain. She'd never seen him this close up before. Her skin crawled with the sight of him. His shirt was open, revealing a large, bony chest. The cord of the Hoover had been pulled from the wall socket in the collision, and its engine whined down to silence. Somehow, Emily's watchband had caught on Ned's big white shirt. He scrambled to get up.

"Wait!" Emily said, her arm being pulled.

With a tearing of cloth, a few buttons flew off of Ned's shirt and skipped like stones across the carpet.

"What happened to you?" Emily called, her wrist free. Ned cowered, then scrambled to his feet. Emily picked up the buttons from the carpet. "Did you fall?"

He rapidly shook his head. It occurred to her that perhaps Ned couldn't speak. He was, it seemed, mute. Now he tried to form words, but all that came out was a trembling, "Nnnnuh, nnnnuh . . ."

She'd heard retarded kids talking before. His speech was like that. The sort of speech that children sometimes cruelly mocked.

She stood now and approached him, but he bent in fear, tripping over his own feet as he tried to back away.

"Please be careful," Emily said. "You're already hurt."

She reached out and took hold of his huge arm.

"Nnnnnuhhh!" he warned.

"You've got to clean that cut on your lip," she said. "I'm not going to hurt you, Ned."

He reminded her, oddly enough, of a frightened deer. His eyes, something queerly beautiful in a face marred by scars and wartlike red welts. Up close, his buzzed-off yellow hair and furrowed brow started to take on a more childlike aspect. His breath came rapidly in and out, through long yellow teeth. But he didn't run away. He stood near her.

Emily opened the bathroom door and ran some water. She took a cloth from one of the cabinets. He seemed to calm down as she wiped the blood from his chin and neck.

"It's a nasty cut, but not too deep," Emily said. "You probably don't need stitches. Maybe you should let Dr. Temple take a look at it."

Ned reared back, shaking his head. His eyes widened with terror.

Emily frowned. "Why are you so afraid?" Then she thought a moment. "Did someone do this to you?" she asked.

Ned started to back out of the bathroom.

"Wait a minute, Ned," Emily said. "I have your buttons." She held out her hand. Ned looked at the buttons, then into her eyes. Slowly his own gnarled and big hand came up. Emily turned her hand and let the three small black buttons fall into the big hollow of his hand.

His lips trembled, and he managed, "Thahhh—" He swallowed and tried again. "Thahh-nk . . . yoooo. . . ."

Emily felt heat in her face, the heat of anger and

embarrassment. "Are you sure you don't want to tell somebody about what happened to you?" Emily said.

"P-Please!" he said. "N-no . . ." And he turned away and ran down the hall, his heavy footfalls resonating through the plaster walls.

That night Emily and Beth went to the Leonora Public Library together. Emily told Beth about what happened to Ned, and Beth shook her head in disgust.

"Another reason to get out," Beth said. "Abuse of the retarded help. We should just quit. I should just quit."

"Easy for you to say," Emily said. "I still have to redeem myself in the eyes of society."

"Yeah, and I have to make enough money to leave," Beth said. "Besides. We have the midwestern work ethic here. We don't just run away from unpleasant jobs. We stay and build character while our lives pass us by." She shook her head.

They left the main study lounge at the community college library and went to the microfilm room. For the next three hours they looked at stories about some of the women and girls, and a few young men, who had mysteriously disappeared in Blackburn County over the years. The glow of the microfilm viewers illumined their faces.

The story of Jan Schmidt had dominated the headlines for days. Emily, in her retro black horn-rimmed reading glasses, looked at Beth beside her, reading the illuminated print. The room was dark, and the fan in the microfilm machine hummed softly. The other microfilm machines were covered with dust protectors that reminded Emily of body bags from a war film.

"I guess when you have stories like this in your newspaper every few years, a small matter of elder abuse wouldn't rate much ink," Emily said. "Nor would the mysterious death of Hazel Stern."

"Nobody with any clout would believe it," Beth said. "The Hamilton Home is revered—and feared. The fact that it's so remote keeps its secrets safe. Few people ever visit it in the winter. Sometimes people in other states leave their relatives here *because* it's so remote. I couldn't imagine doing that to my daddy or mama."

"I couldn't, either. I would never leave anyone at the Hamilton Home. Ever."

Emily turned off the machine, and the small room was silent.

The local pizza parlor was buzzing. It was Friday night, about ten o'clock. Kerry and Emily and Gloria came directly from class.

Green Day blared from the jukebox, and in the back of the pizza parlor community college kids shot pool and drank beer. Gloria hoisted pizza slices onto Emily and Kerry's plates. Emily told them about the incident with Ned, and of her suspicions about the apparent beating.

"I was thinking," Gloria said. "The paper said State Senator Allan Pullman is coming for a visit, and the Hamilton Home is one of his destinations. You could do some investigating between now and then. You could make some suggestions to Pullman on how to improve the place."

"I don't have any real evidence to provide," Emily said. "It's all hearsay. And besides, I can't draw a lot of attention to myself at the home. I'm there on a kind of probation. Pullman is more interested in juvenile crime legislation than in nursing home reforms."

"You don't have anything to hide, do you?" Gloria asked, and took a bite of pizza.

Kerry, who was seated next to Emily, and whose thigh was pressed into hers, looked into her eyes.

Emily had not intended to make this confession time. But she felt close to Gloria and, in a way, closer to Kerry tonight, too.

"I got into some trouble in San Francisco," she said. "I was involved with a guy, his name was Danny, who manufactured an illegal substance. A drug. We took it sometimes ourselves. To make a long story short, he sold much more of it than I'd ever suspected. He got caught. I was with him in a van. They arrested us. He's in prison now. I'm doing time at the home."

Kerry put his hand over hers. "I've decided that whatever you were in the past, it doesn't matter," he said. "What matters is that you're here now."

She took her hand from his. "*Who* ever I was . . . I was just me."

Gloria sighed and shook her head, her eyes filled with sympathy. "You seem like a responsible young woman to me," she said. "The past is the past."

"Almost," Emily said.

"It must have been a painful time," Gloria said.

"Not all of it," Emily replied. "Before we got caught, I thought I was having a ball. My therapist just said I was killing pain. But that's what they all say. Poor little me."

"Was Danny killing his pain, too?" Kerry said.

"No," Emily answered. "He was just making a killing."

A crash came from the pool table area. Emily turned to look just in time to see a fist connect with a face. Blood flew. A fight between two guys had broken out. Waiters in red shirts dashed to the scene, along with several of the restaurant patrons.

Kerry stood up, as did Gloria, but by the time Emily had put her pizza down and wiped her mouth with her napkin, the fight was over. Burly patrons had separated the combatants. The perpetrator, a heavyset young guy with a dissipated face, was being led to the door. The spectators returned to their seats.

"So this is what I'm missing, hanging around in the country with my horses and dogs day after day," Gloria said. "Civilization."

"Blackburn County nightlife at its best," Kerry said.

Later, when Gloria went to pay the bill, Kerry reached beneath the table for Emily's hand.

"Well? Do you like me or not?" Kerry said. "I gotta know."

She tried to gently take her hand back. He held tight.

"Whether I like you or not, I'm not going to be here very long," she said.

"Here? You mean in Wisconsin, or among the living, or what?"

"Very funny."

"Yeah, well, it's very funny how cold you can be sometimes, too."

"You act as if I owe you something. I never promised you anything, Kerry."

"You know what your problem is? You're afraid of losing people."

She rolled her eyes.

"You lost your father, you lost your boyfriend, Danny, you work in a place where people check out of life on a permanent basis. You're like *The Goodbye Girl*. You know, that movie with Richard Dreyfuss. You're afraid."

Gloria was coming back.

"You sound like an undergraduate psychology major. Easy answers. You have no right to say these things, Kerry," she said, though she acknowledged that his observations were, in a way, accurate. Here she'd been feeling stronger. Now he was knocking her down.

"I'm here right now," Kerry said. He leaned close to her and kissed her. With all her might she tried not to feel what she was feeling. It was a wonderful kiss, even there in the pizza parlor, with other people around, and Gloria walking back to the table.

Kerry finally let go of her hand.

Emily turned away. "You shouldn't have done that," she said quietly.

Gloria cleared her throat. "Kerry, can I give you a ride to your car?"

Gloria drove Emily home. They made small talk about the chill in the air, and about career paths. They talked about everything but what had just happened, circling around the topic like scavenger birds over the scene of a bad accident.

Finally, Emily said, "Back there at the restaurant, I hope I didn't embarrass you," she said.

"No, not at all," Gloria said.

"Kerry is a nice guy, but he was under the assumption that I wanted to be kissed."

Gloria smiled.

"By him," Emily added.

"I think you established your boundaries in no uncertain terms," Gloria said. She turned into the Jordans' drive.

"Would you like to come inside? Dad can show you his work."

"I don't know," Gloria said. "Maybe another time."

"Oh, c'mon," Emily said. "You want to see it don't you?" Gloria had been impressed when she'd found out that Patrick was Emily's dad. She was familiar with the reclusive painter's work, and an admirer of it. Emily wanted to make up for Patrick's unpleasant behavior at Gloria's the other night.

"He's really a pussycat," Emily said. "Come inside for a minute. I want you two to be friends."

Gloria shrugged. "All right," she said at last. "What have I got to lose?"

Patrick *was* friendly, shaking Gloria's hand, offering her a glass of wine.

"Sorry I was such a pill the other night," he said.

"No need to apologize," Gloria said. "The circumstances might have caused any parent to worry." She put the glass to her lips.

Emily smiled. Gloria always seemed to say the right thing. Did she ever make a misstep? And how the hell did you get to that place?

"I should have known Emily was in good hands," Patrick said. "She told me a little about the class you teach. Fascinating."

The conversation continued on the topic of Gloria's

teaching. Gloria followed Patrick to the stairs. Emily accompanied the two up to the studio, where the big still life was nearly completed. Emily could see that Gloria was very impressed by the work.

After the tour, the three of them sat down in the living room, which had been freshly cleaned that morning by Webster and his wife. Patrick served herbal tea.

Emily listened to the conversation—about painters, and about life in the country versus life in the city— and sipped her tea. She was tired, and she had a long day to put in at the home tomorrow. Another day down, crossed off her list. She wondered if Danny literally crossed days off a calendar, like prisoners in old movies did.

Sitting there, it occurred to her again that she could merely kill time in Wisconsin, or she could make some- thing out of her time here. She could even have a romance, or battle the likes of Eugenia and Herbert Temple, whether their rumored evil deeds were real or imagined. Yet she wasn't at all sure she wanted to jump into life here. She preferred observing it from the sidelines, from a safe distance.

She realized that she was lost in her own thoughts and wasn't listening to the conversation Gloria and Patrick were having. It didn't matter. They didn't seem to notice she was there in room with them.

Once again, Emily and Beth were assigned laundry and housekeeping duty. Everything had to be in top form for the visit by the state senator. It wouldn't do for the senator to walk into a room and see a crusty towel or gray bed sheet. Every cloth and linen was to be crisp and white.

They assisted the regular housekeeping crew in changing bed linens. Doing so took most of the morning and a good part of the afternoon. When break time came, Emily and Beth slipped up to one of the empty rooms in the abandoned wing and gazed out the window.

The grassy hill, sloping down to the highway, was green and lush under the sun. A few of the elms were streaked with orange, but most were fat with green leaves. The day was September clear and cloudless.

Beth was in a foul mood. It was like she needed a scapegoat for her anger and boredom.

"That Herbert is a real fuckhead," she said, puffing on a Marlboro. "He's ripping off patients left and right. And no matter how awful he is, Eugenia is much worse."

"How would we prove it?" Emily asked, sitting on the end of a twin bed. The beds were made in these deserted rooms—cheap bedspreads in a plaid pattern, tightly tucked in, white pillows left to gather dust.

"We could break into the office and look at the records," Beth said. "Obviously the Temples do legitimate business here, to cover up their crimes. For all we know, they've even committed murder."

Emily turned to Beth. "I really do think someone beat up Ned. But he won't talk about it."

"He probably takes a lot of beatings, and maybe even gives out a few."

"I feel sorry for him," Emily said. "What kind of life is it, serving the likes of Herbert and Eugenia?"

Neither Emily nor Beth had heard the bedroom door open, and they were not aware of the presence in the doorway until they heard its voice.

"Indeed, what sort of life?" Herbert said mockingly.

Emily stood up, a shock running through her. Beth pitched her cigarette out the window, which she'd opened a crack to draw out the smoke.

"Dr. Temple!" Beth said.

"Yes, and you are, judging by your name tags, our youthful little candy stripers. Such difficulties you face, lounging in rooms that are clearly off limits, spreading malicious rumors, engaging in idle gossip."

"We're sorry, Doctor," Beth said. "We didn't know you were listening."

"Obviously!" Herbert said with a laugh. "Whom do you think you are? Speculating about *our* affairs! And what of your scheme to steal into our records? Would you prefer I show them to you myself personally—before I call the police?"

Beth's face went pale, all the more pronounced in contrast to her flowing red hair. Emily had never seen Beth so frightened. Emily herself was less scared than angry. Herbert was not particularly threatening in appearance, just a mild nerd. But she resented being spied on, even if she and Beth had violated a rule by being up here in the abandoned wing. And, of course, it's not terrific to be discovered by the subject of your venomous attacks—even if it had been Beth doing most of the accusing and name calling.

"We were only talking, Doctor," Beth stammered.

Emily interrupted her. She cut between the doctor and Beth, and addressed Herbert to his face. "Something strange is going on here," she said, deciding that second to take the direct approach (she might as well, she thought). "You should know about these things, as the staff physician. Someone beat up Ned Fox. And what about the sick old woman we saw the other day, Charity Francis? We haven't seen her in days."

Beth turned, eyes wide, and looked at Emily.

Herbert cracked a bit of a smile. "So things aren't up to snuff here, eh? You foolish, silly girl. We have befriended you here at the home. Now you seek to betray us with preposterous accusations."

"I'm not accusing! But I know what I saw," Emily said. "The people who live here—or maybe I should say *exist* here—are frightened. In fact, I'd say some of them are scared to death."

Herbert crossed his arms.

"You know what you saw, hmm? You didn't see a thing, my dear, not really," he said. He had a persnickety air. "And you don't know what you're talking about. You're not even sure of what you suspect. Now, come with along with me."

Walking down the stairs behind Herbert, Emily stole a glance at Beth, who held her hands tight together before her, to stop them from shaking. Beth grimaced and looked straight ahead. Where was the tough kid of a few minutes ago? Emily thought.

Herbert led them to a small, dark room with a window covered with a old and heavy wine-colored curtain. Potted palms with their fronds frozen in a wave loomed up over them, all the way to the yellow tiles on the ceiling. Stars imploded silently on the black screen of a computer.

"Wait here," Herbert said. He went into an inner office, where Emily caught a glimpse of Eugenia behind a massive desk. Yet another secret way into Eugenia's lair! Voices could be heard through the door, but words could not be clearly made out.

"Are we in trouble, old bean?" Beth asked.

"It looks like it, old bean," Emily answered with a sigh.

Finally the door opened. Herbert had a smile on his lips. His eyes sparkled. He gestured with a sweep of his hand, and Emily and Beth filed past him, like prisoners, into Eugenia's office.

Eugenia smiled sympathetically and shook her head.

"Come in, come in," she said, standing. She motioned them to chairs. When Emily and Beth were seated, Eugenia, too, sat back down in her big leather swiveling chair. She sighed heavily.

"All this frightful talk about people being scared," she said. "Really, young women, I myself don't want to scare anyone, least of all you." She smiled warmly.

Emily felt a little better.

"I don't want you to be unhappy here, and I especially don't want you to labor under the weight of false rumor and innuendo." She looked at Beth, and Beth looked down at her shoes. "Most of all, I don't want you foolishly endangering yourself by breaking rules you might not understand."

Emily nodded.

"We have very strict rules here at Hamilton Home," Eugenia said, "and the rules have been created for the safety of the residents and the workers." She looked at them sternly now. "We have certainly fired people here for less than you've done today."

"But we were just looking around," Emily said. "It's a beautiful building. It's natural to want to explore it." *And explore its secrets, too*, she thought to herself.

Eugenia considered Emily's words. Her eyes narrowed now. "Inasmuch as I admire your interest in architecture, I would still hate to be the one to find what was left of either of you had you fallen through one of the weak and rotted floorboards in the closed section of the home. There is rotting wood everywhere. Deterioration." Her eyes made a tour of the room, to the ceiling, over the shadowy walls. Then her gaze softened and returned, focusing on Emily.

Eugenia stood up, walked around the table, and stopped near her brother. She gazed at Emily again. Again a warm sad smile came over her face.

"The fact of the matter is, you broke the rules. Emily, without going into the details, you must know how damaging your failure here would be. You've been coming along nicely. You are a competent young woman."

Eugenia turned her eyes to Beth. "I might compliment you, too, Beth," she said. "You've been doing a good job. We will therefore let this incident go, although of course we will document it in your personnel files. Don't let anything of the sort happen ever again."

"Yes, ma'am," Beth said.

"Yes Miss Temple," Emily said. She felt the pressure in her chest easing.

Seconds later Emily and Beth were out the door, striding away as fast as their legs could carry them—without breaking into a run, that is.

Ned Fox's room was small and drab, and located at the end of an empty and out-of-the-way hall at the top of one of the home's decayed turrets. He entered it, using his key, and turned on the radio, keeping the volume soft.

The room was pure squalor. No attempt had been

made at decorating. The walls were a colorless, water-damaged gray. The boards creaked beneath his weight.

He went to his dresser. He put his hand into his pocket where he'd kept the buttons given him by the girl, Emily. He took them out and one by one looked at them. They looked shiny on the dresser top. Like jewels.

Funny how a few buttons could become so fascinating. He smiled—or would have if he'd known how. His face kind of cracked, and a crude grunt came from deep in his throat.

Emily, he thought.

He opened up the top drawer and pushed aside his clean, folded socks. Here he found the smooth wooden cigar box that had once, many years ago, belonged to his mother. She'd kept her few meager keepsakes there. She was dead. Long dead. An icy frozen field, uncrossable and ever winter, lay between the feelings of love he'd once associated with another human being and his present wretched existence.

He opened the box. Inside was an old assortment of items. A picture of his mother, old and careworn. She was not pretty. Her face was expressionless. Next to the photo were some acorns and a nail. Next to them were three bullets. Ned closed his eyes. The sound of gunfire—distant, from a far corner of his mind—faded in and out as he touched the bullets. He opened his eyes, wide with terror, and bared his teeth. And the gunfire went away.

There, too, was the silver pocket watch, its ornate cover closed. The strange engraving and ornamentation fascinated him. Stars, the moon, some sort of astrological or zodiac impression. He felt the coolness of the dulled silver. He simply couldn't bear to part with it the night Eugenia had ordered it destroyed. Such treasures were rare in his life.

Ned had never before disobeyed his masters. In fact, he could barely remember a time in his life when he hadn't depended on Eugenia and Herbert Temple. But keeping what another person has discarded was not stealing. It was not, he remembered, a sin. And besides, his keeping something was as good as if it had been destroyed. For the box was secret. And what was in this room was lost to the world.

He lovingly put the buttons inside the wooden box, and gently lowered the lid.

Chapter Five

The Hamilton Home's big ballroom, with its high vaulted ceiling and port-colored carpet, buzzed with expectant residents. The curtains were open wide from the tall windows, and bright late-September-afternoon sunlight cheered the otherwise gloomy antiquated room.

The large elms outside the window blazed with burnished orange and russet leaves. The velvety hilltop lawn still held its summer green.

Residents were seated at tables and in wheelchairs arranged along a side corridor. At the front of the nearly packed room a podium had been set up with a microphone. Speakers hummed with static on a corner table.

Emily counted about seventy people. She wheeled in an elderly man. "Will you be able to see from here, Mr. Hanson?" she asked him, positioning the wheelchair.

He nodded. Brown spots covered his bald head.

"I'll be right over there if you need me," she said,

pointing. She gave his hand a pat and put the brake on his chair. Then she moved to a standing-room-only spot next to the back wall, where Beth was waiting.

"Here he comes," Beth said, craning her neck.

Mild applause erupted and spread through the room as State Senator Allan Pullman entered. The thing Emily noticed first was that full, perfectly combed head of hair. Politician's hair. He had the easy smile of an aging jock. Not handsome, avuncular. Yet he had an aura of importance and learnedness about him. Something strangely attractive about that, even as you sensed the bullshit artist in him. And that smile sparkled. At his side was Eugenia, smartly dressed in a black wool skirt, black jacket, and pearls. She smiled as she strode confidently past him toward the front of the room.

Senator Pullman lagged behind, shaking hands, greeting his public. He bent and spoke loudly and clearly into the cocked ears of the elderly residents. Some of the old people smiled back at him. Others merely looked wide-eyed at the politician. They'd seen his breed before. And still others looked warily at Eugenia Temple.

A woman followed behind Pullman, a pretty young aide. She wore a hand-lettered name tag marked STAFF. In smaller letters, below, was the name Kay Mathers. Her healthy, long-brown hair, parted on the side, was combed perfectly. She wore a short dark-green skirt, green-black jacket over a white blouse, and black heels. A gold necklace glimmered in the sunlight against the white cotton fabric below her throat. She looked the consummate professional young woman, radiant and serene.

"Look at *her*," Beth whispered. "Think she's sleeping with her boss?"

"Do you think he's that cute?" Emily said, referring to Pullman.

Beth gave Pullman an appraising, top-to-bottom glance. "He's got great hair, but I'd only give his face about a six."

Eugenia eventually reached the front of the room. She stood at the podium and tapped the microphone. An earsplitting squeal of feedback blared from the speaker. She patiently adjusted the microphone and bent her head toward it to speak.

"Good afternoon," she began in her usual cool, deep-voiced tone.

Her introduction was brief. She mentioned the senator's years of service to the community, and his tireless dedication to helping the home remain open year after economically challenging year.

Emily wondered how many years of service Pullman could have dedicated. He appeared to be young—in his late thirties, she guessed.

Eugenia mentioned that Pullman had been to Washington recently to meet with Wisconsin's congressional delegation about "issues of particular interest to the elderly," including Social Security and Medicare. She concluded by stating that the last "surprise inspection" of the home—inspections of all nursing facilities were mandated by the federal government—had yielded "overwhelmingly positive results."

"It is now my great pleasure to introduce to you our state senator and local high school football great, Allan Pullman."

The small crowd offered mild applause.

"He grew up at least sixty miles from here," Beth whispered, her voice dripping with cynicism. "There's nothing local about him."

Pullman raised the microphone and smiled at his audience.

"Thank you so very much for having me here again as your guest," he said.

His speech was short. He mentioned a few bills pending before the state senate in Madison. And he talked about how wonderful it was to be back in Blackburn County. He'd had coffee that morning near the airstrip outside of Leonora, he told the residents. He'd talked to "the people" at the lunch counter there.

Many folks were out of work, he said. And the younger people who weren't headed off to the University of Wisconsin at Madison or one of the other state system universities were not being properly trained in the local high schools to "compete in a high-tech world economy." He aimed to change all that, to keep old Blackburn County "viable."

Emily noticed that several residents were asleep.

Kay Mathers stood faithfully by, her arms overloaded with manilla file folders. A leather briefcase-sized bag leaned against her leg on the floor.

At the end of the speech, Pullman received more tepid applause.

Eugenia rose applauding from her folding chair. She stepped in front of Pullman, and raised her head toward the mike.

"Now, if anyone has questions, you are invited to ask the senator at this time." She smiled.

A few hands went up. Mathers started taking notes. Each time a question was asked, she scribbled furiously.

Pullman was in the middle of answering a question about the controversial hormone that was used to make cows produce ever-greater quantities of milk when a clatter rose up from the back of the room.

The senator stopped in the middle of his sentence. Heads turned toward the area of the disturbance.

Emily was astounded to see two old woman rush in at top speed. Both were dressed in nightgowns and robes. They wore expressions of panic mingled with determination on their faces. In a matter of seconds they had pushed their way to the front of the room.

Emily recognized one of the women. Charity Francis. She remembered the wild golden hair and gleaming green eyes. Emily's heart pounded with anticipation.

Eugenia rose from chair again, the smile noticeably absent from her ivory face. She stared icily at the interlopers, who now had all eyes in the room fastened on them.

"Senator!" Charity cried out. She gasped for breath. "We have to speak with you!"

Pullman stole a quick glance at Kay Mathers.

"Yes, of course," He said to Charity, his deep voice calm and steady. He was unflappable.

"My name is Charity Francis and this is Maria Kraus," Charity said, gesturing to the trembling old woman at her side.

"I'm pleased to meet you," Pullman said, voice steady as a newscaster's.

"Really, ladies," Eugenia said, her voice intruding like a glacier. "Such dramatics. Bursting in here like this when you could have joined us civilly at the beginning of the program." Eugenia turned her gaze to Pullman.

Emily suspected Eugenia was lying. She could tell by the expression Eugenia gave Pullman just then, a sort of "bear with us" kind of shrug, and a searching out of his reaction. Yet Emily knew these two women had not been wandering the home freely. She had seen Charity but once. She'd not forgotten her. And here at last was the missing Maria Kraus. Emily folded her arms across her chest.

"People will think you're troublemakers if you're not careful," Eugenia scolded the women.

"You butt out of it, Eugenia," Charity said angrily. She turned to Pullman. "This woman is stealing from us. She runs this place like a prison. She and her brother are responsible for acts of unspeakable evil, including murder."

A murmur passed through the crowd.

"That is quite enough, Miss Francis," Eugenia said coolly.

"The financial frauds that have been perpetuated here alone are reason enough to shut this hellhole down," Charity continued, ignoring Eugenia. "You must listen to us!" Charity said, pleading now. "You have to stop them!"

Three of Eugenia's aides, including the cigar-chomping yardman, stood behind Maria and Charity. Patti, Maxine, and Laverne also stood at the ready, their breasts heaving with anger, fear in their eyes.

"That's enough," Eugenia said. "Please escort them out."

"We are prisoners here!" Charity screamed as one of the aides roughly took her arm.

"Just a moment," Pullman said. "I really can't take sides, ma'am. And I am quite aware of the Hamilton Home's excellent reputation. Aside from my many pleasant visits, I know firsthand of the excellent care provided here. It so happens that my own grandmother spent her final years here."

A satisfied smile crept over Eugenia's face.

Maria cried out, an inarticulate gasp.

Charity pointed at Eugenia. *"This woman probably ate the living flesh from your grandmother's bones!"* Charity screamed.

Pullman looked with mild exasperation at Eugenia.

"I think you understand the caliber of her complaints, Senator," she said. "Even here, in this grand old place, we have our malcontents. It's a measure of our civility that we turn no one away." Eugenia turned to Charity. "You two have had your fun this afternoon. You are leaving this minute. You've been terribly rude."

"You old *monster*!" Charity screamed at Eugenia. "Your game is almost over!"

Charity pulled from the pocket of her robe a neatly folded piece of green paper, upon which a letter had been written. She extended it the senator. Eugenia swooped in. But before Eugenia could grab the letter, Kay Mathers, who'd been standing nearby, plucked it out of Charity's hand and casually slipped it into the inside breast pocket of her jacket.

Emily could see the outrage in Eugenia's eyes. Kay Mathers simply smiled at Eugenia.

"Ladies, we will look into this matter for you," Pullman said. "I promise you."

Charity looked across the room as she was dragged out. Her eyes locked on Emily's. Emily felt her knees weakening.

Help us!

Beth took hold of Emily's hand. "You okay?" she said.

"I need some air," Emily said.

"Let's get out of here."

The senator left shortly after the meeting. He toured an abandoned factory near Leonora that some local residents hoped could be converted into a new shopping mall. The project seemed unlikely, but Pullman played along and shook a lot of hands. He gave the mayor a Cuban cigar he'd picked up on a recent trade mission to Europe, sneaked back through customs.

By the time they got to the airport, Kay could see that the senator was getting tired. The sun was already setting. She was hungry and expected that her boss was, too. But he declined her offer to pick up some burgers.

"The flight should have us back in Madison shortly after nine," he'd said. "Let's just grab something there at the hotel."

Great, Kay thought sardonically. It's going to be a long night. She felt a stiff wind blowing in her face.

The pilot's name was Smith. The craft was a blue-and-white single-engine affair, chartered, and Pullman had used its services many times. He trusted Smith, though Smith was a drinker and frequently had a beer or two—as did Pullman and sometimes Kay—while in the air.

High winds were coming out of the west, which could make a flight due south a white-knuckle affair. But Pullman had other things on his mind than the sudden change in the weather.

He had numerous fiscal papers in his briefcase, and if they proved too boring, he'd brought along a paperback his wife had recommended. He thought of calling Angie from the hanger, but figured he'd wait until he got back to Madison. She'd offered to drive to Blackburn County that day, and bring their two young sons along. He'd nixed that.

Kay put her cigarette out under her shoe and walked to the small aircraft. She'd hoped to at least be able to change out of these clothes. But as usual her boss was in a hurry. He walked up to the craft, where Smith stood.

"Not quite ready to fly, boss," Smith said. He wore a good-ol'-boy cap with a red bill.

"What the fuck are you talking about?" Pullman said, looking at his watch. "I've got a bitch of a day in Madison tomorrow. The sooner I get back to the hotel, the better."

Smith looked away, at the sky streaked with orange and purple clouds. The wind blew his cap off, but he caught it in his hand. It was that kind of dexterity that made people find him instantly trustworthy as a pilot.

"You're the boss," Smith said.

"Very good." Pullman loosened his tie and climbed aboard. Kay's heels clacked on the tarmac as she approached the craft. Smith turned to greet her.

"He's in total-prick mode," Kay said.

"Tell me," Smith said.

"I figured you noticed. All fueled up?" she asked.

"Yeah, I had a case of Miller while you all were with the blue heads."

She elbowed him lightly in the ribs.

Kay sat in the back of the tiny cabin with Pullman, who'd donned his half lenses and was paging through a thick fiscal report. He had a five o'clock shadow that made him look sexy. She slipped off her heels, then her pantyhose. Pullman didn't look up from his reading.

Smith turned knobs on the control panels above his head. He started up the engine. Kay Mathers reached into her bag and pulled out a thick, glossy fashion magazine, something to page through on the flight to Madison. The magazine's perfumed scent permeated the back of the cabin as she turned the pages.

The sun had set over the airstrip. Seen from a distance, the tiny plane's taillights blinked red. Lights flashed on the wings as it taxied down the runway. From the dark of the hanger entrance, a puff of smoke climbed into the night air.

Bill Shore, a seedy-looking middle-aged mechanic raised a filthy brown duffel bag in his grease-smeared hands. Tools clanked together inside. He pitched his cigarette out onto the tarmac, then dropped the tools into the back of his rusted truck.

Before getting inside, Shore looked around. From his jacket pocket he withdrew a small, flat, half-pint bottle of whiskey. He twisted off the cap, breaking the paper seal. He put the bottle to his lips and threw his head back for a long drink. The liquor burned pleasantly in his throat.

In the distance, the plane took to the air, climbing

into the night. Its engine's buzz sounded like an electric shaver rounding a jawline.

When the plane was just a bright white dot against the sky, almost indistinguishable from the stars, Bill Shore drove home.

Miles away in Leonora, at the moment the plane was approaching the southbound border of Blackburn County, Emily and Kerry sat down together in a darkened corridor at the bottom of a flight of stairs. In a few minutes it would be time for their class to begin.

It was as though the argument and the unwanted kiss in the restaurant had never occurred. Her attraction to Kerry blotted out her objections. He'd asked her to sit down next to him, and now she was, saying nothing for the longest time. Was it fear and trouble that can make you draw closer to some people? Even the wrong people? She felt she didn't have the time to wonder.

Not that Kerry was wrong for her. It was just that the circumstances were so fouled up. She only knew that she was warmed by his proximity to her. By his body being close to hers.

Finally he leaned in toward her. "Do you forgive me?" he said.

She took in a deep breath. She was upset about the events at the home. "Do I forgive you?" she said. She laughed and rolled her eyes. "Yeah. Do *you* forgive *me*?"

"I wasn't offended," he said. He leaned his head toward her. She bent close to him this time, accepting. Then he kissed her on the mouth, tenderly.

She kissed him back, and a familiar warmth filled her. But after a few moments, she broke away. She turned her face away from his. She was troubled, but not by him.

She said, "What I don't think you or anybody really understands is—"

"Yeah . . .?"

"Something really awful is happening in that home."

Kerry took her hand, and he pulled her closer again. "Don't you think if something really weird is happening, somebody will look into it? How about Pullman? He's a big shot. Don't you think somebody else would be onto it, too? Not just you, Emily?"

"Maybe you have more faith in the system than I do," she said. He kissed her again, and this time she pushed him lightly away.

"What?" he said. "Why are you so cold to me?"

"I'm not being cold to you. I don't mean to be, anyway."

But maybe she had. One second she wanted him, and the next . . . She liked Kerry, but she didn't want to get seriously involved with anybody right now. And she felt herself falling. Falling for him.

"Oh, I get it," Kerry said. "Danny. It's Danny, right?"

Emily's jean-clad legs were still entwined with his. "What is that supposed to mean?" she said.

"It means you're still hung up on him. A drug dealer."

"You don't know what you're talking about. And if that's what you think, you sure don't know me, Kerry Thornton."

He looked away. "I think I'm in love with you," he said.

She shook her head. Love. He'd used that word again. Was that what it was between them? Just like that? She felt herself on the very edge of a dangerous, high cliff. She scrambled for safety.

"People are in trouble at the Hamilton Home," she protested. "That's what I've been trying to tell you! And you're going on about love."

He looked at her coldly. "What a fool, huh? Guess we hicks never do see the big picture."

At that moment Kerry's friend Ralph rounded the corner, his camera around his neck. He looked right at them. Emily could see the surprise in his eyes when he saw them together, legs entwined.

Usually she didn't give a damn what other people thought. But suddenly she was embarrassed, as though she'd given away a secret by accident—the wrong secret, the wrong impression. She struggled to free her legs.

"Oh," Ralph said softly, backing up a bit. As if he could rewind this like a loop of film. "Here you are." He was wearing a letterman's jacket, and he plunged his hands into the pockets. A backpack was slung over his shoulder. "Excuse me," he said and started to back away. "I didn't realize you two . . ."

Emily got up. "Neither did I," Emily said.

"Christ, Emily," Kerry said and sighed.

Emily was ashamed of herself for being ashamed. But she took a deep, bracing breath. Too many complications. Can't think about all of this now. She looked at Ralph, whom she didn't know at all, and then at

Kerry, whom, she thought, in a brief mad flash through her mind, she wished she'd never met.

Was it possible her feelings were so naked he could read them? Kerry hung his head down in an exaggerated expression of weariness.

Emily left them. She tried to clear her throat, but it was dust dry. She was, she knew, quite in the middle of things here in Blackburn County. Things that were beginning to weigh upon her too heavily.

The flight was almost an hour under way when Kay heard the first strange rattle, followed by a sickly grinding. Her eyes rose from an article she'd been reading, and she looked at the vibrating ceiling of the cabin. Then she looked at Smith, up front. His shirt was sweated though in the armpits. She looked over at Pullman, who glanced up and then back to his report, dour expression unchanged.

Kay turned a page of her magazine. She noticed her palms were sweating. The plane, at that moment, seemed to drop out from under her and rocked to the side.

"Fuck!" Smith whispered, correcting the plane. Pullman's papers came loose from his grip and were soon all over the back compartment.

"Smith, what's going on?" Pullman barked.

"If I knew I'd tell you!" Smith snapped back. Kay knew that Pullman was not accustomed to be shouted at that way.

Pullman asked in a voice filled with irritation, an unpleasant voice Kay had heard many times, "Do we have a problem?"

Smith laughed bitterly. "I'd say we sure as fuck have a problem."

Kay leaned forward. She was surprised that her hands were actually shaking. Pullman reached for her hand and clasped it tightly in his own.

"Stay calm, Kay," he ordered.

She pulled her hand free of his.

"Smith, can you pull us out of it?" Kay said. She wondered if it was the weather that was causing the problem. Outside the window she could see the moon, clear and bright.

"I could try and put her down in a cornfield," he said.

The plane was rocked again, as if plucked from the sky by a giant, demonic hand. This time both Pullman and Kay were battered around the back seat, heads slamming up against padded walls.

"Oh, Christ!" Kay screamed. "Do something!"

The engine whined hideously.

We're going to die! Kay thought. Strange thoughts filled her head. What am I doing here in the first place? She thought of her mother, her mother's face. She did not think of the letter in her jacket pocket, the one written on the back of the flyer that announced Senator Pullman's visit. She thought: *God, help us!*

"I don't believe this," Pullman said. He was bleeding from the bridge of his nose, where his glasses had been smashed off. He held the glasses in pieces in his hands.

"Come on, you son of a bitch!" Smith screamed at the controls.

It was as though they had stopped in midair. As

though the hand of the giant that had plucked them from the sky was holding them up for a closer look. If Kay looked out her side window, would she see its great, gleaming golden eye peering in at her? An angry flash of teeth? They were being turned this way and then the other way, rocked, jerked. And finally . . . dropped.

Kay could smell the smoke before she saw it. She began to pray harder. Thick black smoke billowed in from the vents, blinding her. She could no longer see anything, and she held her breath. She could feel in her stomach the sudden downward pitch of the aircraft. It seemed to take a long time, that unspeakable roll forward. At last she had to take a breath. She gasped and choked. For a moment she felt as though her insides were on fire. But it all ended quickly, in sudden blackness.

The plane soared like a bright, smoldering meteor over the dark valley, trailing smoke across the moonlit sky. It pounded into an apple orchard and exploded into a great fiery orange-and-black mushroom cloud that seared the grass and glowed in the eyes of a thousand startled creatures.

The explosion was deep and thunderous. Some distance away, through the blue murk of night, an upstairs window in a nearby farmhouse was filled with yellow light.

The old farmer blinked, raised the window shade, and put his glasses on. Was it a kind of miracle? Or a sign? Up the hill, in the apple orchard, the trees danced with fire.

Chapter Six

The next morning, headlines across the state exclaimed the story of the senator's tragic death. Also reported killed in the fiery crash were the pilot and the senator's top aide, Kay Mathers—final confirmation pending a dental records examination. An investigation was underway to determine the cause of the mysterious crash.

Patrick lowered his newspaper and looked across the breakfast table at his daughter.

"It's truly shocking," he said. Steam curled upward from his coffee mug.

Emily nodded, trying to appear brave. Her arms were crossed over her chest. She wore a baggy black sweater.

Patrick stood up from his chair and came around the table to where his daughter was sitting. He bent and hugged her close to him. "You just never know when a tragedy like this is going to happen, honey," he said. Blue whimpered at the front door. He wanted to go outside into the clear and sunny fall day.

"What if it wasn't an accident?" Emily said. "What if Eugenia and Herbert were behind it?"

Patrick grimaced, raising a skeptical eyebrow. "Really, now. Do you think the Temples can command an airplane out of the sky?"

Emily went to the door and let Blue out. He tore across the lawn after a squirrel and treed it. Emily didn't give her father an answer. She stared into the distance. She breathed deep into her lungs the cool country air, fragrant with pine needles. She fought back tears.

"There's going to be an investigation, Emily," Patrick said. "If anything suspicious happened, like a bomb or something, it will come out."

But would it? How could he be so sure?

"Those two women," Emily said. "What's going to happen to them now?" She stared out at the rolling hills. Many of the treetops had turned already, leaves a papery blaze of yellow and crimson. Most were at the halfway point. In the breeze, leaves fell in a glittery golden light. "Will Charity and Maria disappear? People disappear from the streets of Leonora and the farms of Blackburn County. Nobody seems to pay much notice." She covered her face with her hand. The tears came through her closed eyes.

Patrick put a reassuring hand on her shoulder and squeezed tenderly. "I don't want you spending any more time at the nasty Hamilton Home," he said. "We'll work out another deal of some kind."

Emily pulled away. "But it's too late for me to leave," she said. "Even if I could get out of my court order . . . they need me."

" 'They'?"

She turned away. A fat white cloud was blowing over the blue mat of sky, toward the sun. She had never verbalized that feeling before—*they need me*. But it was true. Her heart was held in the grip of this knowledge.

"Honey, I want you to come with me to New York next weekend for a few days," Patrick said. "I want to get you out of this place."

The gallery opening. It was next week. A chance to be with her father in New York. Was that what she wanted?

"I don't know . . ." she began.

"Emily, I really want you to come with me. Please come along. For me. I promise it will do us both good."

Gazing out at the treetops, she thought about it. She thought of autumn in Central Park. Maybe a weekend in New York would be a good way of gaining some perspective. She was too confused.

She turned to him and said, "Okay. Maybe you're right. Maybe that's what we both need."

The news finally made it all the way to the subbasement of the Hamilton Home. The senator was dead. Charity sat down heavily on a cot in the barred room that was an actual jail cell, left over from the bad old days when the Hamilton Home had been a county poorhouse. Eugenia wasn't taking anymore chances where Charity was concerned. The smell of mothballs rose from the bedding.

"This is indeed a setback," Charity said. Fighting back tears, she laughed bitterly. She'd come too far to give up. Even though the situation was more grim than she'd ever imagined it could be.

She looked at Maria, who set down a bowl of foul-tasting soup beside her own cot. The shadow of the bars crossed over her face. Her eyes brimmed with tears. Charity came and sat next to her and held her hand.

Gloom came from the hallway beyond the cell they now shared. The occasional brown mouse scurried by. It was cold down here, the floor slick with puddles and scum, and Maria was falling ill. Charity could feel the fever rising in her friend's flesh.

"You must lie down and save your strength," she said. She caressed Maria's face. To the touch, her companion was on fire.

Maria shook her head, eyes filled with worry and terror.

"I have to get the pocket watch back," Charity explained again. "I'm powerless without it. It's the only option we have left."

Maria nodded. Then she shrugged, eyes wide with questioning.

"How indeed," Charity said with a sigh. "It's time to tell you. We still have a hope. There is *another* here," Charity said. "A true budding sorceress, though young and inexperienced in the ways of magic. She is our salvation. She's got to be."

Charity cast out her mind to search like smoke through the rooms of the Hamilton Home for the girl. But something—someone—pulled her back. Someone needed her immediate attention.

Maria was fading. Charity gently helped her under the covers. "Sleep, my dear. Everything that was stolen from you shall be returned. I promise you, my dear. Yes, everything."

Maria calmed down and eventually fell into a deep sleep. Charity went to her own lumpy bed. She felt weary, nearly exhausted. Despite her words of encouragement, she was uncertain. For the first time since undertaking her avenging mission, she was filled with real doubt.

"If only I could be certain of my convictions," she murmured. The dark, windowless room offered no consolation within its heavy cavelike walls. She closed her eyes. "Emily . . ." she whispered. "Come to us. Help us, Emily. . . ."

The next night, Emily and Beth shared a work shift at the home. Before six o'clock, when Eugenia usually went back to the caretaker's house, they stood nervously outside her office on the main floor.

"Are you sure you want to do this?" Beth said. She was having a "bad hair day." She had tied back her long red locks with a fat elasticized fabric with a pattern that reminded Emily of an old Hawaiian shirt.

"Do we have anything to lose?" Emily said.

"Did Pullman and his aide?"

Emily ignored that. "We have a right to ask where Charity and Maria are being kept."

Emily's snooping efforts had not paid off. After being scolded once for going into restricted areas, she was eager to avoid getting caught again. They had looked around but failed to find the old women. Now they would try the direct approach.

Emily walked into the outer office. Eugenia's door was half open. Emily knocked.

Eugenia looked up from her desk, where she'd been going over some papers with a ballpoint.

"Emily," Eugenia said, a trace of surprise in her voice. "Come in."

Emily started in, and Beth hid behind the door. "I wonder if I could talk with you for a minute," Emily said.

Eugenia frowned and covered her papers. "Why of course. Miss Hanes, too? Do come in." Beth walked stiffly in. She attempted a friendly smile, which melted under Eugenia's penetrating glare. Emily nervously cleared her throat.

"It's about Charity Francis and Maria Kraus," she said.

Eugenia's expression became a degree more stern. "Yes," she said, her tone like a snake rearing its head back to strike.

"I want to see them," Emily said firmly.

Eugenia set down her pen. She was wearing one of her severe wool suits, and on her lapel was a metallic broach—twisted twigs and leaves, encrusted with tiny rhinestones. It looked to Emily like something dead and mummified.

"I see. So, you're worried about them?"

"I want to know that they're okay," Emily said. Her eyes flashed. "And I want to know what they were trying to tell Senator Pullman."

"Do you?"

"I have a right to ask questions," Emily said. "Under the circumstances, you're probably being asked a lot of questions."

Eugenia raised her eyebrows and gave a small, kittenish laugh. Emily was chilled by the sound of it. "I don't know what you mean, my dear," Eugenia said coolly.

Emily almost lost her composure. She swallowed hard. "Just let me talk to Charity."

"What if I told you Charity was ill?" Eugenia said. "What if I told you her immune system couldn't stand a visitor, that your visit could even kill her?"

"You're making it up."

Eugenia's eyes narrowed.

"And you, Emily, are a meddlesome child," Eugenia said. She sighed. "It's obvious, looking over the record of your brief life, that you have a talent for seeking and finding trouble."

Emily looked down at her shoes. Scuffed Doc Martens.

"Do you really think you have some kind of moral authority here?" Eugenia asked. "To society's eyes you're nothing but a piece of, well, *drug scum*, Emily. A terribly twisted little girl. Or, I believe a maladjusted *child of divorce* is what the experts are calling your syndrome these days. Psychologically abused. Abandoned. You went looking for love and found something almost as pleasurable in a chemical laboratory. And with a common criminal."

Emily felt herself shaking. Eugenia smiled; she was just warming up.

"Now you want a second chance," she said, her tone as calm and warm as it had been the day she'd welcomed Emily here. "And here we are, trying to give it to you. Maybe you're smarter than we thought. Maybe you know that real second chances don't come along too often—and never come without a high price."

Emily started to say, "You have no right," but it came out as a barely heard whisper.

Eugenia rose from her desk.

"Haven't I? Where do you think you'd be if I dis-

missed you from this job? You are perilously close to
the brink, Emily,'' Eugenia's eyes flashed with genuine
anger now. ''Think about it.''

Emily turned and ran, running past Beth, who was
terror struck. Emily ran down the main hallway, into
the tiny main-floor bathroom. She slammed the door
shut. Then she leaned over the sink to cry.

She's wrong! She's twisted everything around!

She looked up at her face in the mirror. She saw a
girl there, a bit of mascara streaked on her white cheeks.

Was her life really stained—irreparably—as well?
Had she done something so terribly wrong? Did they
own her now?

I am innocent! She thought fiercely.

Emily, help us!

She gasped. She wasn't hearing this. She was not
going insane.

She splashed cold water on her face. And when she
looked up, she did not recognize the blurry face she
saw in the mirror. She jumped back in horror. She
quickly dried her face, and took another look into the
mirror.

Now she saw her own reflection. So what had she
seen a moment ago? She tried to recall it. It was as
though a hazy memory flashed in and out of her mind:
Eugenia, dressed in the old-fashioned garb of pilgrims,
a musket at her side, blood on her hands.

Emily gasped again. Impossible. It had to be her
imagination working overtime. She hadn't seen such
an image anywhere before in real life.

Someone was pounding on the door. Emily unlocked
it, and Beth tried to rush in. But Emily ran past her

and out the front door of the home. She ran as hard and as fast as she could over the hill. And when she reached the biggest and tallest elm, she stopped, chest heaving. She looked up through her tears and clenched her fists at her sides.

Help you? Me? How can I help anyone?!

The sun pierced through the blue heavens, and its shafting beams pulled her gaze deep into the blinding eyelike orb. She covered her face with her hands. The red glow behind her eyelids faded to black. A sudden calm swept over, like a mild breeze. She straightened her back. She could breath again.

Yes, she would help them. She wanted to. She *had* to. She had to stop Eugenia. She would, she swore to herself. She swore to the sun and to the pale, transparent moon.

Beth caught up with her. "Are you okay?" she said, taking Emily's shoulders and shaking her. Beth panted, out of breath. "That really was the last straw. I'm quitting. I'm not coming back here again."

Emily looked at her friend. "You can quit if you want to," she said. Her face was composed in anger and determination. "I'm staying. I'm staying until I stop those two."

Beth pulled Emily's arm. The home loomed huge behind them, a vast, listening presence.

"You've got to *get real*, Emily," Beth said. "Nothing is worth putting up with this bullshit."

Emily took some deep breaths. "I need some time to get my head together about this. I'm going away for the weekend with my father," she said. "When I come back, I'm going to find out exactly what's been going on at the Hamilton Home, from the financial frauds all the way down the line. And I'm going to expose them."

"You want revenge," Beth said.

"Yes," Emily said. "And I want to save Charity and Maria, wherever they are."

Beth looked up at the blue autumn sky. "This is crazy."

Emily nodded. "Yes, maybe it is. Are you with me?"

"We could both get killed."

Emily shrugged. Was it possible—could they really be murdered, as Emily suspected the senator and his aide and the pilot had been?

Beth pursed her lips and kicked at a great wad of dirt that turned out to be the remains of a large ant hill. She kicked at the grass, staining her shoe green. Emily thought that if Beth had the strength to uproot a tree just then she would have done so. She would have pulled all the big elms out of the earth.

Exhausted and still panting, Beth turned and looked Emily square in the eye.

For a moment that seemed frozen in time, they looked into each others eyes. Thin clouds streamed high above their heads, like foam rolling on hard blue surf.

"Okay, I'm with you," Beth said softly, and slapped her hand into Emily's. They embraced. "I must be crazy, but I'm in," she whispered into her friend's ear.

Eugenia and Herbert sat at their candlelit dining room table and finished a sumptuous meal of roast pork. Gretta cleared away the dishes, and Herbert emptied the last of the merlot into his wine glass.

He sighed. "We could easily get rid of both girls," he said to his sister. "But I've gotten used to thinking of them as our little reserve account. They are sitting ducks, especially the one with the wild reputation. Thank goodness for girls with bad reputations," he mused. "Everyone is only too willing to believe they had it coming."

"At least we've learned that much," Eugenia said. She looked worried.

"In all these years we've learned pretty well how to survive, I'd say," Herbert replied.

"I still want to throw a scare into those girls," Eugenia said. "I want to put them on notice. Put them at the very edge of the cliff, as it were. And then hold them by their hair."

Herbert leaned in close, examining his sister's face. "Do I see a new line forming?" he said, peering at her up close.

Alarmed, Eugenia held her hand to her face. "Maybe you'd better conjure a new batch of the *remedy*," she said.

He chuckled wolfishly. "Afraid the boys won't find you attractive, dear?"

She stroked her face. How long it had been since she'd been with a man?

"The remedy," she said.

"We're in low supply," Herbert said. "I'm afraid you'll have to do with a few signs of wear and tear."

She stood up. The worried look vanished from her face and she laughed at herself. As usual, Herbert was playing to her fears for his own amusement.

"Damn you, brother. Stop playing silly games. We'll survive, as we always have."

"So, too, will your vanity."

"Hush, now. I want to tell you my plan. My plan to shake up those meddlesome girls."

He lit one of his black cigarettes. "I'm all ears."

"I'm going to call Emily's father. There's been a theft, you see."

He tilted his head, savoring her words. The tip of his cigarette glowed bright orange as he drew on it.

"Yes, a theft at the home," Eugenia said, eyes gleaming. "A pharmaceutical theft."

Kerry positioned himself in the Leonora High library entryway and waited for Beth. He wore his cap low, over his eyes. He felt like a private eye. His assignment: the Case of the Human Hearts.

When Beth finally appeared in the hallway, her long hair still wet from her morning shower, he picked up his pack. She stopped dead in front of him.

"Can we go somewhere and talk?" he said.

She cocked her head slightly. "I have to study for a history test," she said. "Sorry." She started to move on. He blocked her way.

"Please. This is important."

She sighed with annoyance. Then she looked around. The hallway streamed with students. The din they created was deafening.

"Let's make it quick," she said.

They went out to his Mustang parked in the gravel lot behind the school. He switched on the radio. It was near the top of the hour, and the radio call-in show was all about the senator's untimely death. Perhaps a UFO had been responsible, one caller suggested. Outside, a bracing chill was in the air. The sky was overcast, threatening cold, gray rain.

Kerry turned the volume low. "It's about Emily," Kerry said. "I guess you know I'm . . ." He searched for words, couldn't find any.

"Yes I know. You're very fond of her."

"I'd do anything, anything at all for her," he said. "But she doesn't give me the time of day."

"That's not true. Anyone can see you're becoming good friends."

Kerry looked out the car window. "Friends . . . is that what we are? There are some complications. Has she told you?"

"Why should she tell me? And if she did tell me, why would I tell you? You have odd ideas about friendship."

"Tell me about it," Kerry said. "I seem to have nothing but misunderstandings with people."

Beth said, "Well, at least you have that." She surprised herself, saying that. It sounded so wimpy and unlike her. She usually didn't allow any self-pity—in herself or others. "What I mean is . . . you're asking the wrong girl. I can't advise you. I gotta go." She reached for the door handle.

"Wait, Beth. You could help me. You could explain things to Emily."

"What things?"

"Tell her I'm really okay. That I'm not trying to rush anything with her. That I respect her, and that I don't mean to come on so strong."

"But you're coming on strong right now. Why force the issue? Why not just let things happen naturally?"

"Because . . . there isn't time!" He looked away

from her. "The point is . . . I'd do anything for Emily. I'd die for her. But she goes days without speaking to me. She doesn't return my calls. She's driving me crazy."

Beth smiled slightly, closing her eyes. Kerry looked out at the parking lot. A few stray drops of rain dotted the window. "I really fucked up my chances. . . ."

"Okay, okay, calm down, and try to relax. You're asking me to try and scam Emily on your behalf—"

"I just want to know I have a chance. For her to know I'm sorry I—But I don't want you to 'scam' her, as you put it."

"Good. I've got news for you, Kerry. She can't be scammed. You'll just have to back off a little. And pray for luck."

He pounded his fist on the dashboard. "That's the stupidest, most worthless kind of help I've ever heard of."

"Hey," Beth said, "don't yell at me. You're the one who asked me to come out here." She opened the car door and started to climb out. He touched her arm, stopping her.

She looked down on his hand, into his pleading eyes.

"I'm sorry." He pressed his lips together. "I never know what to say, how to act. I'm so afraid of blowing my chances. Coach Peterson says the reason I'm such a lousy wrestler is because I'm too impulsive and impatient. I guess he's right. I know what it feels like to be pinned to the mat, and I hate it. Beth, can you help me?"

She had to turn away. Dogs with sad eyes had the same affect on her. Yet she almost felt angry with herself for what she was feeling. He was melting her inside.

"I don't even know you that well, Kerry—not well enough to know these things about you. I've watched you wrestle, though. Did you know that? You win sometimes, and you lose sometimes, and that's life."

"No, that's sports. This is life," he said. "When you care about somebody."

"It's still a kind of game," Beth said. "If it wasn't, would you be talking to me now?"

He turned his face away from her.

"Don't get me wrong," she said. "I like you and all. But you've never really given *me* the time of day since we were little kids. That's twelve years. You have always run with the popular crowd, ignoring the Beth Haneses of the world. Now you want to use me to try to convince Emily of something she's apparently already made up her mind about."

He winced, hearing that. "She's gotta give me a chance."

"I can try to be your friend," Beth said. "I can listen to you, and even keep your secrets." She put her hand on his. It was a bold thing for Beth to do. He looked into her liquid blue eyes. "But help you?" she said. "No, I don't think I can do that. You're the only one who can help you."

Patrick sat in Eugenia's office, his legs crossed. He rarely wore a tie. But today he'd found one—Day-Glo green—thrown it on, and a jacket, too. Gray wool. He sat across the desk from Eugenia Temple, listening.

Normally, he'd never have left his studio in the

daytime. He took a long look at this strange, tightly wound woman. She looked the consummate professional.

Earlier in the day he'd received a call from Eugenia. Emily had been out with Webster in the yard. He'd seen her through the front window, the telephone receiver pressed to his ear.

"We have a serious problem at the Home," Eugenia had said. "It may involve your daughter. I'm reluctant to call the police. I wonder if you could see me in my office at once."

Emily had been leading Amber by a rein while Webster watched her, smiling. She'd been dressed in jeans and boots, and wore an old plaid jacket of his.

"Of course," he'd answered.

When he later emerged from the house, showered, shaved, and dressed twenty minutes later, Emily had been astonished and asked where on earth he was going.

He'd told her flat out he was going to the home, and why, which upset her terribly. He'd tried to calm her, but she flew into a rage. It was true she and Beth had been in some areas of the home that were expressly off-limits, she'd confessed. But they were only "snooping" and had done nothing that would warrant calling the police.

"She's a liar!" Emily had cried.

Patrick had hugged her. "I believe you, Em. But I'd better go see her."

"She's a pathological bitch," Emily had said, making Webster's eyebrows rise.

Patrick had given Emily a kiss good-bye. "We have to play by her rules. Just a little longer, dear. It can't hurt for me to meet with her. She's got to listen to reason. I shouldn't be gone much more than an hour," he'd said. He'd watched his daughter in the rearview mirror as he left the drive. She stood with defiance in her body, a hand resting on Amber's powerful neck. How he'd hated leaving her like that, but what choice did he have?

Now he was sitting in this stuffy office, trying to be polite to this control freak, Eugenia Temple.

"I'm so sorry to have to call you here today, so I'll get right to the point, Mr. Jordan," Eugenia Temple said. "There has been a theft of some pharmaceutical materials, some tranquilizing drugs, from the home. It occurred during one of Emily's shifts."

Patrick listened, expressionless.

"Normally I wouldn't jump to conclusions," Eugenia said, "but I thought you should know we've been having some difficulty with her, and with another girl she's become friendly with. I would go as far as to say Emily's personality has changed since her arrival."

She seemed to be waiting for him to say something. Coffee she'd offered him steamed in a styrofoam cup on the desk between them.

"Emily's history makes her a prime suspect," Eugenia added.

"Did she have a key to the pharmacy?" Patrick asked. "Don't you keep that stuff locked up?"

"Yes, of course we keep it locked up, but keys are not difficult to acquire if you know what you're after. Nor is breaking into a cabinet or room terribly difficult. If you know what you're doing."

Patrick felt anger kindling in his gut. "You said you don't normally jump to conclusions," he said. "What are you doing now if not that?"

She smiled in response. "Under the circumstances, I think my theory is credible."

"I think it sucks."

Eugenia again produced that ironic little cat smile. "If we terminated Emily's community service project, she would probably be sent back to California." The words hung in the air. She looked as though she were admiring them, or waiting for them to echo back.

Patrick was speechless now.

"Do you understand me, Mr. Jordan? That could mean jail. Or at any rate, an environment far worse than this."

"You don't have any proof," he said.

To this, she smiled. "Now you are wearing my patience a bit thin, Mr. Jordan. Whom do you think the court would believe? Whom do you think her own mother would believe?"

Patrick stared at her, astonished.

"Now I want to ask you a question," Eugenia said. "Do you want your child to continue here at the home for the duration of her assignment?"

Patrick sneered in disgust. "You really think you have us by the balls, don't you?"

"We are very discreet here, Mr. Jordan. We keep meticulous records. We watch our backs, as the saying goes. Now, I want, as a condition of Emily's continuing on here at the Hamilton Home, a promise from you that she will come into work on time and keep her nose in her business—and out of ours."

He took a breath. "I don't think you know Emily very well at all." He wanted to say more, but she interrupted him.

"And how well do you know her? I looked her

record over carefully, Mr. Jordan, before I agreed to take her on—to take her on at your request, may I remind you. You, a distinguished member of the community."

"Yes, and I am grateful—"

"She is a complicated child, and she was involved in a dangerous game in California. She has a taste for drugs, and for bad company. She's smart, but in all the wrong ways, it seems. To a drug addict, this establishment might appear to be a kind of candy store."

"I simply cannot believe—"

"Are you in therapy, Mr. Jordan?"

Again, he was astonished by this woman's audacity. "What business—"

"I am not kicking Emily out," Eugenia said. "Just putting her on notice—and you, too." She stood up. "Family counseling wouldn't hurt, Mr. Jordan."

Stunned, he stood up, looked at her extended hand. Absently he shook it. Her grasp was firm, cold.

At the door he turned and said, "You're wrong about Emily."

"Just the same, Mr. Jordan, I hope you have a long talk with your daughter while you're away in New York. She must learn to observe and obey *our* rules. She mustn't stick her nose where it doesn't belong. When Emily comes back here, she will be treated well. But things cannot and will never be what they were."

Patrick didn't drive straight home. He was too upset. Aside from the troubles with Eugenia Temple, he always had a bad case of nerves before a big show in New York. And his return trips to the city always reminded him of his reasons for leaving.

He'd loved New York, and some of the happiest

days of his life had been when Emily was a baby and
Cathleen and he were in love, and young. That time
existed in a frozen-in-amber memory, muted and warm.

Now he was returning to that great city with the
person who mattered most in his life, a daughter who
had followed his footsteps into a chemical wilderness.
She'd been hunted and captured. God, how he wanted
to believe the past was really the past, over and done
with; that its damage was merely a memory or a lesson,
and not something that could reach out into the present,
like some monstrous claw.

As an absent father, he'd hurt his daughter, he knew.
He still felt a tremendous amount of guilt. The pain
he experienced when Cathleen and Emily moved out
to the coast had been his excuse for the coke, of which
he'd consumed so much. But he'd cleaned up his act
. . . and hadn't Emily, even at her tender age, found a
better way to live?

He felt a moment of doubt. What if Eugenia was
telling the truth? What if the last thing on earth he
wanted to believe had an element of truth to it? Emily
had managed to get herself into hot water at the home,
hadn't she? *Something* was up. . . .

Yet now, driving a rolling country highway more
beautiful this fall than at anytime he'd ever remembered
it being, even in his boyhood, he was unconvinced that
Emily had done anything wrong. She'd told him so,
and he believed her. That was it. That was what he
had to go on.

He arrived at Leonora Tech at about noon, and
walked against the tide of students exiting the main
building. At a public information window he asked
where he might find Gloria Munson.

He found her eating a sandwich at her desk in a tiny book-crammed office. Gloria wore glasses with aviator-style frames, and was deeply absorbed in a book. She looked up, slightly startled, when he knocked on the open door.

"Oh, hello," she said, folding the book into her lap.

"I wanted to talk with you about Emily," he said.

She swallowed the bite of her sandwich, and placed the white bread down on a piece of plastic wrap. "Excuse me," she said, clearing a stack of folders off the chair next to her desk. "Please sit down." She removed her glasses.

"I'm sorry to disturb you," he said. He was fidgeting and flexing his hands nervously.

Her eyes measured his distress. She was wearing a black sweater and jeans, both of which showed off her trim figure. Her slightly graying black hair was tied back loosely, a few wisps floating freely about her oval face.

"No, you're not disturbing me at all," she said. She gestured to the empty chair.

"Thank you," he said, taking a seat.

He wanted to tell her about Emily, to seek the advice of a mature woman, someone who he knew cared about Emily, too. He sat down and before he realized what he was doing, he began to tearfully pour out his entire soul to her, a complete stranger.

That night Emily took a long time to get to sleep. Her father had kept telling her he believed her side of the story. He trusted her, he'd said, and he knew she was innocent. She'd ended up crying in his arms.

Stroking her hair, he'd told her that the trip to New

York would be fun, a way to get away from the craziness of the home. He'd said she should just put her time in and get it over with. They were—she was—in a trap of sorts. But there were only several weeks of community service left to perform. The end of this ordeal would come soon. She would have to be patient.

And of course, she didn't really want to leave the home—not now. She told her father she couldn't leave the women there.

"Someone has to help them!" she'd said. He'd looked on, concerned, brow furrowed. It had disturbed her greatly to see him look at her like that. She could not explain herself to him. She could not explain what was not explainable even to herself.

When sleep came, her dreams were fitful. Eugenia appeared, monstrous and huge. Herbert perched on her shoulder like a parrot, snickering. A stream of blue smoke trailed from his tiny nostrils.

And then, the dream took an even stranger turn. The mouth of a deep pit opened wide. A pit beneath the mighty structure of the Hamilton Home. And from inside came the call: *Only you can save us now, Emily. Hurry.*

Hurry . . .

The room was stone cold. Charity woke with a start. She could see the steam of her breath in the blackness, picking up light from a distant lamp, beyond the barred cage of her room.

The room was eerily quiet.

Her bones were stiff, and she felt a considerable amount pain as she rose from her bed.

"Maria," she whispered to the dark form on the cot on the other side of the room.

Maria did not answer.

With her heart beating frantically in her chest, Charity walked to the bed and pulled the covers back. Maria's eyes were slightly open, gaze fixed beyond the ceiling above. Her chin did not tremble.

Slowly Charity reached for Maria's hand. She touched it. Cold as marble. Charity felt frantically for a pulse in her wrist. There was none.

She turned away, rage and terror filling her chest.

"No!" she cried out. Her voice echoed through the strange chamber beyond the bars. "No!"

Then she fell and wept over Maria's lifeless body.

"No, no! We needed more time! We needed just a little more time!"

Chapter Seven

Emily and Patrick Jordan stood on the sidewalk on West 57th Street and watched the late-morning traffic stream by. Overhead, the office building windows reflected the autumn sun. On the sidewalks, people hurried along by the hundreds. Emily and her father watched in silence for several minutes.

They stood together next to a newspaper stand, slightly out of the way of the main human flow.

The gallery was just up the bustling, crowded street. Patrick was due there in about a half hour, to meet with the dealer and see how the paintings had been displayed. He sipped steaming coffee from a white paper cup. He had already loosened his tie.

Emily wore a billowy navy-and-white dress. A cream cashmere sweater was draped over her shoulders.

It was wonderful to be back in New York City. She had visited several times since she and her mother had moved to San Francisco. But the number of visits had tapered off over the last few years. Now memories rushed back on every cavernous block. Some impressions could never change: the yellow cabs lurching through intersections, the shadowy canyons stretching for endless blocks between the towering buildings, the shoppers and businesswomen with their bags, tourists craning their necks, some with apprehension, others with delight . . . all took her back to childhood, when New York was—to her, at least—a safe and enchanted place.

They were staying at a small hotel on the Upper East Side. Wanda had recommended it. It was clean and pleasant, the rooms large and sunny.

Emily felt her apprehensions and anxiety leaving her. And not only because she was away from Eugenia Temple and her dungeon, but because she was thinking now of a strategy to find Charity. The thought of Charity had played strangely on her mind all through the evening flight. She and Patrick had arrived in New York late the previous night and taxied to Nadine's, a restaurant in the Village, rather than straight to their hotel. She'd had a glass of wine with dinner, and when she slept, she dreamed of black rooms and a wild sylvan search through the night.

The morning was sun dappled, the air crisp and refreshing.

"Remember this street?" Patrick said now. "You liked it when you were little."

She smiled. No, she didn't remember this street specifically. But she did remember her hand held tight in his, and the streets and avenues of a different New York, a child's New York of bakeries and toy shops and trips to the zoo, afternoons spent in the parks.

"Did you get enough breakfast?" he said.

"I'm fine."

He finished his coffee. "Let's go," he said, and they walked to the gallery, where two young men and a young woman in a ponytail and white T-shirt were cleaning up.

"Roger's in back," the girl said. She gestured with her chin, and her ponytail swooped around.

Roger was Patrick's art dealer, and the owner of the gallery. Emily followed her father through the gray-carpeted room, past his paintings, one of which she'd seen from its inception as a series of sketches.

Roger was a stout, handsome black man of about sixty, bearded, with a friendly smile and wise eyes. A gold stud gleamed in his chubby earlobe. He kissed Patrick, then Emily, though he'd never met her before. He held both her hands in his.

"The very image of your mother," he said with a jolly laugh.

When he was through visiting with Roger and finishing up on last-minute details, Patrick told him they looked forward to seeing him at the opening tonight. The two old friends warmly shook hands.

"See you tonight, kids," Roger said, and gave a wink to Emily.

They walked over to the Museum of Modern Art to see the current exhibit, a retrospective of twentieth century Latin art.

After that they went for lunch at a small Italian restaurant. Patrick spilled red sauce on his tie.

They stopped in a big department store and picked out a new tie. Sitting on the steps of St. Patrick's Cathedral, eating a pretzel, Patrick Jordan announced he was tired and wanted to go back to the hotel room for a short nap before the opening, which was scheduled for 6:00 P.M. That was probably a good idea, because he was much too anxious about seeing old friends, and about the social aspect of an art opening.

Emily wasn't tired. She wanted to explore the city. Patrick gave her fifty dollars, and she cabbed downtown to the East Village, where she took a long stroll.

The skies over New York were mild and blue. Burnished leaves fell through the air like great snowflakes, then scraped along the dirty sidewalks in the soft breeze.

Emily walked by a Ukrainian café bustling with activity, and past numerous odd shops tucked into the ground floors of the tenement buildings. Eventually she found herself at the Strand Book Store.

The Strand was bustling, and the crowd inside was, like the crowd of people she'd seen outside on the street, mostly young, dressed in hip sloppy clothes.

The Strand's ceilings were high, and everywhere tables were stacked with books. Handwritten signs noticed the multiple categories of books.

"Finding everything you need?" someone said behind her. She turned to see a girl with a shaved head and a small silver ring in her nose. She wore a loose white T-shirt, heavy black boots.

"Yes, thanks," Emily said.

"I been watching you. Anything in particular you want?"

Emily shrugged and smiled. "I'm just looking."

"Where you from, honey? I can see you're not from around here."

"Well, I'm actually from San Francisco, but now I live in Wisconsin."

The girl nodded. "Wisconsin, huh? Never been

there." She scratched her head. "I think there's a few copies left of a cool book called *Wisconsin Death Trip*. Over in the travel section. No, wait a minute—it's in the photography section. Want to check it out?"

"Well, I'm really just browsing, but thank you."

"Wait a minute. I know what you need. This could be your lucky day. There's a sale on Anne Sexton remains."

"Excuse me?"

"Did I say *remains*? I mean *remainders*. It's a steal. You like Anne Sexton?"

"I guess I'm not that familiar with her."

"It's time you were introduced," the girl said, and she led Emily over to a table stacked with remaindered books and secondhand paperbacks. Judging by the worn condition and outdated graphics of the volumes for sale, Emily guessed they had been published in the 1960s.

Emily picked up a paperback volume of Sexton poems and paged through it.

"You can't go wrong at that price," the young woman said, tapping her finger on the book. She smiled and crossed her arms over her chest.

"Well, okay, I'll take it," Emily said. "Can I cash a travelers check here?"

"I got no idea, I don't work here," the young woman said. She smiled crookedly.

"But I thought . . . ."

The woman shrugged and took several steps backward. "Someone needs me," she said, pointing behind a stack of books. "Over there." She ducked behind a shelf.

Emily decided to get the volume of Sexton poems and

move on, quickly. She was ready to leave when another book caught her eye. It was shoved haphazardly to the back of a table. She could easily have missed it.

The *Witches' Guide to Sorcery* was rather beaten up, with a dog-eared black cover. It was only fifty cents. Emily picked it up and slowly turned the pages. There were chapters on spells and talismans and astrology, on white magic and black. And several illustrations of fallen angels and evil demons.

Impulsively, she purchased both books.

She emerged on the street with the volumes and looked at her pocket map, which she kept in a black leather bag, hung over her shoulder. She walked over to Fifth Avenue, then to Washington Square Park.

She remembered the fountain. She was tempted to retrace her steps (tiny ones they must have been) back to the old apartment, not too far from here, but she sat down at the edge of the fountain, instead.

Dozens of people, mainly kids, milled around the fountain's edge. A young black man sat on her left, reading the *Village Voice*. A cigarette smoldered between his fingers. Two white girls were coloring a boy's hair magenta. The boy was about seventeen or eighteen, Emily guessed. He sat at the edge of the fountain as they worked the color into his hair. He wore cut-off shorts, no shoes, no shirt. His skin was almost sickly pale.

It was unseasonably warm, and the sun shone with a glorious autumn intensity. Occasionally the light breeze would send some of the fountain spray over to the part of the circle where Emily, and a dozen others, sat. The light spray felt good.

She read some of the Sexton poems, which struck her as being about a woman held prisoner, not only metaphorically, but truly. Emily could not help being reminded of Charity's plight. Perhaps she should not have come to New York after all. She had, she now knew, a mission in Wisconsin. The women in the home. No voices called to her in her imagination here.

Though she had taxi fare, Emily studied the subway map—she was an expert in maps—and took a subterranean ride back uptown. It had been more than a decade since she'd been on the subway with her parents. For most of the ride uptown, she read about witches. The book had a number of disturbing old engravings reproduced inside. One depicted the burning of a witch, Anne Heinrich, in Amsterdam in 1571. Emily shuddered at the sight of it. The woman was tied to a ladder that was being raised up from behind by some ragged-looking men; a fire raged where the ladder would fall forward.

She continued paging through this strange book. The atrocities piled up one after another. Incredible cruelties inflicted upon so called witches and sorcerers though the centuries. She read about the Inquisition in one passage, and then read another long passage about the mysterious witches at a place called Bamberg.

She was oddly absorbed in this book that had all but called out for her attention. With a start she wondered if she might have missed her subway stop.

Emily looked up at the other passengers in the car, all of whom seemed as though absorbed in some kind of blank-faced waking dream, and the car rocked back and forth in a din of heavy, hurling metal.

* * *

The gallery was filled with people in elegantly cut clothes of dark shades and expensive fabrics. They sipped wine and whiskey and amber-colored fluids from clear plastic cups, served from a portable bar on wheels.

Patrick talked into a microphone held by a woman who wore her tape recorder; it was strapped to her shoulder and hung at her side. She had long legs, displayed from a short gray skirt.

Emily's face felt hot, and she was perspiring under her dress. People said hello and smiled. Someone gave her a glass of ginger ale, which she quickly drank. She stood next to one of the paintings, an explosion of wildflowers in coffee cans, and munched a piece of ice, an empty clear plastic cup in her hand.

A woman who could only have been Wanda came swooping into the room, her long blond hair cut off bluntly at the ends, her moist brown eyes filling with tears as she kissed and embraced Patrick.

"There's someone I want you to meet," Patrick said to her. He kissed her and looked around the room for Emily, who stood near the portable bar, watching. Patrick led Wanda, who wore beige wool, across the carpeted gallery to his daughter.

She gave Emily a kiss on the cheek, then rubbed away a lipstick smear with a series of birdlike flicks of her thumb.

"Let's have a look at you," she said, stepping back and surveying Emily. "I think I could find some work for you here in the city," she said. "Maybe a little short for the runway . . . Hmm. Have you considered moving to New York?"

Emily looked at her father, who smiled.

"We're nestled in at the old farmstead in Wisconsin, at present," Patrick answered.

"Has she done any modeling?" Wanda said, disregarding Emily now.

"For me," Patrick said. "But not fashion modeling."

Wanda, who under that spectacular flaxen head had harsh if classic good looks, rattlesnake cheekbones, and an unusually long neck, put her hand on Emily's face and turned it from side to side.

"Hmm. Yeah, I think I could line something up for you. Something a little . . . offbeat, yet fresh."

Emily wasn't impressed. She raised her empty cup.

"I need a refill of ginger ale," she said.

Later, after the sun had set, Wanda accompanied Emily and Patrick to a French restaurant. The staff wore impeccable white uniforms. Tall black candles burned at every table. Wanda had insisted from the outset on paying. Emily thought maybe that was why she was also dominating the conversation. She literally never stopped talking.

First she gave a detailed list of everyone in New York, in Patrick's old circle, who had died. Some had died of old age, some had died of other things. Wanda told each story, no matter how sad, with relish. Emily looked up at the high black ceiling of the restaurant and saw that the pipes had all been painted black, in an effort to disguise them. But they were there. Like hovering snakes.

Wanda reached across the little table and took Patrick's hand. "I could have really used you around here when Lowell kicked," she said. She caressed his hand with her thumb.

Wanda followed Emily to the bathroom and wanted to help "fix" her makeup. Emily obliged her, but hated the result. She thought Wanda's "help" made her look sick, with nearly blackened eyes. She felt she looked like one of the stereotypical witches from her book.

"But it's the rage this year," Wanda said. "Frankly, I think you should take my advice."

Back at the table, Wanda babbled and giggled and gossiped. When the young busboy came to the table again, she chewed him out for being slow to refill her water glass. He stared helplessly at her.

"Some kind of refugee," Wanda sneered when the boy had gone. "Don't get me wrong, I love New York's ethnic diversity. But, my goodness, sometimes you just want to scream, 'Speak English! This is America!' If you know what I mean."

Emily politely ignored these comments, though she was tempted not to.

Dessert finally came. Emily had a small cold disk of custard dripping with caramel.

Patrick and Wanda ordered coffee and aperitifs, and Emily began to yawn.

"Could we give our little angel here some cab fare back to the hotel?" Wanda asked.

Patrick looked at Emily. She looked down at her plate.

She drew the tines of her fork lightly over her empty dessert plate. She *was* tired. And her ambivalence about Wanda was turning to active dislike.

"Be a sweetheart, Emily," Wanda said, teeth bared in an unattractive smile. "You look . . . *ravaged*—and who wouldn't be after a big busy day in our wicked little hamlet." She turned to Patrick. "Me, on the other hand, I'm bursting with energy. What an old warhorse I am. I feel so alive with your dad back here in New York where he belongs. You never should have left here, you know, Patrick. We all thought you were nuts to leave. Some people still do—though I can't say who, please don't ask. But you must return to us, darling. You know that, don't you?"

That did it.

"What," Emily asked, eyes downcast, then focused hard on Wanda, "do you think my father would want to come back to New York for? You?"

Wanda looked sort of dumbstruck. She smiled. Patrick was frowning, looking away, embarrassed. He sighed.

"God this has been a long day," he muttered.

"I think it's cute when little girls get jealous of their father's friends," Wanda said. "It means there's something really there. But you mustn't feel threatened, dear." She gave Emily's hand a pat.

"Yeah, well I don't think it's too cute when grown women talk like fourteen-year-old bimbos," Emily said.

Wanda sat back in her chair. She wiped the corners of her mouth with her napkin. "I'd forgotten that your daughter spent a lot of years with Cathleen," she said, eyeing Patrick.

"Oh, you knew my mother?" Emily said. "Did she think you were a bitch, too?"

Wanda's napkin was slowly lowered to the table before her.

Patrick finished his port and looked around for a waiter.

"Where's the check?" he murmured.

Wanda looked at him for a long time. He finally turned and looked back. She cleared her throat. "You're just going to sit there, aren't you, Pat?" she said.

Emily leaned back in her chair. She gripped her napkin tight beneath the table.

"We're all tired, Wanda. Maybe we should just call it a night."

"I see," Wanda said. "Well, you know where to reach me." Tears filled her eyes. "But then I guess you've always known that." She moved her chair back and stood up.

Patrick said softly, "Wanda, I'm sorry, I—"

"Okay, then," Wanda said, interrupting. A brave smile appeared on her red lips. "Well." The smile faded, the voice became a whisper. "Good-bye."

Wanda gave Emily one tearful glance before turning and walking out, her flaxen mane waving.

Emily turned to look at her father, whose expression was grim.

"What on earth did you ever see in her?" Emily said.

Patrick shrugged. He wiped his fingers over his jaw. "She was young and ambitious and stoned to the gills when I was young and ambitious and stoned to the gills," he said. "She's an old friend, and you had no right to treat her like that."

"She's in love with you," Emily said. "Or with something she'd like you to be."

He looked away, shamefaced.

"Don't you think you should have told her that you don't love her?" Emily said.

He looked sadly at his daughter. "Do you want to go home?" he said.

He could have meant a lot of places. The hotel, even. Certainly Wisconsin, or San Francisco. Or even the Greenwich Village of a decade ago, a far different place than now.

"I want to go to your house in Wisconsin," Emily said.

"*Our* house in Wisconsin," he said. He reached for his wallet. "We'll leave in the morning." A waiter delivered the check, folded in a leather-bound book. Patrick paid it.

Back at the hotel, Patrick took a long shower. Emily sat down on her bed and read some more about witches and sorcery. What impressed her most was that countless scores of innocent people must have been slaughtered over the centuries because of rumors, fears ... mostly ignorance. In school she'd learned a bit about the Salem witch trials. But it all seemed to be presented with a kind of a chuckle, as if humanity had progressed so far away from senseless cruelty. Had we? What about the way old people were treated these days? Emily wondered. What about the poor old men and women in the Hamilton Home? And all the frail and poor and weak of the world?

She closed the book feeling frustrated. She wandered through the suite, picking up magazines, stacking them neatly on the table by the door. Through the window she could see the crescent moon over the skyscrapers of a luminescent Manhattan. The great sweeping city view was breathtaking. But she felt sad.

She missed her friends in Wisconsin. She missed Beth. And she missed Kerry, despite herself. But most of all she missed Charity, a woman she scarcely knew, and had barely even seen on just a couple occasions, both brief. Her heart pounded. She just knew Charity was in danger.

The Wisconsin night breeze was cool and the sky cloudless. A crescent moon rose over the fields. Beth leaned against the passenger-side door, watching Kerry drive. He sped over the old county highway that led to the Hamilton Home and the cemetery.

Here I go again, Beth thought. But how could she turn him down when he'd called, leaving messages at her home all day long? He'd begged her to come out tonight. Her only other option was staying in and watching the late movie with her kid sister, Amy.

Weird as it was, she wanted to be with him—wanted to and didn't want to. So here she was.

Emily was expected back from New York in a few days, and Beth was eager to see her. Ever since the senator's plane went down, Beth's bad feelings about the home had intensified.

"I think Emily is right about that place," Beth said. "It's evil."

Kerry pulled the car up the drive that led to the cemetery. He wasn't really listening to her. Beth looked out at the dark hills, the nearly bare trees.

Evil. It lurked out there.

"There are so many things about Emily that I don't think I'll ever understand," Kerry said. He popped open a cold can of beer, handed it to Beth, popped open another for himself.

Beth took a sip and watched as the Hamilton Home came into view, just beyond the graves and tombstones, and bare, bent trees. It glowed, windows burning gold under stern eaves. The October chill in the air perme-

ated the car. Beth shivered. Kerry parked the car in
the nighttime shade of a towering old elm.

The wind coursed through the dry, rustling leaves.

Kerry tuned in a radio station, let it softly play. The
car's heater had been on all the way from Leonora.
But it still wasn't warm in the car.

"Emily has a lot going on in her life right now,"
Beth said. "Most of it isn't that great."

"I could help," Kerry said.

"Maybe she doesn't want you to."

She immediately regretted saying it. He looked hurt.
Had she meant to be hurtful? *Why am I such a bitch?*
she thought. *Why did I agree to meet him again?* She
drank down half the beer. At last it was beginning to
get warm in the car.

"You really don't like me, do you?" he said.

Oh, quite the contrary, Beth thought, feeling the
alcohol buzz coming on. It didn't take much. *Kerry
Thornton, alone in a car. With me. It pays to have
friends. But what does it really pay? What's the divi-
dend?*

"I thought we were here to talk about Emily," Beth
said. "Give me another beer."

Kerry obliged her. "I'd really like to be your friend,
too," he said.

"To get to Emily?"

He winced and looked out the window. A low bank
of fog veiled most of the cemetery. All but the tops of
the taller grave markers. They poked up through the
fog like the tips of icebergs. The amber light of the
home's windows glowed through the night mist. In the
car, the golden light from the radio gleamed in Kerry's
eyes.

"Beth, you don't have to be so cool with me."

Why did this sudden rage flash through her mind? "You've been cool with me for more than a decade, Kerry. You've known me since we were in kindergarten, and I can't think of two conversations we've had until this year."

"And are you still the same person? An angry kindergartner?"

She shook out her long red hair, then unzipped the front of her jacket. She felt too warm. And she felt too fat. Too ugly. Too *Beth*. "Touché," she said.

"I feel like I'm not even the same person I was last year," Kerry said.

"Schizophrenia is not pretty," Beth said.

He looked a little surprised, but then he laughed. He clinked his beer can against hers. She smiled. She felt warmth inside, too, despite herself. Melting ice.

"Let's just make a pact, then," Beth said. "Even if Emily doesn't fall head over heels in love with you, let's help her and protect her, because I think that bitch Eugenia Temple and her loony brother are really out to get her."

He smiled. "All I really want is to be her friend."

"Sure," she said, and she tried to stifle a giggle, but couldn't. She turned to look out her window and laughed. She felt his hand on her coat, pulling it off.

"Why don't we try and relax?" he said. She slipped her arms out of the sleeves of her coat.

He took his coat off, too.

He opened two more beers for them. He was drunk and rambling. He kept talking about Emily. Beth watched him talk. She liked his lips. They were awesomely cool. Funny what you notice when you're with someone alone, up close like this.

"You don't know what it's like, Beth. To want somebody. Somebody you think about all the time. But who you think you're just not going to get. Maybe it's not in the cards. Maybe you're a fool and you're kidding yourself." He let his head fall back against the headrest. He sighed.

Beth thought, *That's right, I don't know what it's like. Beth Hanes couldn't possibly know.*

"Maybe you'd settle for saving her life," she said, feeling quite drunk now herself.

"You think it's that dangerous in the old poorhouse? Well, if it is, I vow to help you save Emily from the Hamilton Home," Kerry said. And he gave the finger, aiming it at the home. He laughed.

"You don't believe us. You don't believe two women are being held prisoner up there, do you?"

"I believe it," Kerry said. "If you say it's true, I believe you, Beth. I'll make a pact with you about it, if that's what you want. I'm serious. I will die for you—you and Emily both, I mean."

"Maybe Emily doesn't deserve you," she said. She just blurted it out. Why was she betraying her friend like this? She took a long draft of beer. *Why should I feel guilty?* she thought. *This isn't my fight. And what's more, this isn't my love life. Why am I always in the middle?*

Assholes.

"I'd do anything for her," Kerry said. He closed his eyes and lay back his head. "That's a vow, a solemn pact. I guess that makes it love. Sweet, crazy love."

"Love!" Beth said. "Pulleeeeeez! Why did you bring me out here? Why am I in a car with Kerry Thornton, the golden boy of Leonora High—"

"Aw, c'mon!"

"—Mr. Hot Shot, Mr. Cool . . . Why should I help you, Kerry? Why should I help Emily . . . or anyone, why—"

She stopped herself. Her eyes had filled with tears.

Kerry popped open the glove compartment and rooted through the maps and paper and junk until he found a squashed box of Kleenex. He handed it to her.

"God, I am such a mess," she said, and wiped her eyes. "Screw both of you. Hand me another beer. I'm getting drunk. I just don't care."

Kerry pulled out another beer and popped it open. He handed it to her. She dabbed at her eyes with the Kleenex. It was very quiet in the car, but for the soft music on the radio. She blew her nose. Then she turned and looked at him. His expression was pleading. Tenderness for him pooled up inside of her.

"I do care about you, Beth," he said softly.

She hated him but, God, she liked him. She tried to shake off the feeling . . . an ancient feeling within her. She stifled a sudden impulse to burst into tears.

"We can't always get what we want," Kerry said. He held up his beer can, toasting the crescent moon. "Damn."

"I doubt you're ready to give up on Emily," she said.

"I doubt I'll ever be. Life sucks."

"Life . . . or just love?"

He looked over and smiled. It was a smile to melt

icebergs, especially those lodged inside the heart. Beth closed her eyes, imagined tendrils of ice falling from her heart.

No, I am not going to cave in to this. She shook her head, sat up violently and laughed.

"You okay?" he said.

She looked at Kerry with a crooked smile. "Let's seal the pact," Beth said.

"The pact?"

"Your promise to help us defeat Eugenia and Herbert Temple," she said. "You haven't forgotten already, have you?"

"Of course not."

She felt as though she were recklessly crossing a snowy border, fueled by alcohol.

"This is a pact of friendship," Beth slurred. "Of secrets . . . and of secret love."

She couldn't believe she was being so brazen. She thought that for once she was really taking control— and with someone who a few short weeks ago was echelons above her in social status. She felt power, and she liked it.

She felt something else, too, something taking over. She leaned close to him and smiled. On the radio, the first slippery, cool notes of a Ray Charles song rang out on an electric keyboard, gathering rhythm.

"Do you feel a little better now?" he asked.

"Yes. And you?"

"I'm . . . fine."

"Let's seal our pact of friendship and loyalty and honor, Kerry."

"How," he asked, "shall we seal the pact?"

The voice of Ray Charles grew louder. Beth touched the radio dial. The sexy beat of "What'd I Say?" filled the car.

She smiled. "With a kiss, of course."

She leaned in closer. She had kissed a couple boys before, not boys she'd really liked. Like the boy who had taken her to the homecoming dance last year. Both of them had wanted to go, probably to avoid the social disgrace of not going. At the end of the evening, at her parents' front door, he'd kissed her. It had not been a kiss to remember. It had been a kiss to wash away with toothpaste and Listerine.

This was different.

"I . . ." he said. "I . . . can't."

She cocked her head.

"I mean I shouldn't," he said. "You shouldn't."

She smiled wickedly.

"We shouldn't kiss," Beth said. "We should definitely not kiss. You should never have to kiss a girl like me."

"Beth. Don't say that."

"Don't say that. Don't kiss. Don't, don't, don't."

She was definitely drunk. She turned her head away from his. She laughed, tears catching in her throat.

He put his hands on her shoulders, and she turned her face to him. His eyes were heavy lidded, half closed.

"Please," he said. "Beth, you are . . . you're selling yourself short. You're a beautiful—"

"No," she whispered. And she more or less fell into him, into his kiss.

Their lips met, and they kissed for a long time,

deeply. She felt his tongue slip past her lips, into her mouth. The taste of beer . . . a feeling like fire.

When they parted, the sleepy look in his eyes had taken on a reddish cast. She felt something that she did not, for once, confuse with love, or even with the crushes she'd had on boys at school. It was overwhelming. He was, she could see, feeling it, too.

Once upon a time, in junior high, she'd had a major crush on Kerry Thornton. That had been eons ago, and it had been followed by long years of actually disliking him.

Now this was happening; pieces seemed to be fitting together. Her hand felt right in his. His touch. Thoughts of what they were doing crowded her brain, only to be swept away by this overpowering, increasing desire.

She'd always imagined that she would—maybe even wanted to—lose her virginity in a car. Now it was going to happen.

His hand moved up beneath her sweater, cupping her breast, straining against her bra. She moaned. His warm hand felt so good there.

He sighed. "Beth . . . we should . . ."

She pulled up the front of his shirt and looked at his bare stomach and chest. It moved in and out with breath, alive. In a flurry, clothes were stripped off. When they were both naked and he moved on top of her, she was surprised at how warm—hot, really—and smooth his shoulders felt in her hands. Behind her head was a pillow made of their heap of clothes.

He'd had a rubber in his wallet for ages, a lubricated one with a special reservoir tip. She felt such tenderness for him, watching him bite the foil-and-plastic wrapper.

He put the condom on, his eyes glazing over, lips parting. She watched him secure the latex, saw the slick, foreign glow of it. Then, with some struggle, he put himself inside her.

It hurt, of course. He was unsure of himself. She pressed her face against his neck. He moved up and down on top of her. It didn't take very long for him to finish. He gritted his teeth, then opened his mouth wide and let out several gasps.

Then he collapsed heavily onto her. At first Beth felt it was a bit uncomfortable to have all this dead, sweaty weight upon her. Yet it felt sexy, too, and she moved her hands across his nude body.

It was getting cold in the car. He started to snore. Beth's head throbbed. She felt completely spent. She closed her eyes and promptly passed out.

Later, when she woke, she found that he'd covered her with the pile of clothes. The car was freezing though he had the heater back on, blaring. He sat there in his underpants, sipping beer on his side of the seat, a great gulf between them.

"I guess I'd better get you home," he said.

She sat up, modestly holding her sweater over herself. Her teeth chattered, and she felt that awful spinning sensation. He gathered up his clothes and stepped outside into the chill of the night to dress. She felt fat, ridiculous, and her head pounded with an early hangover.

She tried to balance her weight, grasping the cold black naugahyde seat cover with a hand she noticed was filmy with sweat, despite the frigid temperature in the car. Lifting her hand, she saw her moist fingerprints shrink from the naugahyde surface and vanish.

She scrambled into her clothes, trying to ignore that awful, familiar feeling that she knew meant she would soon have to vomit.

While Emily and Patrick were away in New York, Webster had brought in the Jordans' mail and attended to his usual chores around the Jordan place.

Upon their arrival home, Patrick found, among the stack of bills and magazines left on the kitchen counter, a letter from California, addressed to Emily. The return address was strange. It took him only a couple seconds to realize that the letter had been sent from a California correctional facility. The letter was, in fact, from Danny.

He tapped the envelope on the table. This morning's homecoming was not going to be as restful as he'd hoped.

Emily came into the room from outside, carrying her suitcase. She'd run up to the barn to see Amber before coming inside. She was smiling.

Patrick sighed. "It's a letter for you," he said. "It's from California."

The bright expression faded from her face. She walked over and took the letter. She looked at her father. He cleared his throat and left the room.

She tore open the envelope. Quickly she scanned its contents, written in a haphazard scrawl.

Babe,
  Disappointed I haven't heard from you, though I can hardly blame you. I never intended for you to get caught up in my mess. You've got to believe that.

She really didn't believe that at all. She'd been naive . . . but he'd used her, she believed. In so many ways.

She felt a kind of heartburn sear her chest. She read on.

> You can't believe how lonely it is here. You have no idea how lucky you are to be running free. If I helped in anyway by keeping my mouth shut, I'm glad.

Bullshit. He hadn't kept his mouth shut. And she hadn't asked or expected him to. When the whirlwind had hit, she faced the consequences honestly.

> I think of you, free, living at your old man's place, the place you always talked about. Do you ever think of me? If you do, it would be so nice to hear from you, to get a letter or a card.
> I'm sorry, Em, I swear to God. And I still have feelings for you. I just wanted you to know that.
>
> > Love,
> > Danny

Her first impulse was to tear up the letter. "Feelings" for her! Did the word *love* ever enter the equation? She sighed heavily and folded the letter. She put it back into the envelope. This was the past catching up with her again, all right, she thought. It was over and done with, wasn't it? They were both paying the price, in their own ways.

She wouldn't answer him.

She thought of Kerry. How uncomplicated this guy seemed in comparison—immature as he was.

Emily tucked the letter into her pocket and carried her suitcase to the stairs. Patrick was seated on the sofa, paging through a news magazine. He looked up.

"Okay?" he asked.

"Fine," she answered. "Thanks. Everything is fine."

The October day was bright, and the Hamilton Home was filled with golden autumnal light, at least on the main floor. Emily came in unannounced and unexpected. She had not been scheduled for work, but had insisted to Patrick that she wanted to get back to the home the very day they returned from New York.

She knocked on Eugenia's office door and was admitted.

"Emily," Eugenia said, surprised. "Back so soon?"

"I'd like to get back to work today, if you don't mind," Emily said. "I'm grateful for your decision to allow me to finish my community service here. I'm going to do the right thing. May I sign on to the volunteer roster for today?"

Eugenia, dressed in one of her conservative dark suits, a strand of pearls around her neck, gave a slight nod. "I'm glad you've come to your senses, my dear," she said. She looked away, back to the papers scattered over her desk. Emily silently exited the room.

Beth was not on the schedule all day, and Emily worked by herself, very hard. She helped dispense medicines with Patti, Maxine, and Laverne though they eyed her suspiciously throughout the afternoon.

And when mealtime came, Emily helped deliver meals to the residents who were too sick to leave their rooms.

One old woman needed to be spoon-fed, and Emily gently performed this duty. The old woman had milky blue cataracts over her brown eyes, and no teeth. Emily tenderly wiped her chin with a napkin after each bite.

In the laundry room, she folded towels for two hours. When she was finished, the sky had darkened and the windows were black.

The aide with the unlit cigar ever-hanging from his mouth came to deliver the fresh sheets to their storage closets, located on each floor. They were loaded up in carts on rollers. The destinations were written on note cards that had been pinned to the cart's cloth sides.

Emily saw that one of the carts was headed toward the tower. She approached cigar man.

"Let me give you a hand," she said. "I'll take this one."

He looked at her with suspicion. Emily gave a just-trying-to-be-helpful smile, and he, lazy as ever, gave her the job.

The wheels of the cart squeaked, and that made Emily nervous. She did not want to be seen or heard tonight. Not when she'd just told Eugenia Temple she was going to keep her nose clean and stay out of trouble. She was, in fact, looking for trouble. She was trying to listen for it, too, but the home was eerily quiet.

The rear service elevator was a long time in coming to the basement. Emily pushed the cart in and pressed the button marked 4. She patted the cart, her insurance if she were to be caught up on this floor.

The hallway was dark and empty of people. *A nice place to store linen, up here in the dark*, Emily thought. As she passed each closed door she listened—but heard nothing.

At last she made it to the end of the hall. She opened the linen closet, half expecting Eugenia's head to be in there, smiling wickedly.

"Gotcha!" the imaginary head might have said.

But no head was in the closet. Just empty wooden shelves, which she began to fill with fresh linen.

When she finished stacking the sheets, she looked around. All clear. She thought about the building's exterior. *This is it*, she thought, *this is the place.* She pushed on the black door that she knew led to the tower steps.

The door didn't open, so she pushed harder. Finally it gave way with an awful creak, revealing shallow, barely visible stairs that rose past tall, grimy windows, black with the night. She took a deep breath—and one more look behind her in the hallway.

She'd just passed through the door and was ready to take the first step when a hand took hold of her wrist. She tried to scream, but another big hand was clapped over her mouth. She looked into the angry eyes of Ned Fox.

"Shhh . . ." he admonished. He removed his hand, but held her wrist tight.

"Please let me go," Emily said.

He shook his head.

"Ned, please. Don't take me to Eugenia. I need your help. There are women being held prisoner here. Do you know who I mean? Charity is being held against her will somewhere in the home. Is she up there?"

He looked up the long flight of stairs. He shook his head no.

"Please, Ned! Don't you care?"

His words came slowly. "Y-You stay away from here. . . ." he said, gesturing to the stairs.

The wind blew open a pair of shutters with a scream of strained hinges. Ned cowered down, releasing Emily, who was almost as startled as he was.

Slowly he turned back to her. "Bad magic in the house," he said. "Evil . . ." He pointed a gnarled finger and shouted at her, "Go!"

She started to back away.

"Go!" he cried out again, and she ran down the hall to the main flight of stairs, which she bounded down, running as if for her life.

Later that evening the police and the FBI, represented by two men in gray suits and one woman in a gray skirt and jacket, concluded their investigation at the home. They had no reason to suspect anyone at the home, but Eugenia had made a special point of opening her doors to the authorities and offering her assistance.

"We are absolutely convinced there was no foul play involved in the airplane crash," the woman said. "When the blood tests on the pilot were completed, we found traces of alcohol and evidence of marijuana use. A little checking around confirmed Smith was a habitual user of illegal substances and occasionally flew while intoxicated. Not what you'd call a role model. A combination of weather conditions and pilot error were, we've concluded, the cause." She wore her brunette hair short, and her glasses were owlish wire-rims.

"I'm so pleased to hear that it was, then, just an accident," Eugenia said. "Though it does not lessen the tragedy by much."

"No, Ms. Temple, it doesn't," the younger of the two men said. He sported a crew cut. "But sometimes it does put to rest crazy rumors."

"Rumors?" Eugenia said, arching an eyebrow. "What rumors? What do you mean?"

The older man stepped in. "Not a thing, Miss Temple," he said. "This case is closed. We'll get out of your hair now."

"Thank you so much for all your good work, Lieutenant," Eugenia said.

When she was sure they were gone, Eugenia left the home, too. She went to the old gray Mercedes that was parked outside the garage of the caretaker's house. The walkway was dark, and the sliver of moon cast faint light. Eugenia rarely drove anywhere, rarely left the home. But tonight she was expected to attend a memorial service being held at the Lutheran church in Leonora, a memorial for Senator Allan Pullman.

"Miss Temple," came an unexpected voice from behind. Eugenia's blood froze. She turned her head slowly. She saw the dark figure of a man standing in the shadow of an elm.

The man stepped out of the shadow. A film of sweat covered his lip and brow. His hands were stuffed in the pockets of a heavy dark and ragged coat.

"It's Bill Shore," the man said, and she recognized the mechanic. Her expression of mild alarm was replaced with a relaxed if wary smile.

"Mr. Shore," she said. "I didn't suppose we'd be hearing from you again so soon."

"Never crossed your mind, did it?"

"I thought we'd closed our latest deal."

"It's still preying on my mind, Miss Temple," Shore said, taking a few steps closer to her. He whispered, "You got quite a bargain. And me . . . I caused the deaths of two men and a beautiful young woman."

"Yes," Eugenia said, her voice as soft as she could make it. "And now you want more money."

His face was pinched. "You got any idea the pain I been in?" he said. "I haven't slept. I been suffering. And what I got out of the deal, it wasn't worth it. I want a lot more, Miss Temple. I want a helluva lot more to save you and that brother of yours what I'm going through."

"But you did an excellent job, Mr. Shore. Nobody suspects a thing. The evidence burned with the plane. Pilot error . . . a tank full of fuel. Our secret is safe."

"You want to keep it that way, don't you Miss Temple?"

She nodded. "Come inside, then, Mr. Shore."

He followed behind her. Herbert was seated in the living room, a glass of cognac in his hand, a Wagner CD on the stereo. Herbert's expression did not betray a whit of anxiety in seeing the sweating, shaking Mr. Bill Shore follow his sister inside. She loved him for that.

Herbert stood and turned the music down.

Shore trembled badly. Eugenia stepped aside as Herbert slowly approached the mechanic.

"Don't come any further, Temple," Bill warned.

Herbert stood back, and smiled. "Whatever you say. But do you really think you can play this little game and win? Against us?"

Shore's eyes widened. He pulled out the handgun he'd had gripped inside his jacket pocket, and he pointed it at Herbert.

"Try and remain calm, Mr. Shore," Eugenia said. She lowered her arms to her sides. Unseen, she slowly slipped a hand inside the pocket of her drab, dark coat.

Herbert took another step toward Bill Shore. Shore suddenly raised up the gun up and brought it down hard, striking Herbert in the face. Herbert fell down to one knee, a deep gash on his cheekbone.

Eugenia raised her hands. "There's no need for that, Mr. Shore," she said. "Please put the gun down." She reached her hand out.

"Stay back, goddammit!," he cried. He pointed the gun at her, then at Herbert.

Eugenia felt a surge of pure adrenaline rush to her brain.

As Shore looked at Herbert, she sprang. In her hand was a long gleaming needle, barely visible. In one perfectly executed stroke, she gouged the needle through Shore's right eye. She drove it to the hilt, cleanly up into his brain.

Shore went stiff, and the gun fell from his slackened hand to the carpet. Eugenia withdrew her tiny spear, splattering blood and brain fluid, and watched the mechanic fall to the ground. At the end of the needle, like a large olive on a toothpick, was the mechanic's hazel eye. She plucked it off and let it fall to the carpet, where it rolled over to rest by the snubbed barrel opening of the handgun.

She looked at Herbert, who rose unsteadily to his feet and dabbed a white handkerchief to the cut on his face.

Then Eugenia bent down over Bill Shore's dying body. She aimed the strange needle at the thick blue cord of vein in his throat. She pierced the vein, raising a drop of dark blood. Then, using the needle's sharp point, she sliced the vein open like the belly of a fish. A pencil-thin fountain of blood rose up several inches, over which she knelt and drank.

Soon she could feel Herbert's expectant body beside her, his hand gently but persistently pressing on her's.

At last she turned to Herbert, whose face was upturned toward hers, as if in anticipation of a kiss. His lips were parted, his jaws opening. With eyes rapturous and belly sated, Eugenia opened her mouth, and from it spilled a quantity of the mechanic's blood into the mouth of her brother. Herbert received his feast of blood like a newly hatched raven, neck straining, eyes wild with greed and ecstasy.

Chapter Eight

The countryside seen through the windshield of Beth's car reminded Emily of one of those gift-store snow domes. Except instead of snow, fiery leaves fell and floated in golden light, for miles. They blew across the still green hills of Blackburn County and around the stately Hamilton Home, which towered to the sky and seemed to grow taller as Beth's car climbed the hill.

It was late in the afternoon. They were headed in for an evening shift, having given Patti, Maxine, and Laverne the excuse that Emily was making up hours lost while she was away in New York.

They had another, darker plan.

Beth was oddly quiet on the way to the home. It hardly mattered; Emily talked the entire way. She told Beth about the New York trip, interspersing her remarks with plans for saving Charity and Maria Kraus.

"Oh, God, didn't you hear?" Beth said.

Beth's tone of voice sent a shiver through Emily. She tried to brace herself. "Hear what?"

"Maria Kraus is dead."

Emily flinched. She looked away from Beth, to the resplendent fall scene. Rage burned inside her, and she clenched her fists.

"How did it happen?"

"Do you think they'd tell me the truth? They hush these things up, you know. Don't want the other residents dwelling on it." Beth pushed her hair out of her face. "You know what Maxine and Laverne told everyone? It was just old age that killed Maria. Her time had come. A bad cold turns to pneumonia. No surprise to anyone."

Emily sighed and leaned her head back. At the Hamilton Home your time could come—would come—not at all unexpectedly. Eugenia was setting the clock, Dr. Temple was providing all the medical documentation. That was Emily's best guess and darkest suspicion.

"And Charity?" Emily said.

"Hasn't been seen. Sure you want to miss class tonight to join me at the lovely house of horrors."

"I don't care about missing class tonight," Emily replied. "Kerry said he'd take notes for me, and explain to Gloria."

"How nice," Beth said, eyes on the road.

Beth was really touchy tonight. Better not call her on it, though. Emily thought instead about Kerry. That would be a safer topic. She looked over at Beth, who stared ahead at the road. "Can I tell you something?" she said. Beth didn't answer. "I missed you guys a lot when I was in New York. And don't laugh, but I missed Kerry, too. I think I really do have a crush on him," she said.

"Really? Maybe you should tell Kerry about it, not me."

"Hey, chill out, Beth."

"You're right," Beth said. "I should just mind my own business. I could stay out of a lot of trouble that way."

Emily sighed. Beth parked the car. Before they got out of it, Emily put her hand on Beth's arm.

"You're mad at me because I'm dragging you into this, aren't you," she said. The home loomed before them.

"I make my own decisions," Beth said. Still pissed. "And I was here before you came along."

"So you're with me, then?"

Beth seemed to smile despite herself. Whatever it was that was bothering her seemed to fade. Emily felt that for once she was really getting through to her hard-edged young friend.

"To the death," Beth said.

They laughed, but Emily said, "Let's not jinx ourselves."

Inside, Eugenia was preparing to leave for the night. She wrapped her dark coat around her strong shoulders. Emily pushed a rolling tray of milk and tea into the community room area. She felt eyes upon her. She looked up into the hawklike stare of Eugenia Temple.

After hearing Emily's explanation for being here this late, Eugenia adjusted her scarf and put on her gloves. "I'm so pleased you're taking such a strong interest in your work, Emily," Eugenia said. "Have a good, safe evening." She swept out the through the kitchen.

Safe evening. Sure. Emily delivered the milk and steaming tea to several residents.

As the night wore on, the lights inside the home were extinguished or dimmed until the place resembled a mausoleum. A gloomy, rose-tinted light filtered through the quiet halls.

Insomniac residents sat watching television, frozen in postures of blank existence. One of the old men Emily saw held his head in a frail hand. He seemed to have been watching her intently all evening. He wore a wine-colored robe and sat in a wheelchair with his back to her. She couldn't quite place where she'd seen him before, or whether she'd actually noticed him before at all. It was one of *those* nights, and Emily was getting creeped out.

She was in another room all together, away from the strange wheelchair-bound man, when she realized she'd been seeing this scarecrow of a man in various rooms all day long. Then she realized, her heart racing, who this strange old man was. He was Herbert.

She rushed back into the television lounge, but the old man was gone.

Was her mind playing tricks on her? Had it been Herbert? Had he been spying on her in various disguises? She knew those eyes. She strongly suspected it had been him.

Emily sat down to catch her breath. It occurred to her that perhaps she was being paranoid. Yet she wouldn't put it past Herbert to spy. She just didn't know anymore what was real and what was imagined in this haunted place.

She closed her eyes and ran her hand wearily through her hair.

Emily . . .

It came as a distance voice, traveling on a wave through time.

"Charity?" Emily said, eyes open.

Help us!

Emily sat bolt upright. She tried to listen for the voice.

"Show me how to find you?" she said softly. An old woman in a cheap black-shag wig glanced over at her. Emily stood up, ignoring the old woman's look of wonder.

The woman watched Emily back out of the room. In the hallway she turned and began to run. She had to find Beth.

It was close to midnight, and in an hour—with luck—they would be driving down the hill homeward. Emily found Beth in the laundry room with a couple of the maintenance crew. The stench of cigarette smoke and stale coffee was in the air. All eyes were glued to a small black-and-white television set tuned into a late-night talk show.

"Come on," Emily said.

Beth groaned. "It's almost time to leave, Em," she said. "Let's give it a rest for tonight."

"I think I know where Charity is," she said. "C'mon, don't be scared."

Beth stood up. "Who said I'm scared?"

"You're not?"

"Petrified is a better word," Beth said. "Do you want us to join the parade of missing girls so soon?"

"Of course not, not now or ever," Emily said. "But if we were missing, we'd want someone to rescue us, wouldn't we?"

She held up a laundry bag. The contents shifted silently inside.

"What's that?"

"Tools," Emily said. "Borrowed from the maintenance department. They might come in handy."

They entered a dark basement hallway. The floor was made of concrete, which had buckled and cracked. New paint couldn't hide the faults and deformities in the walls; the home had settled, and the basement bore the scars of time. A damp, musty smell of dust and stagnant water permeated the air.

As the young women made their way deeper into the labyrinth basement of the home, the light diminished. Emily could hear engine sounds. The heating system? An electrical transformer?

And she heard another sound. A human sound.

Emily . . .

And a moaning cry. Quite distant, judging by the sound.

"She's down there," Emily said.

Beth crept along behind Emily, a flashlight in her hand.

Emily felt her heart pounding. But with each step she also felt more determined. They were so close . . . they had to keep going.

At last they came to a door, heavy and wooden. Paint peeled from its warped and misshapen face.

It gave when Emily pushed it, but with a loud squeak. Narrow steps—thirteen in all—led down. Aiming the flashlight beam in front of them, Emily and Beth descended the concrete staircase.

At the foot of the stairs they came to another heavy door, painted black.

"Charity?" Emily whispered.

She was answered with a distant cry that sounded more like that of a cat than a human being.

Beth looked around behind them.

"I think we'd better get out of here," Beth said. "This could be a trap."

"We've come this far," Emily said. "Come on, help me."

They pushed and pulled on the old black wooden door but found it was locked.

Emily reached into the tool bag and extracted a large screwdriver, which she used to pry the lock from the door. Some of the rotted wood around the lock fell away in chunks. With an awful creak the door opened. The dark mouth of a cavelike room loomed before them.

Emily looked at Beth.

"Maybe you'd better stand guard."

"Sure. And if someone comes, what do I tell them? We're on a coffee break?"

Emily pulled a large claw hammer out of the laundry bag and handed it to Beth. "Bop first, explain later," she said.

She entered the dark room. She had a disposable cigarette lighter in her hand, and she flicked it twice, producing a flame.

The faint, echoey sound of dripping water was all that could be heard in this cavernous room. That and a scurrying sound of tiny claws on concrete, which soon faded away. Emily took careful steps, but couldn't avoid the cold puddles that pooled on the floor.

"Charity?" she said softly.

Giant shadows were cast on the walls. The ceiling,

high above, looked like a nice hangout for bats. Stalac-
tites of dust and grunge pointed downward like dull
spears.

The tiny flame cast a glow over the walls. Emily
came to the black mouth of a tunnel. She had to stop
to catch her breath. With trembling knees she passed
through the tunnel's mouth, a cobweb clinging to her
face. She brushed it off, disgusted, goose bumps rising
on her flesh. The tunnel led to another room, which to
her surprise was lit by a tall white candle on a plate.
A golden cave of a room. At the far wall was a barred
door.

Her heart thumped. This was the place. She reached
out, and found that the door was not locked. It gave
easily. She opened it and was greeted by more golden
candlelight.

There, behind the bars of a cage—bars from floor
to ceiling—seated on a tiny cot, was Charity Francis.
The old woman peered out at her, the candlelight
gleaming warmly in her eyes.

"I knew you'd come," Charity said, and she smiled.
The wild, glittering strands of her hair caught the light
and made her appear to Emily like some kind of aged
medieval fairy princess.

Emily rushed to the bars.

"It's true! You *are* a prisoner here!"

"Not only me, child," the old woman said. "Many
more. And you, too, are in grave danger."

Charity gathered up her skirts and rose with difficulty. Emily could almost feel the weariness in the old
woman's bones. Charity walked to the edge of the cage
and reached through the bars. Emily took her hand.

It was as though an electric current shot through

Charity's touch. A surge of energy flowed into Emily. The energy had a momentary calming effect.

"You see, my dear," Charity said, "you have the power to free not only me, but the other prisoners. Not only of this wretched home, but of the prison of time."

Emily felt a tremor of fear ripple over her skin and settle in the pit of her stomach.

"What can I do?" Emily said. "I don't understand."

"I am a witch, so-called." Charity smiled wearily. "My powers are waning. But your powers are strong and new."

"*My* powers?"

"You have heard the cries for help?"

Emily nodded. "Yes."

"They are key to reversing the evil that has lived for centuries in the hearts of Eugenia Temple and her brother."

Emily blinked her eyes. "Are they witches, too?"

"No, they are monsters," Charity said. "Once they were human, but that was a long, long time ago."

Emily felt the cold dampness of the basement room. It seemed to seep into her bones, chilling them.

"You see, Eugenia and Herbert are thieves and ruthless killers. They have kidnapped and murdered upwards of a hundred people in this community. You and your friends are targeted to become their next victims. Just like Maria, and dozens before her."

Murder. Emily held tight to Charity's hand. "What do they want from us?"

"The very essence of time and life force. They want your youth, my dear," Charity said.

Emily was skeptical. She turned and looked at the darkened doorway behind her. She knew Beth would be waiting, terrified. She had an impulse to turn and run.

"My friend is waiting," Emily said. "Is she in mortal danger, too?"

"I fear so," Charity said.

"If what you're saying is true, how can I help?"

Charity again smiled. "By helping me take from Eugenia and Herbert what is not rightfully theirs. Through us, the spell can be reversed."

Emily gave Charity a puzzled look.

"They will not be easy to kill," Charity said, "because they have ceased to be truly alive. They exist. They do not age. Their youthfulness, such as it is, persists and flourishes because they steal it, and they must feed like vampires off the blood of the young."

"And you want me to stop them." Emily felt a bit faint.

"For yourself, and for all of the others."

From the distant corridor came a cry. Beth.

Emily's eyes widened with fear. "I have to go to her."

"Yes," Charity said. "Run to safety."

"But when should I come back?" Emily said. "What should I do?"

"There's no more time to talk," Charity said. "Hurry. But do not forget us. We all depend on your actions. Have faith that in time you will understand and do what is necessary. Now, hurry. You are not safe in this place."

"But . . . how can I leave you here?"

"You must. These bars are strong, and neither of us has the key, not yet. Now is not the time, dear child. Run!"

From a dark corner of the cell, unseen by either Emily or Charity, an eye peered through the gloom from a small hole in the wall. Herbert Temple observed and listened.

Emily ran out the door, stopped, returned, and closed it. She hoped that in the gloom all would appear as it had before she'd stolen into this secret place. Her shoes were soaked through with ice-cold water.

At the end of the corridor she embraced Beth, who was tearful with fright.

"We have to get out of here," Emily said. Together they ran out of the basement and into the relative safety of the main floor.

"I can't explain now," Emily said. They threw on their coats and fled into the night, toward Beth's car. Stars filled the sky, and the shadows of clouds moved over the watery landscape of night.

In the hours before dawn, Eugenia ordered Charity's cell opened. Eugenia watched as the old woman came awake, eyes blinking. Herbert stood silent, next to his sister.

"Killing you would be easy," Eugenia said. She watched for Charity's reaction.

Charity kept her expression plain. "Bury me and you bury my secret," she said.

"Burying your secret is exactly what we intend to do," Herbert replied, his little black cigarette smoldering in his fingers. "Just as soon as we discover it."

"That would be wonderful for you," Charity said. "To have your mortal enemy's plan in your grasp. You've always been such a cunning opponent."

Eugenia gave a sneer of a smile. "You speak as

though you know us," Eugenia said. "You're bluffing."

"Perhaps I'm more a witness to your crimes than you know."

Eugenia absorbed that with her typical skepticism. "I'll give you a chance, Charity," she said, removing a short, thick, black whip from her bag. She gave it an obscene caress. "What is this secret, this key to our destruction? If you know, you must speak now. If you don't know, if you're only bluffing, you're going to pay for this little game."

"I've already paid my debt to you, brother and sister of the night," Charity said. "I'm here to collect on what is owed me, and owed to all of your innocent victims."

"We could always kill the girl," Herbert said in dark whisper.

"As if you didn't intend to?" Charity said. "That is, after you've sucked the life blood from her. You need her as much as you need me. You need troubled youth, so-called bad girls whose disappearances fit into your clever, murderous schemes. You are both so weak in your need. You are the slaves of your own devices."

"Is that your answer?" Eugenia said.

"That, Eugenia, is the truth."

Eugenia's eyes became slits of hate. "Very well," she said. She stepped forward, raising the whip.

Beth cried, wiping her eyes as she drove.

"It's going to be okay," Emily said. "Please, Beth, get a hold of yourself."

Beth abruptly pulled over to the side of the road.

Stopping the car, she shifted into park. She then turned to Emily, eyes bright with rage.

"I changed my mind. I want out of this," Beth said. "I'm never going back to the home! And after tonight, I don't think we can be friends anymore, either."

Emily reached out to put her arm around Beth's shoulder. Beth turned away violently.

"I don't understand," Emily said. "Earlier you said you were with me to the death. And now you're telling me we can't even be friends anymore?"

Beth wiped here eyes with her sleeves. "I have to tell you something," she said. "And I think you're going to hate me for it."

Emily felt a strange prick of anxiety in her chest. "I know you're scared," she said. "But you can tell me."

Beth swallowed hard. "I saw Kerry while you were away in New York," she began, not looking Emily in the eye. "We went for a drive, to talk about you. We were drunk. Hell, we were smashed."

Emily listened. She was barely breathing.

"We ended up kissing," Beth said. "We were blasted out of our minds. You said you didn't want him . . . and for a moment . . . I did."

Emily sat back against the car seat. It was confusing to be hearing this now. She'd trusted Kerry, somehow. Believed him when he'd said how much he loved her. Or thought she did.

And Beth. What about trusting her?

"I'm sorry," Beth said. "It just happened. We did it, we had sex. I haven't even seen him since. It was nothing." She broke down in tears.

Emily looked out the window, into the deep, black woods. She had a conflicting impulse to both comfort Beth and flee from her, leave her crying alone in the car. But at last she only sighed.

"I don't blame you," she said.

"You *should* blame me," Beth said. "Don't just blame Kerry."

"I guess I'm the one who should decide who I want to blame here, Beth," Emily said, laughing. But tears came into her eyes. "Did he beg you not to tell me?" she asked, after a while.

"He didn't have to. I guess I'm the betrayer of all time."

Emily smiled sadly. "I can't think about this stuff right now." She closed her eyes tight. "Listen, Beth, we can't worry about boys or about anything else at a time like this. I didn't come here planning to fall in love. In a way, this revelation might make things easier." She swallowed a lump in her throat. "All I care about now is Charity. I want to save her. I need your help, even if you say you won't ever go back to the Hamilton Home."

"What do you expect me to do?"

"I want you to get help if anything should happen to me. If I should happen to disappear—"

"Disappear!"

"Like the missing girls."

"Oh, God, Emily. It would be better to go back to California and spend your time in a detention center."

"No," Emily said, feeling stronger now. "No, I know what I have to do."

The truth was, she felt awful. But something about feeling so terrible made facing the Hamilton Home easier. She felt like taking risks now. What, she wondered, did she have to lose?

"Take me home, please," she said.

"Emily, tell me you forgive me," Beth said.

Emily looked over at her friend's sad face. "I forgive you. I'm not even mad at you. You deserve better than what you got out this deal. You deserved a lot better than Kerry. And so do I."

They looked at one another, then abruptly burst out laughing. But the nervous laughter was short-lived.

"God," Beth said. "Poor us. May we both have better luck next time."

"He's history."

They drove the country roads back to Patrick's house. Lights from the house cast a yellow glow across the lawn. A familiar Mustang was parked in the driveway. It was Kerry's.

"What the—?" Emily said.

They could see that the driver was asleep. Beth's headlight beams swept through the car's interior, and the sleeper stirred to life. Kerry blinked and rubbed his eyes.

"Oh, no," Beth said.

Emily was out of Beth's car as soon as it stopped. She slammed the door hard behind her.

"Emily!" Kerry cried, emerging from the Mustang.

Emily strode up to him, trying to hold back an impulse to swing, to punch him the jaw.

"Get out of our driveway, Kerry," she said, loud but calm.

Kerry looked past Emily at Beth, who shook her head.

"I'm sorry!" she called, standing next to the open

door of her mother's car. She put her hands on top of
her head, and then over her mouth. The composure
she'd mustered a few minutes vanished in tears. "I'm
such a shit. This is all my fault!"

"It's my fault," Kerry said.

"Yes, it certainly is," Emily said. She looked him
up and down. What a spoiled child. What had she seen
in him? He was a indecisive little brat, a popular jock
who took advantage of the love and adoration of his
best friends. Emily saw it all now, so clearly.

He tried to speak. "Emily . . . I'm sorry, I—"

"You owe an apology to Beth, not me," Emily said.
"She's the one you fucked, remember?"

"Emily!" Beth screamed.

"Aw, Jesus, Beth," Kerry called, approaching her.
She turned and bolted back into her car.

"Forget it!" Beth cried. "Just forget all of it! Fuck
both of you!"

She revved the engine and backed out of the driveway, Kerry calling after her. The rear wheels of the
car spit gravel and dust as they spun, and then the car
roared up the drive to the highway. A second-story
light went on in the house.

Emily walked toward the front door. Kerry came up
close behind her.

"Can I talk to you?"

"What could you possibly have to say?"

He grabbed her arm, and she wrenched it away.

"I know I'm totally fucked up," he said. He fell
down on his knees. Was he drunk again? Was he going
to blame alcohol for all his foul ups? Emily almost
felt sorry for him. He looked ridiculous in the scant

moonlight, tears streaming down his handsome, twisted face.

They were under an elm. In the dark, leaves blew around them on a light breeze. Inside, Blue was barking.

"I love you," he whispered. "I know it now. And I know I'm not worthy—"

"Please be quiet, Kerry," she said. "You're going to wake my father."

"You're torturing me! You know I love you, and you're just . . . God, Emily, you're making me crazy."

"You're making yourself crazy! Look at you. You don't know what loving someone is . . . you can't even *see* me. You've never bothered to really look inside anybody, especially yourself. You don't know what other people are!"

He fell to the ground and covered his head with his hands.

"If I can't see you"—he cried into the ground— "if I can't love you, Emily . . ." Slowly his face rose up, and his eyes shone in the moonlight. "Then I hate you. *I hate you!*" he screamed at her.

Emily backed up, as though astonished by the acts of a madman.

He threw leaves into the air. "Why did you have to come here? Why don't you go back where you came from? You're a witch! You're a fucking witch!"

That did it. She came up close to him and grabbed him by the collar of his jacket.

Tears sprang from her eyes. "I don't ever want to see you again!" she yelled. "Ever! Now, get out of here before my father comes out here and kills you!"

She released him and turned back to the house, and he staggered after her.

"Emily!" he cried, a child again. *"Emily!"*

She stabbed her key into the front-door lock, and entered the barely lit room. He reached out, but she slammed the door behind her, in his face. Patrick stood at the foot of stairs in his bathrobe. His hair was a mess, a look of sympathy chiseled on his face.

"Is he leaving?" Patrick said. "Do you want me to go and talk to him?"

"I want you to drive your car over him!" Emily said, fighting her jacket off.

At the top of the stairs came the soft footfalls of another person. Emily looked up. There, in one of her father's robes, was Gloria Munson. Her hair was down, flowing softly over her shoulders, and she looked sleepy eyed.

God, Emily thought.

"Hello," Gloria said with a sheepish smile.

"Hi," Emily said quietly.

Gloria came down the stairs. "Do you want me to leave you both alone?" she said.

There were many things Emily might have said to her father, to Gloria. But she was tired. More tired than she'd ever been. Outside, a squeal of tires over gravel heralded Kerry's departure. Blue ran to the front door and barked, hair rising on his back.

"I think I just want to get some sleep," Emily said.

She kissed her father on the cheek, gave Gloria a warm smile.

In her bed she trembled.

I've just got to be strong, she thought. *I've got to*

forget about all this crazy relationship stuff. Am I going insane? Maybe I am.

Emily sat up in her bed. Outside, the branches of the trees swayed slowly in the wind. Was it hate that was motivating her? Or was it love? Could she possibly love Charity? A person she scarcely knew?

She had to find out. She lay her head back down on her pillow. The room was so calm and familiar. The light was shimmery, a silken blue-black. She was beyond being tired, too tired even to sleep, too excited and frightened. She listened to her pounding heart.

Soon, she knew, she would have her answers.

Chapter Nine

Emily gazed up into the clouds.

She lay upon her back on the dry yellow grass, indifferent to the coldness of the ground. She could feel the chill of the frozen earth through her leather jacket, but could not be bothered by it. She was lost in her thoughts. Blue nudged her hand with his nose, and she stroked his soft, shiny coat.

She felt as though she were flat up against the world, barely clinging to its surface. When she was a kid, sometimes when she'd looked up at the sky, on her back or hanging upside down from a swing, she imagined the earth letting go of her and a long fall into the big, blue, empty bowl of space. She had that woozy sensation now.

October light collected overhead in the papery boughs of the trees. The last of the leaves had turned from green to a bouquet of crimson and orange; they fell softly in twos and threes, spiraling slowly to the ground. Beyond the few high clouds that drifted by, the sky was blue and hard, polished by golden rays.

It was, she thought, a day to contemplate the death of love or the death of friendship, or even the real death that might await her in the dark, evil heart of the old Hamilton Home.

Webster called for her, and she picked herself up and waved to the hired hand, who stood off in the distance. He motioned to her to accompany him.

Down in the barn she helped him throw some hay in for the Sally, the cow, and for Amber, who neighed expectantly.

"Your daddy is right worried about you," Webster finally said, cutting through the silence.

Emily wiped dirt from her hands. "I guess that's how a father is supposed to be sometimes," she said.

"I have some family up in Canada," Webster said. "If you want to run."

She smiled. "I haven't got that much to run from, have I Webster? A juvenile record in California. A shady past."

"I didn't mean that. I meant, if you want to get away from *them*."

She turned and looked into his face. His usual grizzled, friendly good looks had been replaced by a mask of doubt. Fear gathered like dark clouds in his eyes. He frowned.

"Do I have much to be afraid of?"

He cleared his throat. His voice cracked when he spoke.

"Yes. I think you should stay away from that place."

She turned and embraced him. She felt his rough hand patting her head, and when she looked up, she saw he had tears in his eyes. Then she took a few steps back.

"I have to go back there and . . ."

She stopped. And free Charity? If she told, would the police be called? Would Eugenia and Herbert kill Charity, as they had killed so many others? The Temples were poised to spring their trap, to frame her on the bogus pharmaceutical theft.

Webster wiped his eyes with the back of his gloved hand.

"If anything should happen—" Emily started to say.

"No—"

"If anything funny happens, call my friend Beth." She saw a notepad on the workbench and several pencils. She wrote Beth's phone number down and handed it to him. "She can tell you everything I know and everything I suspect up to this point."

"Emily, you don't have to go."

She shook her head. She felt her heart pounding. "I do," she said. "I love you all, but I do."

The hilltop loomed over the silent valley at dusk. The trees that lined the walkways were nearly bare of leaves. Around back, piles of leaves were strewn between the headstones of the small cemetery. Above the hill, the sky was itself the color of a weathered tombstone. The home, in its massiveness, could now be seen through the woods, from the distant and rarely traveled highways.

When Emily arrived at the home, she took a quick careful look around the grounds. What a fortress the building seemed! The windows of the lower floors looked like the best possibilities for escape, if need be.

She gazed up through the bare branches of the tree. How deathlike they had become. Mere bones. And yet after winter, the trees would bud and bloom again. Year after year the cycle repeated itself. She took a little comfort in knowing that.

Yet spring was a long way off. The black branches began to move in a sudden wind that blew up from the valley. There was something wicked about the way they waved. Was it a warning? Was her imagination working too hard, or was she being mocked by every being, alive, dead, or half alive on these cursed grounds?

Emily paused with her hand on the doorknob of the old Hamilton Home's side entrance. She closed her eyes and took a breath. Up till now she'd been playing it relatively safe.

But she was sure she wanted to go on. She stepped inside to a warm, stale mass of air.

The corridors were veiled in gloom and shadow. Emily watched carefully, hoping she was not being observed as she crept to her destination: the basement door that would lead to Charity. She was very frightened.

At last she came to the basement stairs. The door had been closed.

Crazy . . . turn and run . . .

But she was compelled to go on. Turning the doorknob, she felt a screaming in her mind. She was in a sense defenseless. No weapons, no gun or dagger— not even a baseball bat. Nothing but sheer guts and determination to go on.

And not a friend in the world . . . No, that wasn't true. She had Webster, and she had her father and Gloria. As for Beth and Kerry, she thought . . . but then thought better of it; this was not the time to take an accounting of loyalties.

She closed her eyes and swallowed hard. Oh, this would have been so much safer with Beth and Kerry at her side. The young and strong and fearless . . . but she was all-too alone.

Emily took a last look up and down the hall. Then she quickly descended the stairs. In the basement, she encountered the familiar damp smell and the half-lit gloom of the corridors.

The halls were empty of people. No nurses in their hospital whites. No high school volunteers or minimum-wage earners.

Turn back! a voice seemed to call. Or was it her own fear speaking to her?

No! she answered in her mind; it was too late for turning back.

She began to run—not away, but deeper into the black pit of darkness that lay ahead of her. Soon she was running as if being chased, flinging doors open and rushing through them.

''Charity!'' she whispered.

At last she reached the subbasement. She passed storage shelves crammed with folding chairs, cardboard boxes, tools. She picked up a hammer. Too heavy. She dropped it, and the clatter echoed though the black tunnellike corridor.

She chose instead a small screwdriver. She lunged out with it, as though fending off an attacker. It felt fine in her hand.

Down here, the strange whine of machinery could be heard through the clammy stone walls. At the end of the corridor, new puddles had formed. She saw her frightened reflection in the black water at the foot of the final door.

Emily reached for the door with trepidation. She was surprised to find that the locks she had destroyed had not been fixed.

The door creaked. In the candlelight, Emily saw Charity, seated on her cot, behind the bars of her cage.

"Charity!" she cried, rushing into the room.

Charity, whose eyes had been closed, stirred to life. She jumped to her feet, eyes wide.

"Run!" Charity screamed. *"Run away now, child!"*

Emily stood frozen. The door slammed shut behind her. Her heart seemed to fall three stories to the bottom of her chest. She dropped the screwdriver, and it rolled over to the tip of Herbert's expensive, shiny black shoe. He kicked it away.

"Nowhere to run, child," he said calmly. "Not any more."

Eugenia stepped out of the shadows, hands hidden in the pockets of her jacket. Herbert raised a small pistol and pointed it at Emily. She ran to the bars of the cage in which Charity was kept.

"Oh, God, Charity!"

"Never mind," Eugenia said. "She can't help you now." Eugenia took a step toward her.

Emily turned to Eugenia. "Why are you keeping her here?" she screamed. "Do you really think you can get away with it?"

"You both have something we need," Eugenia answered with a sneer.

"Don't surrender!" Charity cried to Emily. "Never give up!"

Eugenia lurched out at Emily, clawing. Emily screamed and raised her arms. Eugenia caught hold of her wrist in a bone-crushing grip.

"Let her go!" Charity commanded.

But it was too late. Eugenia now reached out and wrapped her cold fingers around Emily's neck. She was surprisingly strong. Her grasp paralyzed Emily. Now Emily couldn't breath. Her heart was slamming in her chest. *Am I going to die? Are they really going to kill me?*

And then she saw Herbert coming toward her with the needle. She felt the needle enter her neck, like a bee sting. Instantly she felt a cold fog envelop her. Her vision blurred. She felt herself slipping from consciousness.

The last thing she saw, hovering over her, were Eugenia's gleaming eyes, black and cold as stones.

Beth began to worry when Emily didn't show up for her shift at the home that night. Knowing she was probably being watched herself, she thought about making plans to leave, of feigning illness if necessary.

She had debated with herself all evening about whether to come to work at all. She'd sworn she wouldn't set foot in the home again. At last she decided that she'd come in, but avoid Emily at all costs.

When Emily didn't show up, Beth couldn't keep her mind on anything else.

All evening she'd been asking around about her. In the lobby, by the magazine rack, she asked nurses and cooks and maids if Emily had called in yet. She casually asked some of the girls if they'd seen her. No one had. No one knew where she was. No one had heard a thing.

Beth hid her face behind a copy of *Life*. She was sitting in the break room on one of those slippery doctor's-office sofas, the kind that seem to be covered with rubber and pick up strange black skid marks. This one was bright orange.

There was nothing to do but call Emily's home. She fished into her jeans pocket for change.

She dialed Emily's number, and when Patrick answered, she tried to disguise her voice.

"Emily there?" she whispered.

"No . . . she's at work."

God.

"Okay," Beth said in a frog voice. "Thank you."

"Wait . . . who is this? Beth?"

Beth hung up the phone.

An icy chill washed though her. It was happening. They had Emily, she was certain of it. Emily would not have been absent without an excuse—not after the false accusations Eugenia had leveled against her. There was no other place in the world she would be at this hour but here at the home, searching for Charity.

Beth paced up and down the tiled floor that led to the kitchen. The slightly nauseating smell of onions mingled with the fumes of some industrial-strength cleaner. She wanted a cigarette. She wanted to scream. What could she do? Whom could she call?

Kerry seemed the logical person. But how, after the row the other night—not to mention after that night at the cemetery—could she speak to him? She bit her lip in exasperation. She would just have to swallow her pride. Tears brimmed in her eyes. Her hand shook as she dropped more coins into the pay phone. After several rings, he answered.

"Something is wrong," she said. She fought back tears. "Emily is missing. She's been kidnapped."

"Beth? What are you talking about? Maybe she's just playing hookey from work."

"I wish that were true," Beth said. The worst had happened, she was certain.

"Beth, you've got to calm down," Kerry said.

"How in hell can I be calm! How can *you* be so cool? The girl you claim to love so dearly is in big trouble! You've got to help me. You've got to bring help!"

"The police?"

"No! Not the police. We can't count on them. The police would only ask a few questions, and Eugenia would pull the wool over their eyes. We need to rescue Emily ourselves, if she's still—"

"Alive?"

"Oh, God, Kerry . . . I'm really worried."

"Okay . . . Just stay where you are."

"No way . . . I'm on the work schedule for three more hours. But I have a sudden cramp, if you catch my drift."

"I have an idea, too," Kerry said. "I'll need some help."

They agreed to meet. Beth found Patti and Laverne, both dressed in their immaculate hospital whites. She explained her "illness" and need to go home at once. The two nurses looked at one another with skepticism. A large red pimple or wart had surfaced between Patti's eyes. Before they could reply, Beth was pulling on her denim jacket.

She fled out the door of the home, terrified that she would feel the pull of hands from behind her, the grasp of the Temples. But she made it to her car. She started the engine, and looked out over the dark hills. It was an unseasonably cold fall night. Beth pulled her collar up around her throat. She sped down the hill, toward Kerry's house.

As soon as she had stopped in the Thornton's driveway, Kerry was on his way out to the car.

Despite herself, she felt a glow in her heart at the sight of him. For once he didn't look to her like Mr. Straightlaced Innocent from a milk advertisement. He hadn't shaved, and a shadow of whisker stubble grew over his chin and jaws. His eyes were red, desperate with worry. So human after all.

He came up to the driver's-side window, which she frantically rolled down.

"Beth, I wanted to say I'm sorry for—"

"We have to put our differences behind us," she said, taking in a deep breath. "At least for the time being." She said it as much for own benefit as for his. Her hair was pulled up, tied with a rubber band. Over her hair she wore a Milwaukee Brewers cap. She pulled the bill down low, almost covering her sapphire eyes.

He looked down for a moment, ashamed. But then he looked at her with determination in his eyes.

"Agreed," he said. "Now, tell me what's going on." He climbed into car, next to her.

She told him what she'd seen in the basement of the home, and what she knew from Emily. She told him about Charity being locked up behind bars in a cage, about Emily's suspicions that Herbert and Eugenia might have been responsible for the senator's plane crash. She also told him that she herself suspected the Temples of running elaborate financial scams at the

Hamilton Home. Emily, having stumbled upon these facts—and even more—was now in grave danger.

"We have to tell her dad," Kerry said. And then he turned and looked out the window. Beth could see the anguish on his face. His brown eyes were brimming with tears and anger.

"I'll kill that fucking whore Eugenia Temple myself!" he said through clenched teeth.

"Don't forget Herbert," Beth said.

"I'll stomp the shit out of that slimy little lizard," Kerry added.

"That's fine. But first we have to find Emily. As of now we don't even have proof she was kidnapped by those creeps. If Dr. Temple and his sister are really as sinister as I think, don't you think they've already planned for an assault on all fronts?"

Kerry nodded.

"We really need a better strategy," Beth said. "And we might want to let the cops in on it after all."

After some further discussion, they devised a plan. Phase one: If Emily was not returned safe and sound by ten that night, they would report her missing, and they would point the finger of blame at Eugenia.

At eight that evening, the telephone in Eugenia's office rang. She was seated at her desk, going over a financial report. Number crunching soothed her ragged nerves. Of course she'd been expecting a clamor over Emily's disappearance. Removing her glasses, she picked up the receiver and answered.

"We know you have Emily," someone said, the voice of a young man.

"Who is this?" Eugenia asked evenly.

"This is your death if you harm one hair on her head," he replied.

"I'm afraid I don't know what you're talking about. I'm calling the police," Eugenia said, and she hung up the phone.

Her first impulse was to bite a nail. But then she thought about it. Children. Mischievous children. Not worth getting excited over them.

New blood was soaring through her veins. Already she felt replenished, years younger, and strong. It's silly to let little worries get to you, she thought. Herbert is right. At my age, I ought to be a little less concerned, a little less worried about the trivial. She looked at her hand. The skin tone was perfect, taut and smooth. The looseness she'd noticed this morning was gone. A thrill rippled through her entire body. The effects of the injections were in full swing. She found herself smiling, then giggling nervously. It took a couple minutes for her to compose herself. Then she turned her attention back to the numbers on the page before her.

At ten-thirty that night, the nurse's station buzzed Eugenia in her office.

"Miss Temple?" She recognized the voice of one of her favorite of the trio of nurse-henchwomen: The one Beth called "Maxine."

Now what? Work was going so well, her mind flush with renewed energy.

The nurse announced that some angry visitors had arrived. "They insist on seeing you," she said.

Eugenia had, of course, half-expected this, though not quite so soon. But before she could answer, Patrick stormed though the office door. With him was a woman

Eugenia didn't know, a woman who, while pretty, had let her dark hair pick up a smattering of gray. Gloria Munson. The nurses followed, clucking like chickens whose nests have just been robbed of their eggs.

"I want some answers!" Patrick thundered. Behind Gloria, a third person entered the office. He wore a wide-brimmed hat. A badge stone on his chest. The county sheriff, Chip Drummond.

Patrick Jordan was frantic. Eugenia might have expected that. Other parents had had similar reactions. But she'd only seen them ranting on the TV news. Never had they been this close.

Bad girls. Their parents were always slightly ashamed, the police always slightly dubious.

Eugenia stood. Calmly, she extended her hand. Out of the corner of her eye she saw Beth and a stranger, a young man. They entered the room now, too, accusation in their eyes. That explained the earlier phone call.

"Good evening," Eugenia said, and smiled. "Quite a posse you've put together, Sheriff."

"Now, Miss Temple, we have to consider everything," Drummond said. His gray-flecked brown mustache twitched. He had a strong lantern jaw and sad, dark eyes.

"That's why you're here accusing me of having something to do with Emily's sudden disappearance?"

"Then you know about it?" Gloria said.

Eugenia smiled at Gloria. "One of these youths made an obscene phone call earlier in the evening. They accused me of kidnapping Emily Jordan. Preposterous. Emily Jordan is a troubled girl, Sheriff."

Eugenia produced a file, and handed it to him. Patrick's eyebrows were raised in alarm.

"Not only did she traffic in drugs in San Francisco, her presence at the home coincided with a rash of pharmaceutical thefts," she said.

"Liar!" Patrick said.

"Your daughter has chosen an unsavory crowd to run with," Eugenia said. "It has happened around here before. There's always one person to blame, and that person is usually a thrill-seeking little ... *girl* who almost always winds up missing or dead—or in even deeper trouble."

"She's my best friend," Beth said. "You stupid old cow."

"Your loyalty is impressive. You are suspended for one month."

Beth took another step forward, leaned in closer to Eugenia. "Like I'd come back here. You're not going to stick your fangs into my neck, too."

"Now, everybody settle down," the sheriff said. "Emily has not been missing all that long. Technically speaking." He held the file in his hand, as if weighing it. "Maybe we ought to all go home and try to consider our options."

"I'd say that's a good idea," Eugenia said.

"Don't fall for it, Sheriff," Kerry said. "Ask to take a look around."

"You may keep the file and return it at your leisure, Sheriff Drummond," Eugenia said.

"Sorry to have burst in on you like this, Miss Temple. But the kids, they ... well, they're worried, as you can see."

"I'm quite worried, too," Patrick said angrily.

"Well, I came up here with you, didn't I, Mr. Jordan?" Drummond said, looking angry now, too. "You didn't tell me Emily had some problems already." He shook the file folder. "There's always another side to these stories. Now, go home and cool off."

"I can't believe this!" Beth said. She fought back angry tears.

"Oh, what woe one little girl can cause us," Eugenia said. She gave Patrick a look that he had to turn away from. An accusing look.

"There are other questions to be answered," Gloria said. She looked at Eugenia. "What about the claim that women are being held here against their will?"

"Goodness," Eugenia said. "My patience is really being tried this evening. Sheriff, really . . ."

"You're right, Miss Temple. I'm sorry."

"But—" Gloria tried to speak.

"No more buts," Drummond said. "We came here to ask about Emily Jordan, not launch a full-scale investigation. Now, come on. We're leaving." He tipped his hat to Eugenia. She gave him a thin-lipped smile.

Kerry put his arm around Beth's shoulder and led her out of the office.

The vanquished group filed through the main hallway, led by the sheriff. The hall was dimly lit. And despite the relatively late hour, a few of the elderly residents were seated here and there.

Just before he reached the front door, Patrick's eye was caught by a slowly approaching old woman. She came from the day room, and leaned heavily on her cane as she walked. Something about the urgency with which she struggled toward him made him stop cold in his tracks.

"Wait . . ." the woman called to him, her voice paper thin, a mere rasp.

The woman was, Patrick guessed, at least ninety. Her hair was white, wispy, and she raised a frail, trembling hand. Her old, watery-bright eyes stabbed at his heart.

"I . . . I know you. . . ." the old woman said. Her thin eyebrows rose at the center of her face. She desperately tried to speak, to search for words.

But Patrick did not exactly recognize this old woman. Was she a former grade school teacher? She was terribly distressed, and now she began to cry. After all the upsets tonight, he just couldn't face this awkward scene.

"No . . . I'm sorry," he said. "I'm so sorry."

The woman tried to speak, but it was too much for her. She shook her head, as though this action would fire her fogged memory. She gasped for breath. Gloria and Emily's friends stood near, watching on with stoic expressions. Beth did not recognize the old woman. In fact, she would have sworn she'd never seen her before at the home.

From behind this group came Eugenia, demurely clearing her throat. All heads turned.

She approached, smiling, showing teeth. "Ned," she called out, and the tall, ghoulish man—who must have been standing nearby—lumbered into the hallway.

"Please take the poor dear to her room. She has confused Mr. Jordan with someone."

The old woman cried out as she was gently led away. She looked at Patrick with eyes so desperate in their pleading that he caught a little sob in his throat. Gloria put her hand on his shoulder.

"It's very sad," Eugenia said, drawing his attention back to her. "Many of our residents have so few visitors. They often mistake young men for their own sons. Sons who cannot or will not visit. We take care of these poor souls. That, friends, is our mission here, a mission you have so cruelly misconceived."

Drummond nodded sadly.

Patrick turned away, haunted by the woman's face. Now his mind was playing a trick on him. He felt as though he did indeed recognize her—but from where? That was all he needed now, he thought angrily; now, when his mind was so consumed by his lost daughter. Emily was all he could think of. He turned and embraced Gloria. They walked like wounded soldiers to the door. At the door, Patrick turned and looked back at Eugenia, whose regal frame eclipsed the light of the hallway. She appeared as a faceless black shadow.

"Help me find my daughter," he said to her. Then he shouted. "Help me find her!"

Ned Fox firmly escorted the frail old woman into a small room.

"Please," she said. "You're hurting my arm. . . ."

He led her to a chair, not bothering to turn on a light. He pushed her roughly down into the chair, and she let out a groan of pain. For a second, their eyes met. He looked searchingly into her face.

"I know you. . . ." she said. "You—"

"Shhh," he said. He touched her hand.

"You're Ned!"

"I-I . . . don't know you. . . ." he said. "You're nuh . . . *new* here." He turned and walked awkwardly out of the room. He closed the door soundly behind him, leaving her in almost total darkness.

Slowly, her eyes adjusted to the dark. She had been

so confused, today . . . so confused she could barely hold a clear thought in her mind.

Where am I? What's happened to me?

My name . . . What is my name?

And the faces she'd seen today . . . the face she'd seen downstairs. Her mind reeled.

All at once it came to her, as eyes adjusted to darkness and began to see. *That man downstairs . . . the man with the pleading eyes . . . is my father!*

I am Emily Jordan! I am seventeen!

Dear God, what have they done to me?

Hours passed. It was night when Emily awoke from a strange slumber. She felt weak, cold. With all her strength she lifted herself from her chair and walked to the bathroom, where she turned on the light.

The full horror swept over her like a cold and heavy Atlantic wave. *That strange woman in the mirror . . . it's me.*

She put her hand to her face, and felt.

I'm old.

The skin clung loosely to the bones of her face. Deep lines and fine cross-hatching made a map that traced time. Yet she'd not lived the years associated with such a face. Yesterday she'd been a girl.

Only her blue eyes had remained vibrant and recognizable. Her fine mane of black hair had become brittle as straw. It gleamed in its whiteness. Her wrists were skeletal. Her small breasts sagged beneath the nightgown she wore. Her bones seemed to creak as she moved her arms.

Is this what Eugenia and Herbert Temple had been

doing to the young girls of Blackburn County? Sapping away their youth? What kind of monsters were they?

And will I die now? As others, like Maria Kraus, have died?

Her eyes glistened, but the expression of distress with which she gazed at herself dimmed the familiar brightness. She touched her pure-white wispy hair.

She touched her face. Her chin sagged ever so slightly. This was not a dream. And this was no mask, it was living flesh. She showed her teeth and saw that they were longer, but intact. Her lips had grown thin, her nose a bit larger. Still, the effect, if shocking, was not entirely displeasing, she had to admit. She would be—was—a handsome old woman.

I'm not ugly. I'm old, but I'm not ugly.

She turned her head from side to side, looking at all her aspects. Her skin was translucent, every fine vein showing dimly through to the surface. She opened her gown to look at her chest, and quickly closed it again.

Her hands were white and skinny, knobby at the knuckles, dotted with liver spots. Thick blue veins crisscrossed over them. Her fingers were not at all straight, as they had been yesterday. She rolled up her sleeves. More thick blue veins protruded.

Now she had at least a part of the answer she was seeking. Eugenia, Herbert, even Charity—none were what they seemed. And the hint of black magic that had loomed over the Hamilton Home since her arrival now announced itself darkly.

Her youth—and the youth of how many people?— had been stolen. How to get it back? *Could* she get it back?

She walked slowly, each step an agony. The door was locked. Even if she had the strength, she wondered if she could escape. And escaping this room was not enough; how would she escape this body? Was this dark magic reversible?

Tears filled her eyes. Now she had some of the answers she'd sought. Now she understood the fate of the old people of the Hamilton Home. She guessed that many of them had suffered this same strange curse.

Emily had long sensed that this place was under an evil spell. The strange callings she'd heard, the sirens in her mind. How long had they been crying out for help from this evil? The full weight of the situation overwhelmed her failing mind.

The night was long, the moon heavy in the sky. Its beams shone down over Emily's little room, her prison cell. The next day was Halloween. How fitting, she thought to herself. Instead of partying with her young friends, she would be rotting in this room. Each day would be as another tick of the clock; surely her body could not hold out in this condition for long.

"Charity," she called aloud. Such a funny squeak of a voice. "Sister," she said, though she'd never thought of Charity as her sister before.

She did so now.

She called out fiercely in her mind, yet no answer came, not through the cold walls of the Hamilton Home or through the telepathic channels that had, she now believed, once linked her mind to Charity's.

When the light of dawn finally broke over the hills, Emily felt that she could sleep. Cold fog hung over the wheat-colored hills. How she longed to run over the grass, to run to her father's house.

She fell asleep, vowing to save herself. Vowing to save the victims of Eugenia, and of Herbert. But all she had was this promise to herself, and scant reason left to believe in hope of any kind. It would take more than mere mortals—her father, the power of the state, her friends—to save her.

On the afternoon of Halloween day the light was fuzzy, casting a surreal white glow over the fields and barn and through the cedar-and-glass house where Patrick Jordan waited in agony for news about his daughter's disappearance.

He drank cup after cup of tea. He kept hoping he would be released from this bad dream. If only Emily would walk through that door. It was terrible that not even one of her new friends had a clue—a reliable, solid clue—where she could be.

Of course Patrick had not worked in his studio today. Gloria, feeling frustrated and rather useless, had finally given him a kiss and headed off to try to get some work done at her office. Light that had barely existed all day was now failing. The days were shorter. He'd thought it necessary to call Cathleen but couldn't find the strength to tell Emily's mother that Emily, some-how, was gone.

He would tell her . . . tomorrow.

He'd watched the phone all day. It rang twice. The first call had been from Gloria. She waited for him to speak, knowing he would have told her at once if everything were all right.

Everything was wrong. The second call came from Sheriff Drummond. It yielded nothing.

Blue sat at his master's boot-clad feet, and Patrick, in tears all day long, stroked the dog's velvety coat.

The door opened, and Patrick jerked his head around to see Webster, face contrite, deeply pained, enter the kitchen. He had a jack-o'-lantern in his hands. Patrick rose and crossed the room, staring at the pumpkin.

"We carved it together," Webster said. He meant he and Emily. It was a beautifully shaped pumpkin, a potential prize winner. "Shall I put it in the window?"

Patrick ran a hand across the grinning pumpkin. "God, Webster, I can't think about a pumpkin right now . . ."

Webster put the pumpkin out on the front porch, on a ledge where it could be seen from the winding driveway. He returned and took a seat. Patrick took two glasses down from the shelf, and poured bourbon into them.

"I wish there was something I could do, Pat," Webster said. "Something I could say. I'd kill with my bare hands anybody who harmed that precious girl."

Patrick watched Webster, a man as tough as any he'd ever known, turn his head to hide his tears. Webster accepted the glass of bourbon Patrick held out to him.

"I just can't believe she's gotten herself into any trouble on her own," Patrick said. "She's had some trouble before . . . but I believe she was over it." He thought of the letter from Danny.

"She wouldn't run away," Webster said. "I just know she's gonna be back. Damn that Temple woman and her bastard of a brother!"

"We need proof before we go damning," Patrick

said somewhat harshly. He immediately regretted his tone. "God, what am I bitching at you for?"

"No offense taken, Pat," Webster said softly.

Patrick nodded, and turned his head to drink. He tasted the bourbon. It warmed his throat and chest. He lit a stubbed candle on the table, took it out of its cobalt glass holder, and stepped out onto the darkened porch. The cool breeze was bracing. Darkness had fallen over the hills of his farm, his once happy home. His sad land, he admitted darkly. The jack-o'-lantern grinned devilishly at the encroaching night.

Beth had to avoid running over a gaggle of jay-walking trick-or-treaters. She drove fast to Kerry's, tooted the horn, and watched him run out to the car.

He dropped a sack of tools on the back seat, and the contents clanked together. He scooted onto the front seat beside her.

"I brought this," he said, raising a bottle of sweet vermouth. "For courage."

Beth looked at the bottle. She remembered what happened the last time she went drinking with Kerry. This was different. Tonight they were going to save their friend. They were going into a dangerous place.

She took a swig and winced. "Awful." She handed the bottle back to Kerry. "If courage is what you get from that, I'll take fear."

Kerry took a greedy sip to calm his nerves. He held the bottle up. "Fear could take us both," he said.

They looked at one other. The levity seemed to evaporate. Beth's freshly shampooed long hair shimmered in the moonlight. Kerry looked so good to her, just then, despite everything. She knew that if she were ever to hate him as much as she wanted to, it would have to wait.

"To Emily," Beth said, and she swallowed the impulse to tear up.

"To Emily," Kerry said. "And to us. May God have mercy on us. Especially on our necks."

Beth put the car in gear and pulled away from the curb, heading out of Leonora, past windows glowing with the light of carved pumpkins, and past parents closely watching their costumed kids, who ran eagerly from door to door.

The home cast its imposing shadow over the near-dark hills. The moon was hanging on the horizon, like a great orange pumpkin, glowing, oblong, not full but swollen, climbing a ladder of stars toward the top of the sky.

At the caretaker's house, light shimmered in the windows. Deep within, a strange ritual took place in the glow of a hundred dripping white candles.

Eugenia, her silver hair full and lustrous, her face free of lines but far from beautiful, ran her hands up and down her body, clad in a white silk robe.

She turned slowly to her brother. "I'm ready," she said.

Herbert looked up from a bubbling vat of amber incandescent liquid. Thick curls of smoke rose from the brew.

His face was relaxed, but rather than assuming any of the beauty associated with youth, he'd grown uglier.

From his pocket he removed a strange gnarled charm, a metallic mass of crossing twigs, encrusted with diamondlike crystals. He lowered it into the liquid.

A scorching hiss sliced through the silence of the room. A stench of sulfur permeated the air. Stepping back, he parted the curtain from the window. Moonlight fell across the brew.

Waves of golden light pulsed from the brew, a concoction made from the very blood of Emily Jordan.

With a gold ladle, Herbert poured the magic potion into two wine glasses. He began a strange chant in an unintelligible language, his eyes closed tight.

Eugenia took a long draft from her glass. "Such a heavenly brew," she said, enraptured.

"Hellish, actually, my dear."

"Young blood!" Eugenia whispered, near ecstacy.

"Blood of the lambs," Herbert said.

They raised their glasses and drank.

Eugenia sighed. "Wait here, just for a moment." She ran from the room. Moments later she returned in a black gown. Ornate, with long floating sleeves, and a gleaming black stomacher, the gown perfectly fit Eugenia's slender form.

She turned, letting the dress twirl at her ankles. "It fits like yesterday," she said in a whisper.

"Like a hundred thousand yesterdays," Herbert replied. He stood and took her in his arms and danced her around the room.

"Oh, how much longer can it last?" Eugenia said.

Herbert stopped, drew back. "Eugenia, you poor dear. You're having doubts, this late in the game? Our little Emily is as a dry leaf, my dear, spent and powerless. Not a witch at all."

"And Charity?"

"I think it's safe to say I'll soon slit her throat and cut out her old, dead heart. She's hardly worth the trouble for the few measly dollars we're squeezing out of her. Just another old bag of bones. Now, had we found her when she was young . . ." he gazed wistfully at his sister.

A smile spread over Eugenia's lips.

"I'm sorry I doubted you, even for a second, dear brother."

"Be calm, beloved sister," he said. "And drink. Drink! To eternal life! Eternal beauty!" A smile crept over his thin, pale lips. "To eternal youth and immortality!"

With that they put the glasses to their lips. Eugenia felt the cool burn of youthful life itself, of spring passion, passing her lips, filling her mouth and flowing down her throat. It glowed all along the way, to pool warmly in the cage of her chest, to fill the void where a human heart used to be.

The night Emily's youth had been stolen from her, she'd slipped deeply into a strange dream.

Danny's voice came to her in her bed. He called for help. She woke and found—with a bit of a start— that she'd grown a great pair of wings, gossamer and angelic. A huge window opened to the night overhead, and, with a sense of fate, she flew across the stars to find herself in the skies over northern California.

She looked down upon the dark mountains and hillocks, dotted with the lights of homes, and cast her gaze out to the vast, black Pacific, to silver wisps of cloud threaded into the distant, star-strewn horizon.

The dream fast forwarded like a video, and she found herself wandering, in a long white robe, wings at her back, through a prison cellblock. Concrete walls everywhere, and bars. Scant light. The men slumbered in their cells as she passed by, barefoot, the hem of her white robe trailing behind her.

The dream hurtled forward, and she was airborne again, hovering over a strange white-tiled room, barely lit. She recognized that this must be the communal shower room. Faucets gleamed. The shower was empty, or appeared to be so, and silent. But then she saw something stir in a dark corner.

It only took her a second to recognize Danny, crumpled on the floor, naked. He had been badly beaten. She was lowered over him as if by invisible wires.

He was alive, but his breathing was labored, and he was crouched in a fetal position. His lustrous black hair was sopped with sweat. His eye was blackened, and a deep gash had been cut into his face, from his jaw to his ear.

"Danny!" she cried. "What happened, what have they done to you?"

"They wanted me dead," he said.

"Who? Who wants you dead?"

"You know . . . them . . . Eugenia and Herbert."

She knew she was dreaming this. It didn't make sense that Eugenia and Herbert would have come here to beat Danny. Yet dream logic prevailed.

She touched his warm back. "Oh, Danny . . . how did we let all of this happen? Didn't we love each other enough?"

"It was a good time while it lasted, babe," he said. He rolled onto his back. Beneath him, blood had pooled. His. From his left breast, a dagger protruded.

It was in him up to the hilt. It heaved up and down with his breath. She clapped a hand over her mouth in fright.

"You didn't answer my letter," he said. "You really let me down, babe. And look what happened."

"You think this is my fault?" she said. Tears fell from her eyes.

He grinned up at her. "Happy now?" he said.

She reached for the handle of the dagger.

"Hey," he said. "Watch it."

But, in dream logic, she knew what she was doing. Slowly she pulled the dagger from his heart. Seven inches of metal slid from his smooth skin. He gasped and his head fell backward, the whites of his eyes glowing.

She held the bloody spear before herself. Her chest heaved. Then she raised the dagger skyward. Had a ceiling covered this prison shower? Above them now was the open night sky, filled with a canopy of dazzling stars.

With a flap of wings she rose, away from Danny's crumpled form. She soared again to the brilliant sky, her dagger thrust out before her, pointed east.

Chapter Ten

Charity closed her eyes and tried to call Emily, silently, through a channel of her mind. It took all her concentration. Her wild, flowing hair picked up a fizz of electricity that hummed delicately around her plump old face. The tiny strands of hair pulsed to their ends with this charge, and a strange golden light radiated from Charity's forehead. But just as quickly as the light began to glow and pulse, it scattered and died. She was tired. And this bed she sat on was lumpy, the basement smelled so damp, and there was an unpleasant chill down here. All of this made message sending difficult.

She closed her eyes and tried again.

Concentrate, she told herself. She pressed her eyelids hard together.

This time nothing at all happened. It wasn't working.

Charity rose with creaking bones from the cot that served as her bed down here in the deepest cellar of the Hamilton Home. With a hand on her lower back, she walked slightly hunched to the bars of her cage.

Black shadow stripes slid over her dressing gown and face. She took hold of one the bars in her hand. It felt cold, rough, wrought of unbending steel.

Oh, Emily, she thought. *Maybe it's wrong for me to get you involved in this terrible dilemma. What choice do I have, though? You heard my call, child. For whatever reason, we have a kinship. I need you desperately. I hope someday you'll forgive me.*

If we get out of here.

She closed her eyes. *Stop thinking this way,* she told herself. *We* will *get out of here. Anyway, Emily can't hear you. And it's possible Herbert and Eugenia have already taken Emily and—Curse these thoughts*!

Charity walked quickly back to her bed. *If I have so little confidence, then all hope really* is *lost,* she told herself.

The hour was late. She lay her head on her pillow and closed her eyes.

If I can just . . . If I could only . . .

Her thoughts drifted like fading music.

She felt her head on the pillow. But she felt she was not in this basement cell any more, at least not consciously. She was leaving. . . .

A mass of red light flooded her brain. Blood coursing behind her closed eyelids? She didn't know. She was entering a strange dream, perhaps brought on by exhaustion. Whatever was causing it, she yielded to the dream's otherworldly pull.

The red-light mass, fluid at first, seemed to harden. It grew like a crystal, deepening to a burgundy hue, through which passed a warm, red glow. The red glass rose upward in an immense flat pane, ruby beamed, stretching and shining. And then the red pane stretched to the point at which it could not stretch any more. It shattered in a diamond-white explosion.

The light in this vision seemed to slowly fall just then, like lights dimming in a huge theater. Charity became aware of an odd presence in the dream darkness: a heavy, wet, and pulsing red veil, rich and satiny, luscious with folds, and seeming at once to be both a curtain and a vast, magical eyelid. It rose with a gentle rustle upon a dreamy memory. Suddenly revealed with a vividness that alarmed her—though she was aware she was quite asleep now and dreaming this—was the terrible place she knew so well: a dark wood, a leaf-strewn forest floor, centuries old . . .

. . . three hundred years ago.

The wheels of the horse cart creaked over the old dirt road in the dark hour before dawn. Charity and the other girls in the back of the cart remained silent, as they had been ordered to. In the gloom she could barely even see whom she was next to, a strange girl from the village. The girl wore an ankle-length drab dress like her own, the prim, high-collared, modest apparel of all the village women and girls.

Charity looked up to the bare, gnarled black branches of the trees seeming to pass by overhead. The trees were old and sturdy and tall, with immensely stout trunks. At their upper reaches they leaned toward one another, forming a queer canopy of fat twisting branches over the winding road. The yellow eyes of an owl, stern and filled with disapproval, pierced down though the night blue-blackness, blinking at Charity. His ghostly hoot made gooseflesh rise on her arms.

The faint predawn light seeped eerily into the October sky beyond the tree branches, a bruised gray, like rocks that cover the mouths of tombs. In the distance, a chorus of wolves howled. She imagined their upturned heads and closed eyes. Teeth that flashed in moonlight.

Down here, in the deepest part of the forest, it was black as midnight. The wooden wheels of the cart crunched over the leaf-strewn path. Dry, dead leaves scurried along the ground and swirled upon the chill morning breeze.

Charity clutched at the bed of straw she lay on. Her hands were tied behind her back. So, too, were the hands of the other girls. The cart went over a bump, and a collective gasp was heard.

"Ye be still!" hissed the driver.

Charity felt as though she would vomit her supper. It had been on their way home from a church gathering that the girls had been kidnapped, hours ago. They had walked the usual route toward home, with full stomachs and light hearts, dancing along the path under the stars, holding hands and giggling. And then the rough capture, hands being bound, tears and cries for help as they were pushed into the wagon.

Now her heart pounded. She looked into the wide eyes of the girl lying next to her. The girl, whose teeth were frightfully crooked, swallowed and looked away. The strange village girl she barely knew, called Angelica, was now slightly more visible. Morning was but an hour away.

Up at the bend in the road, an eerie orange light pulsed against the trees. As the cart rounded into a clearing, Charity saw the blazing torches of the encampment, where men and women were bound to trees, their heads hanging wearily down. Others, in black robes, stood nearby. The cart came to a stop. The horse snorted, breath smoking in the air.

"On yer feet," the driver said. He roughly took hold of Charity's arm and yanked her from the back of the cart.

"Blond maiden," someone said. "Stand here." Charity turned to see the face of the physician Templeton, a traveler new to this part of the colonies. He had gained a reputation as a witch hunter, with the added credential of being a man of science. Herbert's long red hair fell to his shoulders. His little mustache and pointy beard gave him a devilish appearance. Beside him stood his raven-haired sister, Eugenia. And beyond them were some of the village elders, and the Reverend Mr. Burrows.

"Methinks you have made a grave error," Charity said.

"Do you?" Herbert grinned.

"If it is Satan's brides you seek, I beg you, you will find none among us."

Charity thought of the travesties of the witch killings going on in the area. She knew well that most if not all of the women put on trial had been falsely accused and persecuted. Why, some of her own friends had been called before the courts, all of them innocent. Nevertheless, many had been tortured into making false confessions or drowned or crushed under boards weighted with stones or burned or hanged.

Finally some of the village elders—none of them present tonight—had called for an end to the purge, the net of which had widened to include members of almost every family.

Yet certain zealots persisted. She looked out among their grim faces. What was it they really wanted?

"Do you know a lot about witches?" Herbert Templeton said, giving Charity a cursory glance up and down. He took a length of her long blond hair in his gloved hand, let it slide through his fingers.

Charity looked down at her feet. She could not speak.

"I thought not," he said. "You are thyself a lying witch."

"No," Charity said. She looked at him. "Let us go home, before it is too late!"

"Methinks 'tis is already too late, lass. Back with the others," he commanded, raising a gloved hand. He looked away. Charity was hustled off to stand among the captured women, young and old. Tall trees circled around them. A bonfire crackled. Someone, a middle-aged woman with blunt, graying hair, moaned softly though her tears.

Herbert stood before them now.

"Who amongst you knows the incantation of eternal youth?" His eyes narrowed, gleaming with torch light.

Charity wearily lowered her head. She knew nothing of what he spoke.

"Heh? Speak up now!" He walked among the women. "Who shall speak first and be spared?"

A young woman cleared her throat. Herbert turned to face her, his eyes flashing.

"You . . . your name?"

"Angelica," she replied in a trembling voice. Charity now saw the maiden whose teeth were so frightfully crooked. Her eyes were wide with terror. Such a ghastly girl, Charity thought. A high, wide forehead; thin hair the colorless color of drab, dead grass, pulled tightly to her skull. A witch?

"Speak now and live," Herbert said calmly.

Say nothing, and we all will die, Charity thought to herself. She began to tremble.

"The curse," Angelica began, "is a blood curse. . . ."

"A blood curse!" Herbert repeated. Eugenia drew closer. The other zealots gathered around.

"What does she mean?" Eugenia said. "Blood curse?"

"Let her speak," Herbert said, holding up a hand before his sister's face. Eugenia pushed her brother's gloved hand aside.

"Let me by, Herbert." To Angelica she said, "Speak the incantation."

"There is a spell. . . ." Angelica said. She was shaking now.

"Yes, girl. Continue."

Angelica closed her eyes. "It is thus—"

"Mercy!" cried one of the women.

"Hold your tongue!" hissed Elder Burrows. He was eager to hear this and drew in a little closer now, too. His long gray hair fell from a loose knot and swept across his stout, wrinkled face. He pulled it aside with exasperation.

Angelica swallowed hard. "When the moon rises, at eventide, extract the blood of maiden or bride."

Gasps.

"Blood," the avid elder exclaimed in a whisper. He looked around at the others. "Extract? But how? In vials? And is it necessary to kill the—"

Herbert turned to Burrows. "Please, Reverend. If you will listen patiently, all will no doubt be explained."

"If maiden or bride are not at hand, drink from the river of the heart in boy or man."

"Ah," someone said, like a scientist observing a colleague's laboratory experiment.

Angelica continued, eyes half closed, entranced.

"To seize ravaging time's golden reins, place the blood of the lambs in your own veins."

"Heavens!" someone exclaimed. "So blood *is* the key!"

"Yes, but there must be a magic talisman," said another. "Mere blood alone—"

"Quiet, please," Eugenia said sternly. "Is a talisman required, Angelica?"

"Thimble, feather, bone, or locket, curse a token from thy pocket."

Each of the elders fished in their pockets for a token of luck. Coins were produced, rings and keys, all flashing in the light of the nearby fire.

The Reverend Mr. Burrows touched his wrinkled chin. A greedy smile spread across his face. Angelica spoke.

"With a talisman touch the cursed red brew, and believe the spell will now come true."

A sudden wind began to howl through the old trees. The men held their hats to their heads. Eugenia looked to the dark sky.

Angelica's eyelids fluttered. Her eyes had rolled back in her head, exposing a shimmering whiteness.

"*Aeternus . . .*" she whispered. Then she moaned the word again, "*Aeternus . . .*"

"*Aeternus,*" repeated the witch hunters. "*Aeternus.*"

Angelica opened her eyes and tears ran down her cheeks. She chanted again, in a barely controlled shriek.

"From the book of black magic's darkest page, comes eternal youth—whilst your victims age!"

The crowd gasped.

"Let's give it a try!" the reverend cried. "Whose blood shall we take?"

The girls began to scream.

Charity and some of the others tried to run. Herbert and Burrows took hold of them.

"Give me your wrist, maiden," Herbert said to Charity, amid the panic that surrounded them. The village elders were chasing the youths with knives raised.

"No, my lord, I beg you!"

Herbert withdrew a long thin blade from the folds of his black cloak.

"Your wrist, my dear. Or your throat."

With that, Charity fell to the ground, unconscious.

Hours later—though it seemed like mere seconds as the familiar, recurring dream continued—Charity awoke on the shore of a steaming pond at the edge of the woods. She shook her head and coughed. Her wrist ached. A ragged bandage was wrapped around it. By whom? Where were the other girls? She blinked in the late afternoon sunlight. Why, only that morning she'd been taken in a horse cart to the deepest woods where she'd seen and heard . . .

She rubbed her eyes. Had she only imagined it? *And how*, she thought, *did I get here, to this desolate place at the edge of a pond*? She smelled the cool, pond-scented air, and the pleasant mingling wood smells of autumn. A low sun hung on the horizon. Absently she caressed her aching wrist. She noticed her feet were bare.

She picked herself up and looked out at the green water. Grassy leaves pierced through the shimmering surface in patches, and closer to the rocks at the shore, paddlelike leaves waved up from the pond's murky floor.

The water had receded from the rocks, which lined the edge of the pond. Algae that had slicked the rocks with green slime in summer had dried like pale green paint in swirls, coating the larger rocks by half. Looking at the rocks, she caught sight of a small furry brown head and sparkling black eyes peeping up through a crevice.

A muskrat!

The little fellow twitched its nose and whiskers and darted back down between the rocks. Charity followed it along the shore. She whistled, trying to catch its attention. Up ahead several feet he emerged again, scurrying over a few rocks, muscles flexing beneath his furry coat. Then he darted back down. *There must be tunnels beneath the rocks*! she thought.

The mystery of how she'd gotten to this splendid place was momentarily forgotten. She was fascinated by the little animal. She called out to it, smiling with delight.

Hurrying after him, bare feet on the cool grass, she found he always popped up over the rocks several feet ahead of where she expected him to be. He traveled fast. Up again came the furry beast. And down again he went. She ran along the grassy shore of the pond, fascinated with the creature. She didn't notice the presence of another. She didn't expect what happened next. Up through the tall grass came an unseen white hand, clutching at her skirts, pulling her off balance.

Charity screamed in horror, falling to her knees. The hand gripped her wrist. She felt herself being pulled down, into the grass. She saw there in the tall grass the white form of Angelica.

"Help!" Charity cried, trying to free herself from the witch's grasp. She'd not imagined the previous night's horror. The elders had taken her to the woods to be slaughtered with the other suspected witches. Somehow she'd gotten away.

Angelica's eyes were limned in red, heavily hooded. Her lips parted, crawling up over those gnarled, crooked teeth. She drew a breath.

"Help is what I offer, Charity. The only help that can save you."

Charity collapsed beside her, her face inches from Angelica's.

"No! I don't want a witch's help."

"What choice have you?"

"I want my mother! I want to go home!" She noticed ghastly wrinkles and veins in Angelica's face, so white in broad daylight. Angelica's prim, high-collared black frock had been torn and was now soaking wet. "What have they done to you?"

"Not only to me. Look at your hands."

Charity tried to pull away but Angelica held her fast.

"I said, look at your hands," Angelica commanded.

Charity held up her hands before her eyes. To her amazement, she did not recognize them. The nails had yellowed and grown long. Skin sagged around the fingers, the bones of which were curiously bent. Thick

veins and brown spots covered the skin of the backs
of her hands and wrists. With horror Charity pulled up
her sleeves and saw the bones of her forearms, the skin
hanging loosely upon them.

She gasped, feeling as though she would be ill.
"What have you done?"

"Not I. The physician Templeton and his sister. They
have your blood and the blood of all they captured last
night. And now you are cursed."

"And what of the elders?"

"All dead. At the hand of Herbert and Eugenia Templeton."

"The Reverend Mr. Burrows?"

"His severed head lies upon the road not half a mile
from here. The Templetons never planned to share the
dark magic."

Charity closed her eyes. A fly buzzed past her ear.
With a shudder she imagined the cloud of flies that at
that moment must have been hovering and roiling over
Reverend Burrows's offended face and red, pulpy
stump of a neck.

"You gave them the spell," Charity said angrily.
This is all your fault! I should like to kill you myself!"

"I am already dying, Charity. It is too late for me.
I have lost too much blood. The Templetons knew not
what they were doing. The victims began to die. That
is not how the spell works. To feed upon us, we must
be kept alive. Alive, until they have had the last drop
of our blood."

"You too are evil! Else how did you come to know
this spell?"

Angelica put her hand over her eyes. "How I wish

I had never learned it. What fools we were to dabble in magic.''

''We?''

''The coven. Thirteen of us, who met in secret . . . or so we believed. To practice not the magic of darkness, but of light . . . to seek cures for the illnesses that have ravaged our colony. But the Templetons and their kind found us out. And now look at what they have done!''

Charity fell back upon a rock and sobbed. ''And what of me? Shall I die here, too? All because of some witch's folly?''

''Would I have carried you here only to let you die?''

Charity looked into Angelica's pale eyes, eyes like death itself. ''*You* brought me here? Why?''

''When they threw our bodies upon the pile given up for dead, you showed signs of life. And something more—a magic glow. I faked my own death in order to live a few more hours. In the light of morning, after the slaughter, I escaped with you with what little trace of strength I had left, to give you this.''

Angelica pressed a small, cold object into Charity's hand. Charity looked closer and saw that the object was a silver pocket watch. It shone in the light. A skilled craftsman had forged an enchanting image of the moon and a cascade of stars upon it. She opened it. Roman numerals shone in black against an ivory face. It was the most beautiful watch she'd ever seen. She looked into Angelica's eyes.

''I do not understand.''

''When I gave Herbert and Eugenia the magic spell, I did not tell them there is a magic antidote. Never lose this charm, Charity. If it leaves your possession for more than a month or so, you will die. With it, you will not get any older—ever. Make it a part of your consciousness."

Charity sobbed, "But I am already turning into an old woman!"

"So you shall be. For as long as you possess this secret watch, unknown to the Templetons." Angelica closed her eyes in a sudden spasm of pain.

Charity touched Angelica's shoulder. "The antidote," she said frantically. "What about the antidote?"

"Find the Templetons and their evil cohorts to undo the dark magic—all of it. They have already fled. Track them down, no matter how long it takes you, no matter how many oceans or continents you must cross."

"Angelica, how can I do this? I am feeling so frail . . . I am scared."

"You must do it to save yourself, and many others, I fear. Find them and insinuate yourself into their lives, any way you can. Then wait. Vengeance shall be yours." Angelica placed a finger on the watch Charity held in her palm, and closed her eyes.

Charity felt the watch pulsing warmly in her hand.

"Place this charm in a sorcerers' hand, on the anniversary of this night," Angelica said, stroking the watch. "Go to the place where darkness sleeps, and whisper in the moonlight."

Tiny liquid sparks of gold pulsed from her touch. They ran like beads of mercury through her fingers, dancing and scattering.

"In the presence of true love will come the retribution of the cursed, for only with true love's passion will the dark spell be reversed."

Abruptly Angelica's hand fell to her side. She gasped. Her hair turned white and her face froze, the color of ash. Her hand, held in Charity's, crumbled to dust, as did the rest of her form, until there was just a trace of white powder in the grass.

Charity screamed.

"Angelica! Where have you gone?"

Some of the white powder was on her hands. She raised them, looking at them in horror. Suddenly she was aware of the voices of birds. The grass was alive with birds, singing. She stood up, fighting tears, and took a few steps back. She fell into the pond.

The water near the shore was shallow, but she managed to soak her clothes and hair. The water was icy cold.

Panic swept over her, bracing as the cold water. She'd dropped the watch in the water in her fall!

With a frantic mind she splashed on her hands and knees in the shallow water, sinking her hands into the silty muck, searching, feeling around for it. The muck enveloped her hands and fingers like cold silk gloves. Her toes sank into the revolting mire. She felt around, pulling up pebbles and rocks and slimy strands of weed, all of which she cast furiously back into the water.

"Help me! Help me find it!" she cried out to no one in particular.

Breaking through the water, several feet from where she groped on her hands and knees, was a small furry face. The muskrat's nostrils flared, spouting a fine mist of water. His brown eyes sparkled and his sleek coat shone. He slipped past her, and with a wary glance at the strange girl who had invaded his pond, submerged himself again. A few small bubbles surfaced.

It was then that Charity's grasping fingers brushed across a cold, smooth object underwater. She grasped at it, but it slipped from her fingers like soap. Clutching madly at the water, with a deafening splash, she caught the watch in her hand and held it up to her face.

She sighed deeply, then raised the wet glistening watch to the blue sky.

"I won't lose you," she said to the watch.

She pulled herself through the water to the grassy edge of the pond. A huge flock of small white birds took flight from hidden places in the grass. She watched them in amazement as they rushed past her through the air. She stood on the bank and felt the water dripping from her clothes.

She began to run, the task before her coming clear. She knew she was no longer of this world. She would be an old woman now, undying. She would have to find Herbert and Eugenia Templeton and reverse the evil spell, no matter how long it took.

If I cannot die, I have time to look, she told herself. *To find them. And I will! I will find them!*

She ran, the silver pocket watch tight in her hand.

Chapter Eleven

OCTOBER NIGHT

Emily slowly came awake, a voice stirring her to consciousness. The narrow room was dark. She raised her head from the hard pillow. She was weak. But she could hear a distant cry.

Emily . . .

"Who are you?" Emily cried out in the dark room. "Charity, is it you?"

Yes, child. I need you. You must come here at once. . . .

Emily now recognized Charity's voice. It came to her clear and strong.

Now is the time; the hour is near. . . .

Emily threw back the covers and pulled herself to her feet. Aged as she was, she had a sudden burst of energy.

"Help me!" Emily cried in a squeaky voice. She made her way to the door. "Somebody! Please help me!"

With trembling hands she pushed and struck the wooden door.

Now is the time; the hour is near. . . .

"Yes, but show me what I have to do!" Emily protested. She banged her fist as hard as she could against the door. To her surprise, the lock clicked over, and the door opened.

She fell back. The huge shape of Ned, the helper, loomed in the doorway.

"Y-You must be quiet," he said in a whisper. She stepped forward.

"Ned! Ned, do you know me?"

With eyes that appeared wounded, he looked at her, squinting. He slowly shook his head. "I don't know you."

"You *do* know me!" she pleaded, coming closer. "Yes, you do! I'm Emily Jordan."

He looked confused. "Emily Jor . . . Jordan is a child."

Emily closed her eyes in frustration. An idea came to her. She looked down at her white gown. With a firm tug, she pulled off a button. She held it up so that he could see it.

"Do you remember?" she said. She placed the button in his hand, and closed his fingers over it. "Remember? I found the buttons from your shirt. I was with you after . . . after Dr. Temple beat you. You do remember that day, don't you?"

Ned slowly opened his hand and stared in disbelief at Emily and then at the tiny button in his huge palm. His eyes glistened. He looked closely at Emily, eyes wide now.

"You . . . ?" he said.

"Oh, Ned, you must know what kind of evil is happening here at the Hamilton Home," she said.

He turned his face away. "You w-were the only one . . . who ever showed me any kindness," he said, his voice trailing off. "And look what they did to you."

"Eugenia and Herbert did this to me," Emily said. "And they've done terrible things to the other residents, too."

He nodded. "I . . . I know," he said with a shiver. "I helped them do it."

He hid his face in his hands. The button fell to the floor and rolled to a dark corner.

She reached out and gently took his hands in hers, lowering them from his tear-streaked face. "Ned, there's no time for this now. You've got to help me. You still have a chance to help undo some of the wrongs that have been done here. You're a prisoner here, too. And now you've got to help me."

"But . . ." he said, "but they'll kill us all."

"No, not if we act quickly. There's still hope. Take me to Charity. Take me to her before it's too late!"

He took several deep breaths, seemingly unable to answer. He looked sheepishly over the grim little room. He spied the button on the floor. Bending, he picked it up and slipped it into his pants pocket. Then he held out his big hand. Slowly, Emily placed her hand into his. His grip was warm and strong.

"This way," he said.

Together, tentatively, they started down the wide, dimly lit hallway, the rose-pattern carpet muffling their footfalls.

* * *

Kerry pried open the basement window that led to the darkened laundry room of the old Hamilton Home. He used the flat edge of a crowbar. With a squeak of wood against wood, and a small, sickening crunch, the window was opened wide enough so that a person could enter through it.

In the dark he climbed through and dropped to the floor. The hardness of the concrete was not lost on him. Pain shot through his legs. The smell of rotted wood and dampness surrounded him. Silently, Beth followed.

"Careful," Kerry said, helping her through the window. Beth's flashlight beam struck him full in the eyes, blinding him for a moment. He felt her hand grasp his wrist as she leveraged herself in.

"God, this place *is* creepy," Kerry said, peering through the gloom. Industrial-size washing machines reflected the moonlight from the window. Straw laundry baskets were stacked almost to the ceiling.

"If you want to go back, this is your last chance," Beth said. "We can't pretend to not be in danger here."

"I didn't say I wanted to leave. I just said it's creepy in here."

"This is nothing," Beth said. She straightened her sweatshirt, which had come untucked from her jeans.

"Terrific," Kerry answered, looking up at the basement ceiling. Ancient plumbing crossed overhead. From deep within the heavy, sweating walls came the distant, muted sound of a huge roaring furnace.

"Come on, then; let's see the rest of it," he said.

The two crept around the corner of the laundry room and entered the basement hallway. The occasional overhead naked lightbulb—low wattage—provided enough illumination to make using the flashlight unnecessary. The cavelike walls had been painted chalk white. Avoiding the noisy elevator, they headed for the stairs.

Beth saw the man on the stairs first. She was too frightened to scream. She stopped dead and gasped. Kerry bumped to a stop behind her.

On the darkened staircase, near the bottom, was the facedown body of an old man, sprawled out, arms above his head. A knife had been plunged into his back. His head was twisted in such a way that his face could not be seen. His dark suit jacket was open, spread out like dead wings on the stairs.

"Oh, Jesus!" Kerry said. He stepped forward.

"Be careful," Beth said. Kerry slowly approached the still body.

Beth took a few steps back. She bumped into something. No, *someone*. Someone alive.

Before she could scream, an icy hand was clapped over her mouth. Turning her head, she caught a hideous glimpse of Eugenia's face, terribly close to her own. Eugenia smiled. The redness of her gums contrasted with the whiteness of her long teeth.

The body on the stairs twitched. Kerry jumped back as the head of the knifing victim jerked upward and smiled. Beth recognized Herbert Temple immediately.

Herbert quickly got to his feet.

"Good evening, kids," he said. He leered at them, brushing off his pants. Then he reached round and pulled the knife from his back. It must have been a fake, Beth thought, her heart pounding in her ears.

"A prop of sorts," Herbert said with a laugh. He held the knife up, ready to swing it.

"What a coup, dear brother," Eugenia said. "Two more prey."

With all the strength she had, Beth kicked at Eugenia. The kick landed solidly against Eugenia's knee. Eugenia cried out in pain, and the firm grip she'd had on Beth began to slip.

Beth wriggled free, kicking and twisting. She screamed as loud as she could.

"She's getting away!" Eugenia hissed.

"And we haven't had a proper introduction to the boy," Herbert said calmly. He didn't move, even as Beth and Kerry scrambled toward the opposite end of the hallway.

Eugenia cried out for her thugs: "Mac! Stanton! Get them!"

Beth and Kerry ran, escaping down the dark corridor.

"Halt!" Eugenia cried out after them.

Yeah, right, Beth thought to herself.

She could hear Eugenia's curses following down the darkened basement. At the end of the corridor was a narrow flight of wooden stairs.

"Up?" Kerry said, out of breath.

"There's no other direction to run," Beth said.

They bounded up the stairs.

At the top, Beth took a quick look back. No one followed. Not yet, at least.

"What do we do?" Kerry said, breathless. They stood in an enormous service entry to the kitchen and garage. Wheelchairs lined the walls. Silently, Beth pulled Kerry into a tall broom cupboard. Pine-scented cleanser suffused the small space. As she closed the door, she watched the last of the light fade from Kerry's face. His eyes were wide and expectant, lips parted, chest heaving. She was completely out of breath, too. The door clicked shut.

Blackness.

For a moment at least, Beth knew they were safe. But she knew it wouldn't last. They had gotten away too easily. Almost as if the Temples had planned it that way.

Ned slipped the key into the barred gate where Charity waited, her hand over her fluttering heart. Emily felt her own heart beating frantically. She aimed the beam of a flashlight at the lock Ned worked on. At last the door swung open with a pained squeak.

"Hurry," Emily whispered. Charity looked upon Ned with supreme disdain. Emily saw Ned looking from one to the other of the two ancient women. What a contrast they made. Emily was the taller and more slender of the two. Her hair was completely white, her arms and legs long, fingers slender. Charity, shorter and stout, had a much wilder head of hair, streaked with gold. Her features were strong where Emily's were fine.

"We haven't much time," Charity said, tottering out of her cage. "What are you looking at, you silly fool?" she snarled at Ned. "Let's get out of here!"

With that the two old women, trying to support one another with grasping hands, prepared to make a run for it. It wasn't easy in the long dressing gowns they wore.

A clatter came from the end of the tunnel. Ned stepped over near the doorway.

Emily and Charity stood back in the shadows.

"Ned Fox!" Herbert called, charging into the room.

His hard shoes slapped through the puddles. "Good man, you're here already. We're expecting trouble." His voice echoed in the dark chamber.

Now Herbert caught sight of Emily, and he started in surprise. A thin smile crept over his lips.

"Well, well—" he started to say.

Another surprise followed. Ned clobbered him hard over the head with his bare clenched fist. Herbert wilted to the floor.

"Eugenia won't be far behind," Charity said. The threesome scrambled into the tunnel, running to what Emily hoped would be safety. Charity led the way.

They climbed the stairs and ran to the pantry off the kitchen. The great kitchen, with its grease smells and glowing pilot lights, was silent.

Emily turned to Charity. She smiled slightly. "The hour has arrived," she said.

"Yes, my dear," Charity said. "At last."

The two women embraced.

Charity turned to Ned. "I ought not to trust you," she said to him. He hung his head down. "But I do," she added. "When I saw you strike your master, I knew I could trust you."

A clatter came from the stairs.

Ned, Emily, and Charity cowered in the shadows as three of Eugenia's henchmen ran by, flashlight beams swooping over the kitchen walls. Emily recognized the stout handyman with his ever-present cigar butt clenched between his teeth. Accompanying him was a tall man with strawlike yellow hair and a bulldog face.

No one spoke until the room was empty and the footfalls of the potential captors were echoing away.

Emily looked at Charity's kind old face. "Are you going to tell me who you are?" she asked softly.

"This is no time for explanations!" Charity whispered.

Emily gripped her hand. "I have to know now! I've waited a long time to understand all this. And I will not die not knowing!" Her lips trembled.

Charity smiled bravely. She stroked Emily's hair. "There, there, my dear. You're right. I owe you an explanation, but there isn't much time. Save any questions for later. And you are not going to die 'not knowing,' as you put it, because you are not going to die in this wretched place. Be confident."

Emily wiped the tear from her eye. "Thank you," she said. Ned sniffed loudly.

"You said you've been waiting a long time, Emily," Charity whispered, a wry smile on her lips. "I've been waiting, too. A *long*, long time. If it hadn't been for you, I would probably have eventually died in that awful cell."

Emily shook her head. "We could still be killed. In fact," she said, trying to be brave, "I think I'm dying. My mind is losing strength. I saw my father the other day when he came here looking for me. He didn't know me! I couldn't speak, I was so confused."

She buried her face against Charity's shoulder. She felt Charity's hands stroking her hair.

"We're going to be all right," Charity said. "There are two of us now. We can complete the task."

"The task?" Emily asked.

"Reverse the spell," Charity said. "You see, this is what I came here for in the first place. Disguised as a resident, I observed Herbert and Eugenia, took an accounting of their crimes and learned as much as I could about their victims. I daresay they turned the tables on me for a while."

Emily drew back. "But Eugenia and Herbert aren't witches . . ."

Charity scowled. "Hardly. They were mortals once, a long time ago. In fact they were witch hunters. They are stealers of magic. Over the course of three centuries they slaughtered many a young witch to gain their power. And countless mortals."

Emily shook her head. "You've been trying to find them for *three centuries*? How did they manage to elude you for all this time?"

Charity frowned and said wearily, "I'm not exactly Sherlock Holmes, if you haven't figured that out already. I'm a cash-poor old woman who has had a great deal of difficulty getting around. Just as you see me now, this is how I've had to live, in this tired old body. Yet I of course had to find Eugenia and Herbert eventually; it's not like I had choice in the matter."

Ned's breathing was labored, but he listened intently as Charity went on with her story.

"When I met Herbert and Eugenia, they hadn't yet changed their names from Templeton to Temple. After our first encounter, they fled to Europe. I've always been at least one step behind them ever since. In London they fed on the blood of prostitutes and waifs. Herbert always had a knack for setting himself up as a staff physician or warden, especially in places like orphanages and poorhouses, prison hospitals and places where the indigent sought help. The Temples had many a close scrape with Scotland Yard—and with me. But they were masters at placing themselves in situations of chaos and poverty, as far from the gaze of the law and respectable society as possible.

"The war times of the twentieth century were particularly fruitful for them. Eventually the Temples worked their way back to the New World, always keeping an eye open for the obscure, out-of-the-way sanctuary. A remote home for the aged in northern Wisconsin provided the perfect cover for their well-practiced deeds. I discovered that they made a mad dash here after a scandal broke out in Toronto, where they ran a halfway house for psychologically disturbed veterans."

"How did you finally find them?" Emily asked, looking around, her heart pounding with fear.

"The usual methods of trial and error. Of course, they didn't know me, or believed me dead if they ever gave me a second thought—and they wouldn't have recognized me. They could have only mildly suspected anyone like me was in pursuit of them. In Washington, D.C., I researched the inspection records of many places I might call human warehouses, knowing the Temples's proclivities. I came across the Temple name, other clues, resumes, and dossiers. Of course, I was tired and weary and a major flop of a detective, having chased down more than a few blind alleys in my time. But I had some money saved, the means to travel. On a hunch I traveled here and insinuated myself into the Temples's lives as just another indigent old woman. A role I daresay I know too well from having lived it in many places, for too many years."

"But how on earth did you survive all these years?" Emily asked.

"Alone. Sometimes living in the streets. I never got

along as well as the conniving Temples did, I'll tell
you that. For many years I was homeless. Or locked
up 'for my own good.' I have such a poor head for
figures I was barely aware of the savings account I'd
kept at a bank in New Orleans. Lucky thing I remembered it. It was my ticket into the Hamilton Home.
Thirty thousand dollars isn't exactly a fortune. But
Herbert and Eugenia licked their chops when I, acting
as a mental incompetent practically on her deathbed,
signed power of attorney over to them. At that point,
I was in. All I had to do was wait . . . until tonight!''

Ned listened, cowering next to the two women. Charity eyed him with suspicion, and he looked away.

''Three hundred years ago,'' Charity said, ''at the
stroke of midnight, the magic was stolen, and the spell
of the moonlight was harnessed by two mere mortals.
With this power, Herbert and Eugenia have been able
to remain young and strong . . . provided they steal the
youth of a steady stream of new young victims.

''For some the process is long and painstaking, and
the poor, wasted souls are kept in reserve, aging until
they are drained dry. This evil house has been the
perfect cover. A tangled spider's web from which the
Temples have been feeding unsuspected for decades.
Tonight I'm going to turn it all around.'' She touched
Ned's elbow.

''Take us to it,'' Charity said. ''Take me to the silver
pocket watch.''

Ned looked frightened.

''I know the watch survived,'' Charity said sternly.
''Had you destroyed it in fire as Eugenia ordered you
to, I would never have had the power to contact Emily.
I would have withered and turned to dust. You were

the last to hold it in your hand, Ned. You kept it, didn't you? I'm very grateful that you did. You needn't be concerned about a petty theft. You've thrown in your lot with us. It's your own life you ought to think about protecting now. We're your salvation.''

Ned looked at Emily.

''Don't be frightened,'' Emily said softly.

''M-My room,'' Ned said, stuttering.

''Hurry!'' Charity said. ''There isn't a moment to lose!''

In Eugenia's candlelit office, Herbert held a cloth to the small cut on his head. Sitting in a big wine-colored wing chair, he told Eugenia about Ned Fox's mutiny. Eugenia paced the floor. Her shadow loomed large over the walls and paintings—portraits of the grim-faced Hamilton clan, ornately framed. Orion Hamilton himself, the great patriarch and builder, scowled down at the Temples. It was as though he shared their worry and disdain about these eventide intruders.

Eugenia stopped pacing for a moment, trying to organize her thoughts, to separate dread paranoia from rational conclusions. Her mouth twitched. After a few seconds, she paced across the room again.

At last, the worst of her fears won out. She could not speak at first. Her brother looked agitated. He gave her that look doctors sometimes gave troublesome patients, an expression of haughty annoyance.

''Well?'' he said.

Her voice was thick with dread.

''The pocket watch!'' Eugenia said. ''Our idiot servant kept the pocket watch!''

Herbert dabbed at his forehead, looked at the spots

of blood on the white cloth. He was not impressed. "That was just a silly fool's trinket along with the junk we took from Charity Francis and burned."

"Yes, I remember, Herbert. I remember how foolish I felt when I told Ned to take it away and destroy it. How I disparaged my fears. How you scoffed at me." She raised her voice accusingly. "And yet the moon foretold the existence of a talisman. Could it have been the watch, and Charity Francis the avenger? Oh, how I wish now I'd destroyed the bloody thing myself! Damn your confidence! And damn mine!"

"I'm not completely convinced. A pocket watch? Perhaps. Yet we've eluded our enemies for centuries. Might you be jumping to conclusions, sister? Falling for a mortal's trick?"

"I might be. Hell help us if my hunch is correct. We can't afford *not* to assume the worst. Not with a house rampant with meddlers and . . . and *witches*! Witches, Herbert!" She pressed a button on her desk, and two of her thugs ran in—the fat one with the cigar between his teeth and the bulldog. Both wheezed, exhausted from their failed chase.

"To Ned Fox's room at once," she said. "Hurry!"

Beth was beginning to think that maybe fleeing the home was the best policy—at least for tonight. Yet how could she leave Emily?

Finally the heat in the cupboard became unbearable.

"Let's get out of here," Beth said. "If they find us here, we'll die like rats in a cage. I'd rather be killed in flight."

"I'd rather not be killed at all, if you don't mind,"

Kerry said. "You have some idea where we should go next?"

Beth didn't appreciate his tone of voice. "Any place is better than this," she said. Although she knew that Charity was imprisoned deep in the basement, she had no desire to return to that cold damp place—not after just fleeing there. She had an idea where she wanted to look next: the forbidden upper floor, the sealed-off wings. "Come on," she said, opening the cupboard door. She squinted her eyes against the pale light of the kitchen. "We're going up."

The third-floor stairs were wide, the carpet patterned with a spray of bloodred roses. A rail overlooked a crude atrium three stories high. Tall windows let in a blue light through ancient panes. From the wedding-cake ceiling there hung an elaborate crystal chandelier. Moonlight beamed brilliantly from every facet.

On the third floor, Beth and Kerry crept around yet another corner of this labyrinth of corners and corridors. Their shadows stretched down hallways, crossing over closed and locked doors. They stopped and started, occasionally bumping into one another, stepping on feet. Each time they advanced, it was with trepidation. They couldn't stay in one place, nor could they be sure what they would find with their next steps.

The smell up here was of rotted wood, burning candles. A breeze moved swiftly through the tree branches beyond the rooms and windows. It whispered and warned.

Beth shivered. Kerry's shoulder was pressed against hers. They crossed a huge, silver-bright window and became black silhouettes against the moonlit sky. Beth glanced out the window and let her gaze fall three stories to the ground. Below, beyond the backyard, the grave markers glowed in the small cemetery, that loathsome potter's field of local legend.

They came to another corner. To round it? Or stop and take another direction?

Beth looked into Kerry's eyes. Fear mingled with uncertainty. Neither of them really knew what to do but to go on, further into the dreamlike silence and gloom. So she went forward, the line of her vision expanding, the doors of the next hallway coming into view, the feeling of the cold air on her face. And then the awful hand that reached out of the darkness before her and dug into her neck.

She had no time to scream. Kerry's flashlight fell to the floor, its yellow beam careering over the faces of the men; the yard men, the furnace men, the men who hauled out the bodies of the dead.

The flashlight went dead with a crack of glass.

A scream came from Beth's constricted throat. She saw the unlit butt of a cigar clenched between small yellow teeth. The thug reached with a another hand and took hold of her hair, viciously hard.

"Help! Someone help me!" she cried, but she could scarcely hear herself amid the sounds of violent struggle.

Her head was held in the thug's vicelike grip. Yet she was able to see, from the corner of her eye, the tall man with the bulldog face deliver a vicious kick to Kerry's leg.

"Hold still, you little bastard," another one of the

thugs grunted at him. This one was squat, lantern-jawed, with a gray crewcut.

Kerry lashed out with his fists and feet, connecting against the pudgy-faced brute. But the blows didn't stop the hulk. Beth watched in horror as Kerry received a vicious backhand to the face. Blood flew from his lip and spattered against the wall, glowing with moonlight.

She kicked at her captor. He kept his tight grip on her throat. Through painful tears, Beth watched Patti, Maxine, and Laverne, in their perfect hospital whites, bound into the hallway with clubs raised. They moved as one beast.

An all out brawl ensued, Kerry throwing wild punches against the men and the vile-faced nurses. Kerry managed to get to his feet. Maxine hit him in the back with a black club.

"Stop! Leave him alone!" Beth cried. The man who held her gave her hair a yank, then struck her so hard across the face she fell to her knees.

Through her tears, Beth saw, at the end of the corridor, the sly face of Eugenia Temple coolly observing the violent assault.

Kerry struggled against the thugs before the tall window. Heavy velvet curtains were opened to the darkness. The squat helper hoisted a baton, aiming it at Kerry's head.

"Look out!" Beth yelled.

The squat helper brought the baton down hard, but missed when Kerry—eyes wide and gleaming in the moonlight—ducked out of the way. Knots of muscle rippled in the thug's forearms as he lifted the baton again. Kerry crouched down in an adept wrestler's stance, then barreled head first at the thug's ample gut. Faint light came through the window behind him. Kerry rammed into the man, whose tongue lurched out of his mouth with the impact. Arms flailing, the brute fell backward against the great pane of glass. It gave in an ear-shattering explosion. The thug's fading cry of horror signaled a long fall. Kerry rolled forward on the carpet, the nurses pouncing at him.

Beth screamed with all her might into the ear of the cigar-butt-chomping yard worker. His face twisted in pain. He lost his grip.

Breaking free from the grasp of the momentarily stunned thug, she ran. The last thing she saw before rounding a dark corner, opposite the one Eugenia stood at, her fists clenched tight, was Kerry, held fast by the bulldog and the lantern jaw.

"Run, Beth!" he screamed. Blood trailed from his nose.

She ran as fast as she could into blackest shadows, tears blurring her vision.

Kerry fell limp to the carpeted floor, which was strewn with gleaming, jagged glass. The yellow-haired thug held him by his shirt collar. Kerry was too exhausted to move or give fight. Eugenia approached him. She gave him a mean, surmising look, then struck him in the face with the back of her hand. The blow stung, but he didn't cry out. His face was numb.

"How dare you come *here*, you little fool," Eugenia hissed.

"What have you done with Emily?" he said through a mouthful of blood.

"What I'm going to do with you," Eugenia said,

menacingly. She assumed a mocking tone. "Oh, whatever have you done with my poor, dear Emily?" She laughed deeply at that. Her breath was coming hard as she bent down to gaze into his youthful face.

"Do you love her?" she asked with a spreading leer. "Do you think you could love Emily if she were ninety years old, instead of seventeen? Old, wrinkled, and ugly as the chattel who live here with us?"

A bruise was already forming around his eye. He took a breath and said, "What have you done with her, you fucking bitch?"

Eugenia turned to one of her henchman. "Bring him with me." She stalked off down the hallway.

The door to the tiny bedroom opened. Emily and Charity rushed in, followed by Ned, who quietly closed the door behind them.

The smell of dust and mothballs filled the room. Charity held the candle over the bureau as Ned opened the drawer. It came open slowly, with a squeak.

Ned withdrew the wooden cigar box. He slowly lifted the lid.

Inside, amid a menagerie of odd things, buttons, a worn gray photograph of a woman, and a few books of matches was the old silver pocket watch, ornately cast. It shimmered in the golden light of the candle. A strange depiction of the moon and stars still gleamed through the tarnish. Charity placed her hand over it. She touched it with her fingertips, like a blind woman reading braille. She held it up for Emily to see.

Her eyes filled with wonder, Emily touched the watch's silver surface with the tip of her index finger.

All at once the door banged open, and Herbert

stepped in calmly. In his hand was a pistol, trained on the threesome. Two of Eugenia's henchmen, a little the worse for wear, stood close behind him. One of them was still sucking on his foul, unlit cigar butt. He rolled it on his tongue and smiled. All were breathing hard.

"Our evening's fun has come to an end," Herbert said. He gave Ned a piercing scowl, and Ned hung his head.

"I advise you to let us go, Herbert," Charity said bitterly. "You don't understand the powers you're dealing with here. Stand aside."

Emily saw the pocket watch in Charity's hand, which she now held behind her back. Charity had hidden it from view when the door banged open. She closed her frail fingers over it. Slowly, she slipped it into a pocket of her robe.

"Let you go?" Herbert said. He snickered. "First give me the watch."

"Stand aside, I said," Charity warned. She stepped toward the window, where a black curtain covered the glass. Herbert watched warily. He looked at the curtain. With an exasperated sigh, he stepped over to the window and shoved the curtain aside. Moonlight glowed through the window. Training his gun on Charity he took a quick glance outside. It was then that Ned lunged forward.

Charity grabbed Emily's hand and pulled her toward the door as Ned and Herbert locked arms in a deadly struggle. The thugs tried to help their master. But Ned, powerful as he was tall, knocked them both away with ease. Herbert freed the gun, and as Ned turned to attack, Herbert fired.

Emily saw the red hole in the center of Ned's forehead.

With wide white eyes, Ned sought Emily out and found her. He stood still by the window. Gazing at her, a strange sad smile played over his lips.

"Ned!" Emily cried.

His eyes rolled back into their sockets. Blood coursed from the hole in his head. Emily watched as the giant's legs folded beneath his great weight, and he crumpled to the carpet. In his hand, she saw now, was the old photograph of his mother. She covered her gaping mouth with a trembling hand.

Charity yanked Emily's arm, pulling her though the door. Ned had fallen over Herbert, pinning his legs and blocking the henchman, at least momentarily, from the doorway.

"Stop them!" Herbert cried as the women escaped the room. "Get this oaf off of me!"

With Charity's hand pulling at hers, Emily ran down the hallway, as fast as her old legs could take her (surprisingly fast, under the circumstances). When they reached the top of the stairs, Emily heard shots, and she felt bullets whizzing by her ears.

As old as her bones seemed to be, she was able to run. Her life depended on it. But now she could hear the footfalls coming closer, and her bones were growing frailer. Charity clutched at her, pulling her along, till they reached the balcony at the top of the stairs.

It was four stories down to the hard, parquet floor. On a table stood a vase. Even from that distance, Emily could see three white roses, three perfect stems. Across the chasm was another rail and some furniture. Beyond the table, a dark hallway beckoned. The men drew closer, feet pounding the wooden floor through the carpet.

Emily looked into Charity's eyes. She followed their gaze to the crystal chandelier. Emily looked back down, four stories. She could see the legs of the grand piano, silent in the main-floor foyer.

Emily knew instantly what Charity had in mind. It seemed impossible.

"You think we should jump across!" Emily said. "But look at me. I'm a ninety-year-old woman!"

Charity took hold of Emily's hand. "You are, my dear," she said firmly, "a girl of seventeen. Now, *come on!*"

Before Emily could protest, she found herself climbing with Charity to the top of the rail. With her feet on the rail, Emily stood up, precariously balanced, her arms flapping like wings. With a scream, they jumped for the chandelier.

Bullets crashed into the glass as Emily caught hold of the chandelier. It chimed wildly as it swooped, carrying two old women over the great chasm to the rail on the far side.

"Let go!" Charity screamed; the chandelier had swung to its farthest distance. Emily's hands were dug into glass and wire—but she let go. She felt herself falling through space, and then bouncing on an old velvet-covered sofa. The sofa softened the impact, no doubt. Pain nevertheless shot through her legs like shards of broken glass.

"Get them!" Herbert screamed from across the chasm.

Emily and Charity were already picking themselves up.

"I think I've broken my foot!" Emily cried. A bullet was fired into the plaster wall above her head, sending down a shower of dust.

"No time to do anything about it now, dear. Lean on me. And run!"

Wasting no time, Emily followed her friend down flight after flight of stairs. They made it all the way to the rear kitchen door. But as they reached for the door handle, a shadowy figure lurched out of the darkness and let out a terrifying, high-pitched scream.

It was Beth. She held an enormous butcher knife before them. Her eyes were wide with horror.

"Beth! Oh, Beth!" Emily cried. But of course Beth didn't recognize her.

Emily watched Beth taking steps backward. "Oh, God!" Beth said. She shook her head, her lips crumpling, sucking for air. The knife trembled in her hand.

Charity approached Beth, hands reaching out.

"Young woman," Charity said, "you must get a hold of yourself. Don't try to understand it now; it will all be clear to you later. We are your friends. This is— you must believe me—your friend Emily. We are all in grave danger."

Beth looked at Emily, then back to Charity. "What the fuck are you talking about? This is *Emily*?" She blinked her eyes.

"Please, Beth," Emily pleaded.

Beth let the knife fall to the floor. She clutched at

her copious red hair, stringy with sweat. *"I'm going crazy!"* she screamed. Emily took her by the shoulders.

"You're not going crazy," Emily said sternly. "Look into my eyes. Understand that you've got to save yourself, and help us save the lost souls of this house."

Beth swallowed hard and gazed into Emily's eyes. Emily could see a shudder of recognition pass over her friend's face.

Beth touched Emily's cheek, gently ran a finger over the mottled flesh of her chin. "You *are* Emily," she whispered. "Oh, dear God, you are. . . . What have they done to you?"

"Never mind that just now," Charity said. She turned to the kitchen window. In its frame was the brilliant white glow of moonlight. "Look," she said. "The moon has risen. We must use the moonlight." She swept past both of them and out the door.

Beth clutched at Emily's arm. The wall on the clock said it was only ten minutes to midnight.

"Emily . . ." Beth said. "Oh, Emily . . ." She lowered her face, tears streaming down her cheeks.

Emily took Beth's hands in her own. She looked down at them, and saw that the contrast was striking. Beth's hands were almost babylike and plump. Emily's were skeletal, mapped with gnarled blue veins.

"You have to help us, Beth," Emily said. Taking Beth's arm, she leaned against her. "Come along now. There isn't time to explain."

"Just tell me we're going to be all right."

"We have to hurry."

"But . . . they have Kerry!"

"Kerry came here with you?"

"He came here with me to find you. He's alive. But they were beating him."

Emily put her hand over her mouth. She felt as though she might retch. But she steeled herself. Her friends, after all, had come to her rescue. Now she had to keep her head if she was going to be of any help to them at all. With a straight back, she guided her friend out the door.

Together they made their way hastily toward the cemetery, where Charity stood with her arms outstretched to the moon. The chill night air enveloped them. The grass beneath their feet was stiff with frost. The cold wind blew through their hair.

Emily shivered. She saw Charity swaying, seemingly entranced, up ahead. *"Charity!"* Emily screamed. "Hurry! They have Kerry!"

Charity did not respond. Emily thought maybe she was unable to hear her. The wind had picked up. Charity opened her sea-green eyes and looked up at the black sky, and, to Emily's amazement, wisps of clouds began to dance around the moon as Charity started to chant.

Strange words came from Charity's mouth. Her voice sounded weird, like a record played backward. Silken mists spun from the ground, shooting up out of the earth and soaring in great arcs in the direction of the moon. Were they clouds? Or spirits? They rippled like poured cream, but flowed upward.

Translucent, these cloud streams took on luminescent pastel colors. Vivid aqua deepened to purple and seeped away to violet as they shot skyward.

A rope of fiery crimson split through the frosted grass, arcing toward the moon. It turned to brilliant pink. Another sprang from the earth—first neon yellow, then crimson, followed by jets of brilliant flowing orange. Emily watched in fascination, only half believing what she was seeing.

The sky took on deep hues of blue and purple, and the stars' brightness grew in intensity. A whirlpool of colors began to spin around the great white egg-shaped moon, slowly at first and then with gathering speed. Charity withdrew the pocket watch, and an electric charge swept through the air. It was short-lived.

"Stop right there," a voice said.

Emily turned, terrified. There, standing only a few feet away amid the bent tombstones, was Eugenia Temple. At her side was Kerry. Eugenia held a handgun to his head. She looked cadaverous, her eyes slits of evil.

The gun in Eugenia's hand shook slightly. Behind her came Herbert, also brandishing a handgun. A red-haired thug and another of the henchman, the fat one with the slight limp, followed, as did Patti, Maxine, and Laverne, each carrying a black club. Patti repeatedly slapped her club into the fleshy palm of her hand. She smirked. Wisps of her lacquered beehive hairdo, mussed up in the struggle, floated around her fat face.

The sky overhead lost some of its intense color, like a pinwheel that had been spinning frantically and was now losing velocity.

We've come too far for it all to end like this, Emily thought desperately.

One of the thugs gave Kerry a shove forward. He stumbled. Blood had dried darkly on his face.

"Kerry!" Emily cried in a whisper. She watched his eyes widen. He was horror-struck at this scene. Did he recognize her? She had to turn away. She looked at Charity, who eyed their tormentors with pure disdain. The pocket watch she'd held raptly in her hands a moment ago was nowhere to be seen.

"Shall we all go inside, quietly?" Eugenia said.

"Go inside? Your time here is almost finished," Charity said in a booming voice. Confident bluffing? Emily could not be sure. She saw the snub nose of the gun pointed at Kerry's head. One of the thugs, the bulldog-faced one, held Kerry's hands from behind.

"It's you and your hapless disciples who are finished," Eugenia said evenly. Moonlight glinted off of the gun metal in her hand.

"You ought to say your prayers," Charity said to Eugenia. "If you know any."

Eugenia pushed Kerry toward Herbert, who cocked his pistol and held it to Kerry's temple. The young man stood frozen. Beth touched her shaking fingers to her lips, terrified.

Eugenia walked toward Charity. She smiled catlike.

"I know you now," she said. "It took me forever to place you. An almost fatal lapse—almost. But now I remember you."

"The centuries have been kind to you, Eugenia," Charity said.

"Yes, they have indeed. It's been a long time since our last encounter. But there was something I should have done the first time I laid eyes on you, Charity Francis. Something I should have done as well the night you came here with your plans to ruin us."

Charity stuck out her chin. "Do your worst," she said.

"Oh, I intend to."

Eugenia pointed the gun at Charity's heart. Emily felt her mind reeling.

"No!" Kerry shouted.

Eugenia smiled and pulled the trigger. The blast was immediate and devastating. Beth let out an earsplitting scream.

Emily felt her own pained legs begin to collapse beneath her as Charity fell backward over a tombstone, a fountain of blood gushing from a hole in her chest.

Beth ran to Charity's side.

"Stay back or you're next," Eugenia said, training the gun on Beth.

Emily saw then what Eugenia could not have seen: the watch being pressed into Beth's hand. Charity's face quickly drained of color. Her eyes looked out to Emily, then to Eugenia, and then back to Emily. Her lips moved but words did not come.

A pearllike tear, swirling with a prism of colors, formed in the corner of her right eye. The tear fell and splashed over the old woman's slightly parted lips.

Emily . . . Emily, save us. . . .

Charity's eyes fluttered closed, and her head fell limply to her shoulder.

Beth scrambled aside. She turned to Eugenia.

"You bitch!" she screamed.

Eugenia laughed and sighed, blue moonlight pooling over her death mask of a face. Herbert pushed Kerry forward, toward Emily. "Fun and games!" he shouted. "The witch is dead! Time for some *fun* and *games*!"

Eugenia, mad with bloodlust, parroted the phrase. "Fun and games. Look, Kerry. Your beautiful little girl, the girl who wanted to help a witch. Recognize her? She's an old hag now. Look at her!"

Kerry fell down on his knees before Emily, who turned violently away.

"Emily!" he cried. But she couldn't let him see her face.

"We'll soon be better off without these meddlesome children," Herbert said. He rubbed the side of his face with the nose of his pistol.

"Two are still fresh," Eugenia said, as if at a market of human flesh and blood. "They'll keep for a long time."

"Emily," Kerry said. "Please look at me."

Slowly she turned her face to his, feeling the moonlight behind her closed eyes. She opened her blue eyes, and tears fell down her cheeks.

"Oh, Emily," Kerry said. "I don't care!" He choked back his tears. He whispered in a choked voice, "I love you! I'll always love you."

She shook her head, and she turned her face away again.

He gently touched her face with his fingertips.

"Please look at me," he said. "Please."

Slowly, she again turned her face to his. His lips were only inches from hers.

She felt his mouth on hers, and his warm kiss. Hesitant at first, she accepted his kiss with her own, putting her arms around his neck. He released her from his kiss and touched his warm fingers to her hair, then to her face, and gently wiped away her tears.

She looked at him, felt his embrace. "Kerry, I'm so sorry I got you into this mess."

"I'm not sorry. I'll stand by you," he swore. He held her tight. She felt his chest heaving against hers, the warmth of his body "To the death I'll stand by

you. I swear I love you, Emily. I'll love you forever.
I'm asking for a chance I suppose I don't really deserve.
A chance to be loved by you. Just give me a chance
to make you love me back. Say you'll take that chance.
Say that whatever happens now, in this life, or the next,
that you'll take that chance."

She lowered her eyes. Would they be alive five minutes from now? Were her feelings for him the feelings
of real love? Would she ever know?

She looked into his pleading brown eyes. She parted
her lips to speak. Her throat was so dry, her body so
racked with pain.

"Yes," she said. "Yes, okay, Kerry . . . I will." She
touched his brow, ran her frail hand over his thick hair.
"My brave boy," she said.

They kissed.

"Finish them off!" Eugenia commanded.

Emily saw the brown iris of Kerry's left eye. It was
as though he were speaking. Something was going to
happen. *Now.*

Everything happened as if in slow motion. Herbert's
steps were like those of an old elephant, slow and
plodding. He seemed to be looming over them forever.
All at once Kerry burst up out his crouching position.
His arms were spread wide, like a hawk's. His hands
were clenched into fists.

Emily's perceptions suddenly dragged almost to a
stop. In slow motion she saw the blow connect; Kerry's
fist met Herbert's jaw. The physician's glasses, shat-
tering in stop-action time, glass blowing out like the
windows of a bombed building, then dropping from
his crumpled face. The glass fell from the frames like

jagged, frozen tears and spilled down the front of his immaculate suit like a glittering little waterfall.

With the forceful blow, Herbert's gun was knocked into the air; it flew, turning over and over, moonlight playing over slick metal.

A hush fell over the hill.

Emily fell back against the tombstone and watched as Beth dove for the falling gun. This simple act seemed to take forever. Beth's eyes blazed with purpose. Echoing screams rang in Emily's ears, along with the sudden sound of gunfire.

Eugenia was shooting wildly, pulling the trigger of her handgun, her jaw clenched, teeth bared. Bullets were fired into headstones, sending plumes of dust into the air.

Beth caught the gun. It made a solid *thunk* in her hand. She raised it, as slowly as if her arms were heavy as cement. Kerry attacked Eugenia from behind, pulling her arms down. She violently jerked free, but lost her handgun in the process. It fell to the black ground, into shadows.

Eugenia's henchman, who had run to assist her, now stopped in their tracks, eyeing Beth.

Beth pointed her gun, slowly, at Herbert, who scrambled to his feet, then at Eugenia, who had withdrawn from her coat a long, shining needle.

Beth aimed at Herbert again as the Temple siblings circled her like wild, stalking hyenas.

All time seemed to exist in a bubble—an enormous, slow, monster of a bubble, floating and rippling in the air. With the suddenness with which this sensation had begun, it stopped. The bubble popped.

Normal time had seemed submerged in water, slogged down; now it sped back to reality, to actual time. Emily's perceptions shifted back to normal time with a shock of noise. It was as though the very air were shaken by the pandemonium of beating wings, of a great invisible flock of birds taking flight.

"Shoot them!" Kerry shouted. The red-haired thug jumped on Kerry's back, tackling him to the ground.

Beth squeezed the trigger. A slug slammed into Herbert's body. Emily saw the pale fluid that shot out of his stomach. He clutched a hand over the damage and kept coming toward Beth.

"The watch!" Emily cried. Beth held it up in her free hand. "Throw it to me."

"No!" Eugenia screeched like a giant hawk. Her clawlike hands were raised in terror.

Beth tossed the watch into the moonlight. It turned over and over as it traveled in an arc through the air, against the night sky, moonlight dancing on its surface. It fell on Emily's gown. The thugs had taken hold of Kerry and were beating him. Patti and Laverne ran toward Emily, clubs raised and ready to strike down, to smash her skull to pulp. Emily opened up the pocket watch.

Blue moonlight fell like a kiss on the white face of the watch. Immediately the spindly black hands began to turn rapidly. Blue swirls of moonlight spun from the watch face, arcing a few feet at first, then several yards into the air. These curved beams grew, emanating from Emily's hand.

Emily gazed up at Herbert's terror-struck face.

"No!" he shouted. Eugenia's thugs looked at one another, awestruck and frightened. They took a few steps back. But as they approached the mansion, a burst of blue light suddenly dawned inside. Every window contained a strange reflection of a sapphire sunburst. The hands of the pocket watch folded together at the stroke of midnight. And stopped.

Emily saw the shadowy silhouettes of the old residents moving about inside the house, passing the windows. Several poured out the doors. Meanwhile, Herbert and Eugenia's remaining henchmen started to take flight.

The watch felt as though it were a living thing in Emily's hand, a cosmic eye. Three blue beams shot out the watch face. They struck their targets—Patti, Maxine and Laverne—now cowering together at the base of a weeping willow. The blue charges seemed to enter the nurses' bodies at their stomachs and surge upward. The wispy branches of the willows shot straight into the air, suffused with electricity. The thuggish nurses' eyes glowed and bulged.

One after the other, their heads blew off their necks like corks from champagne bottles, followed by noisy geysers of foaming blood.

All around her Emily could hear moans and cries. The ground over the graves seemed to bubble with life. A chorus of agony seemed to be sung from the bare branches of the trees, from the unseen shadows of the graveyard.

Eugenia reached for her brother's hand. He took a step back, avoiding her. She clutched at her stomach, as though she would be ill.

The red-haired thug and the fat one started to run, as did the thug with the limp. But they were instantly surrounded by the angry mob of aged residents, who shook fists at them and kicked as the thugs tried to escape.

From one end of the home, smoke poured out of the windows. A fire was spreading. The old residents blocked Eugenia's path as she tried to find a place to run to.

"No!" she screamed. *"Brother, help me!"*

Two great blue arcs of light beamed from the watch like lightning bolts, seeking targets. This time the targets were running. But Eugenia and Herbert didn't get far. Herbert was already badly injured; he held onto a length of gushing gray intestine that protruded from his abdomen.

The blue arcs found them. Herbert and Eugenia were struck on their heads with the light, and they screamed, their arms madly grasping for one another. Electricity surged through them. Blue sparks shot from the fingertips of their wildly shaking hands.

Eugenia fell to her knees, her face running like the wax of a blazing candle. She was aging! She scrambled to her feet. An arm fell off as she writhed, dancing a terrible dance of pain and decay.

Herbert turned around like a spinning top, and he aged three hundred years, skin rippling and running with wrinkles. His face sagged and drooped. And then it fell off.

The siblings jerked and danced their strange death dance, body parts falling from them, what was left of their skin turning green, then black, then white—the whiteness of skulls and bones.

"Damn you, Emily Jordan!" Eugenia croaked. Her eyes rolled in their bloody, bony sockets. Emily held a hand to her mouth, so terrified was she of this spectacle. Yet she held tight to the watch. Blue beams pulsed into the Temple siblings. White halos, like ripples in a pond, radiated from their heads. These cloudlike rings expanded and widened as they rose to the night sky, casting a white light down upon the cemetery grounds. At the upper reaches of the sky, the parameter of the rings could have contained the entire town of Leonora.

At last Eugenia's legs were worn down to stumps. Brother and sister twitched on the ground, skulls grinning at the moon.

Within seconds there was little left to twitch.

Fire crept along the frosted grass. Kerry picked up a long thin twig from the leaf-swept ground. He ignited the dry wood.

He approached Eugenia with that burning stick. Emily saw that almost all of the residents of the home had now fled the burning structure. Within seconds, dozens stood with her in the cemetery, their faces masks of astonishment and fear.

Kerry touched the end of the burning stick to Eugenia's rotting stump of a body. When the flame touched her, what was left of Eugenia's jaw fell open, but not a word came forth, just a sickening hiss. The corpse burst into flames.

With that, a smattering of applause arose from the crowd of the aged. It grew in strength. Hands that had been too weak to rub together clapped with vigor and strength.

Suddenly a great fireball exploded from within the home, and Emily could feel the heat of it on her face. The fire made the scene as bright as day.

Emily looked at Beth, who had fallen to her knees. "Look," Beth said. She pointed. "Look at them."

And Emily saw what she meant. Many of the old women were clutching one another as their wispy white hair blew from their heads like feathers. Thick, luxuriant hair sprouted instantly in its place, rich in the colors of youth and vitality. One woman, nearly bald, spurted out a flaxen mane that fell all the way down her back.

Skin that had sagged drew taut, and wrinkles and cataracts disappeared and faded as these women watched themselves. They were turning into young girls. *Turning back.*

Hoots and yells of joy erupted as they embraced one another, examining hands and skin, and running fingers through their hair.

Emily recognized some of their faces from the microfilm newspaper articles about the missing teenagers. She saw Jan Schmidt, the young mother who had disappeared from her home one day years before. And here, too, were many others, girls whose faces had been plastered on telephone poles and in shop windows. Faces that had faded from the posters and been forgotten.

Two of the older men whom Emily remembered for their timidity and shyness—and occasional crankiness—had become young men.

"Charlie, look at me! I got my youth back!"

And those who truly were old watched on in amazement, shaking their heads with happiness. Secrets and suspicions held for years evaporated into the air with great whoops of joy and freedom.

Emily saw one of the old women who had been extremely infirm. Emily had spoon-fed meals to this thin, nearly emaciated woman on many occasions. Now the old woman stared at her hands as they cleared of spots and wrinkles. Milky cataracts faded until her eyes gleamed. In just a few seconds, she became a girl of fifteen. She even had a spray of pimples on her chin, which she touched and then couldn't stop touching as tears came into her eyes.

Emily rose, her body still racked with age. She stumbled through the smoke. Through the blue curtain, Kerry came to her. He stopped dead. She could see by the look on his face that something strange was happening to her. She felt it. She was being transformed, too.

Strength returned to her arms and legs. Her breath came back. She touched her hair. It was growing full again, in her hand! And she felt her skin. It was smoothing over her face, then across her arms and body. Her foot, which had been either broken or badly bruised, stopped throbbing.

Her very heart seemed to grow. It beat with a new intensity.

Kerry threw his arms around her and kissed her. She closed her eyes and with all her strength embraced him.

Beth ran over, and Kerry and Emily pulled her into their embrace. In the distance, Emily could hear sirens.

Kerry looked up at the home. From the top floor, a dormer collapsed and fell in a shower of sparks.

"Come on," Beth said. "Let's get out of here before it goes."

"What about all these people?" Kerry said.

"We haven't much time," Beth said. "Look, the building is collapsing." Beth turned and ran from person to person.

"You've got to run to safety," she said. "Hurry!"

The residents began to run from the hill, young assisting the old.

Kerry ran toward the home.

"*Kerry!*" Emily screamed.

"We have to be sure everyone is out!" Kerry shouted back. "Meet me in the valley, in Tomkin's cornfield. I'll be there in fifteen minutes."

"But Kerry, you could be killed!"

"I'll meet you in Tomkin's field in fifteen minutes. I promise! I'm not going to lose you now!" He turned and ran toward the flaming structure.

Beth linked her arm with Emily's. Emily shouted as they ran through smoke.

"Charity!" she called.

But Charity was nowhere to be found. People hurried from the scene, as they might have in the aftermath of some great airliner crash. All fled the hill. Even Gretta, the Temple's housekeeper, could be seen running away, hauling a large suitcase, her face spooked beneath a broad-brimmed black hat.

Together Emily and Beth ran from the ghastly place as pieces of the home crumbled and fell in massive fireballs. The home was being consumed in record speed.

Arm in arm they ran from the hill and crossed the highway. They heard the roar of the volunteer fire rig as it barreled down the highway. Its red lights swooped over the cornfield.

When they were safely in the field, Emily reached around Beth's shoulder and held her close. She felt Beth's hand on her head, stroking her hair, comforting her. Beth's face was smeared with charcoal streaks, her hair wild. She smiled.

"We're alive," she said. She choked on her tears. "We made it."

Emily gazed up at the hill, which was bright with fire. Above the blaze, the crater-pocked moon cast its glow over the hill and valley, the dark forests and winding country highway. She saw the light of fire and moonglow reflected on the face of her friend.

With eyes shimmering, they watched as the last of the collapsing old Hamilton mansion leaned wearily over the valley. In an avalanche of sparks and boulder-sized fiery coals, the home spilled down the hill with a thunderous roar.

Chapter Twelve

November Morning

The previous night's horror was replaced by an eerie calm. The hard-blue morning sky was cloudless, and the sun cast a golden light. Only the pines in the valley showed green. The earth and trees around the site of the old Hamilton Home were scorched black. Debris smoldered on the ground.

Emily, clad in a new white coat and long red-and-green plaid wool scarf—both shipped overnight by her mother—walked with Patrick amid a sea of reporters and TV cameras. Cables snaked over the ground. Back at the car, leaning up against the BMW's white doors, Gloria and Beth sipped hot cocoa from white paper cups.

Kerry, whose head and leg were bandaged, limped over from where his Mustang was parked and stood next to them. He held a wooden crutch in one hand and a baseball cap in the other. A reporter had asked him to take off the cap and smile for a photo.

He smiled across the charred distance at Emily. He had a terrific shiner. Emily smiled back. She felt her father's arm around her shoulder.

"I've been meaning to ask you, do you think you'll stay here?" Patrick said they walked along, knowing they were being photographed, but out of earshot of other people. "I don't want to pressure you, but you don't have to go back home to San Francisco right away. The city will always be there waiting for you when you're ready to return to it."

"I know," Emily said. She pulled her collar around her throat. Despite the golden sunlight, a fresh chill spiked the air.

Patrick pulled her close. "With your mother on our side now, things should go a lot easier with the courts."

"I'm not worried about that anymore," Emily said. "Or about Danny. That's history. And my community service hours can be completed here, helping to find new housing for the Hamilton Home residents who really need a place to live. I've thought it over, and I've decided I want to stay here a while."

Patrick gave her a warm, hard hug. They started back to the car, where the others waited. Webster had arrived on horseback. He waved his cowboy hat and smiled. Amber snorted, her breath steaming from her nostrils.

"What we need now is a little peace and a little time," Patrick said.

She kissed his cheek. As she did so, she saw out of the corner of her eye a face in the crowd of people, a face that stopped her heart. Patrick stood back and followed the line of his daughter's gaze.

Standing apart from the hubbub of police and reporters milling around the scene, about one hundred feet away, a woman in a beige trench coat watched them.

"I'll be back to the car in a minute, Dad," Emily said. She saw his brow furrow. "I'll be okay," she said.

"Don't let these reporters bother you too much," he said. He looked at the young woman standing away from the crowd.

"I have to talk to her. It won't take long."

Emily walked through the mists toward the handsome blond woman in the trench coat. The woman, who was not a reporter, wore a leather travel bag over her shoulder. She watched Emily approach. A small serene smile never left her face.

As Emily drew nearer, she saw that the young woman was truly beautiful, and her green eyes strangely familiar. As familiar as she'd hoped they would be.

When they met, the woman put a hand gently on Emily's shoulder. She kissed her lightly on the cheek.

"I thought I might never see you again," Emily whispered. "But here you are, young and alive."

"Saved by an ancient spell, actually," she said.

Emily smiled and felt a strong tug on her heart. Tears brimmed in her eyes, and she laughed at herself, at her own tears. She dabbed them with a Kleenex. "What will you do now?"

"My task here has been completed." She looked around the scene of wreckage, at the burnt black foundation of the Hamilton Home. "I have years ahead of me. So do you, Emily. So do all of the people you saved here last night."

"Are Eugenia and Herbert really dead?"

She nodded. "For all time, my dear, along with their evil. Thanks to your bravery."

"It is I who should be thanking you," Emily said.

The woman lowered her eyes. "Have a beautiful life, Emily, and that will be thanks enough." She buttoned her coat and gave her bag a pat with her gloved hand. Emily wanted to ask a million more questions.

"Are you," she blurted, "are you mortal?"

"Just as mortal as you are, Emily. Good-bye, dear friend. And do have a good, long life."

"Good-bye, Charity," Emily said.

With a smile, Charity turned to leave.

"Oh! Wait," Emily said. Charity's eyebrows rose. Emily fished into the pocket of her jeans, struggling beneath her coat. She held out her hand.

Charity opened her gloved palm. Emily slipped the silver pocket watch into it. Charity's eyes glittered. She held her bright gaze on Emily for a moment. Then she smiled, slipped the watch into her coat pocket, and turned and walked away.

Emily watched Charity walk through the crowd, into the mists of the morning. Several hundred feet beyond the place where Emily stood, Kerry waited with her father and her friends. Emily stood still, as if between two worlds. She closed her eyes for a moment. When she opened them again and looked, Charity was gone. Vanished into the morning.

Emily took a deep breath of the chill, wood-smoked air and began to make her way back to the car.

WITH HIS TAUT TALES AND FAST WORDS, CHARLES
WILSON WILL BE AROUND FOR A LONG TIME. I HOPE SO."

—JOHN GRISHAM

Paleontologist Cameron Malone has discovered a
500,000-year-old man, so miraculously preserved that
some scientists call it a fraud. But Malone firmly believes
in his find—and so does another man, renegade scientist
Dr. Noel Anderson, who has plans for the Ancient Man.
Plans that will prove the theory his colleagues ridiculed,
and shatter the very foundations of modern science.

When Anderson steals some tissue from the frozen corpse
and uses the still-viable DNA to create a modern Ancient
Man, his experiment succeeds beyond his wildest
dreams—and transforms into a waking nightmare. Only
one man, Dr. Cameron Malone, can stop these horrors of
genetic engineering. But can he do it before they are
unleashed on mankind?

DIRECT DESCENDANT
Charles Wilson

Joanna Carr awakens in a hospital after six months in a catatonic state, only to be told that her beloved husband, David, has been brutally murdered, and police are still searching for the killer. Grief-stricken and confused, she flees to the safety of the country home they once shared to try to piece together the crime—and her life. But Joanna knows that something is dreadfully wrong—and that the nightmare is just beginning...

MEG O'BRIEN

I'LL LOVE YOU TILL I DIE

A WOMAN'S DESPERATE SEARCH FOR THE TRUTH PLUNGES HER INTO A WEB OF DECEPTION, DESIRE, AND DANGEROUS OBSESSION.